AF429515

THE BADGE

a novel

Will Caudill

NFB Publishing
Buffalo, New York

Printed in the United States of America

The Badge/ Caudill— 1st Edition

ISBN: 978-1-953610-37-9
       979-8-218-26693-6

1.Title
2. Fiction >Futurism
3. Fiction> Science Ficton
4. Fiction> Technology> Dystopian
5. Fiction> Future Society

NFB
NFB Publishing/Amelia Press
119 Dorchester Road
Buffalo, New York 14213

For more information visit Nfbpublishing.com

WHERE THE AUTHOR CREATES CHARACTERS THAT HE FORCES YOU TO ENDURE, ALL THE WHILE REFUSING TO DO THINGS AUTHORS ARE REQUIRED TO DO; AND I MUST PLAY THE PART OF GUIDE TO SOME OF THE INITIAL CONFUSION.

SOMEWHERE IN THE WORLD, off the main highway, or thoroughfare, or interstate, or even a road, to the west of the pavement in mind, is where this particular tale takes place. We have many options for the exact location, it could be in the deserts of the American Southwest, where the morning air is dry and cool and the sun paints spectacular canvases when it rises and sets. However, the author insists that anyone who has ever stepped foot into a desert should know that water is everything and every living thing has a weapon for either retrieving it or protecting it. As he reminds me, people often say, "everything in the desert hates you, personally." I myself dear friends, have never heard that.

Alas, the desert is too dry and hot a clime for this story

and must therefore be remembered for another time, with perhaps another author. Instead, we could find ourselves among the frozen fields of the Northern Plains, where hardy vegetation and hardier beasts scrap out a life from near-barren lands. To see a sun dog in person is truly a delightful experience. The author also mentioned that Alberta Clippers are fierce and that blah chill temperatures too far left on a number line are not good for tales that venture out of doors, which will be necessary here.

Perhaps we could visit the Southeast, with its history and its friendliness? There are places in the South that have the charm of the whole world, the character of a good play, and the hospitality of a very fine hotel. If we are strategic in our story placement, we can behold the unforgiving and fierce, fierce Atlantic Ocean. Unfortunately, the author felt it necessary to say some things both too sensitive and too inconvenient and that do not bear repeating; thus, we shall not be having this tale there.

We seem to be at an impasse, my good friends. I cannot say anything at all about New England because the author is too biased towards something "in the South," "about the South," or "to the South," for this story to be in New England. It will be "Stupid Yankees," this and, "effing Northerners," that, which will become so burdensome, it will reach atrocious levels. I mentioned the confusion in that last sentence but the author wanted me to leave it ambiguous on purpose; I cannot tell if "atrocious" is a noun or an adjective.

Our impasse is this: we can have the tale in the Pacific Northwest, and if we make it last long enough to avoid the dumpy season, then it would be splendid weather indeed! It would also present a fabulous landscape to behold; towering mountains and lush, green forests. The mighty, mighty Pacific Ocean. We could also have it in the American Midwest, with its incredible vistas of flat plains, its changing seasons, aspen trees in the fall. The mighty, mighty Rocky Mountains. I tell you my dear reader, fall in the Rockies is like hoopla. Summer in the PNW is also like hoopla. Follow your heart, pick your hoopla.

To you, dear readers, I must now confess. The author has told me that this tale takes place in an underground bunker after people have ruined any ability for humans to survive on the surface of the Earth. I will say this for him, it is an incredibly powerful image that he has going on in his head because this place has a democratic system in place where, in any two-party system, the loser has to commit seppuku within six weeks of the official "Declaration of Loss."

If you are anything at all like me, then you will wonder how that works. I asked him and here is what I got: when a system is in place where there is only a two-party vote, then keeping with the "true democratic fashion," it is only right that it is a "winner-take-all" contest. In an election, this means the loser has to "lose all." Initially, the Bunker Dwellers avoided having to actually do this by making the "Declaration of Loss" date so far in the future that no one would be alive long enough for it to matter.

This rule was ultimately rescinded in its entirety after Mildrew wrote a "Bunker News" op/ed piece explaining that although the losers were dead, that did not negate the fact that they were still losers. Since the Seppuku rule was in place to punish the loser, the mere inconvenience of death was not a sufficient cause for not committing Seppuku because you are still, in fact, a loser, just a dead one. Not wanting to make the dead commit Seppuku, the Bunker Dwellers had simply made it that all elections were legitimate three+ party contests. In the Deep Bunkers, where the other Others and the bat-like things live, the dead are constantly made to do things. Truth be told, as bad as being alive in the Deep Bunkers is, the real horror of the place was being dead there. The three plus party contest didn't solve anything because it was still a popularity contest and the original concept, about the perils of a two-party system, weren't at all assuaged by making it a multi-party system. I suggested a Parliamentary system, to which suggestion the author countered by challenging my patriotism.

This story is not told in an underground bunker for reasons that will become immediately apparent to the reader, once we get to the part where the main character is running along the road. That is not a spoiler, in case you were worried about it. The first sentence of the story isn't an epiphany or anything; neither I nor the author expect you, dear reader, to read the sentence, "As Ali was running down the road, he was trying not to think about anything," and then throw the book down and stand up and grab a dude next to you and explain anything meaningful to him on account of having read that then or when/if you read it at the beginning of Chapter Two. That seems ridiculous; I mean, why on Earth would you do that? The point here is that the author's insistence on having all this take place in underground bunkers does not coincide with the fact that the book clearly has the main character, a fellow named Ali, running down a road and not in a tunnel or on an underground treadmill.

As you are probably figuring out, one of the reasons that part of this chapter title is "all the while refusing to do things authors are required to do," is that one of the things the author is refusing to do is get to the part where he "creates characters that he forces you to endure" and also get to chapter two.

To help everything along, I offer you the following: this tale is about a fella named Ali, who has a problem, although he does not know it at first. When we meet him, he will be running along a road trying not to think about anything. Ali is a typical middle-manager in an omni-present Company that does what companies do; which is to say that they exist for the same reason that anything else does. The author claims to know Ali and that Ali is based on a real person. This cannot be true because he has told me things that violate the law of identity with regard to Ali; like that sometimes he's clearly a male and other times clearly a female. I have mentioned that Ali is actually an amalgamation of many people he knows, of all types and shapes and color and stuff. The author simply insists this isn't true. I don't know what to do.

Following the dictates of NE, B1, C6, §1, I will present the reader with the truth, as I seem to understand it. The author's main point seems to be something like this: organizations exist to serve themselves and once a person is in any organization, anything not part of that organization is seen as either negative or as inferior in some way. It is a classic story of, what the scholar-class call, "otherness." As my friends in the "industry" will say, the author seems to be really bad at accomplishing this in story form, which is why I keep interrupting like I am now; which is to say, I keep interrupting him to help you understand what he is doing.

The author continuously makes his point throughout the tale, and he is consistent with what I think his aim is; however, he doesn't always seem to be capable of distinguishing between formal existence and objective existence. This becomes problematic because things enter the story which have no objective existence and the author talks about them as though they do. If you understand the difference between Aristotelean logic and Boolean logic, that will make more sense because of existential import and the status of categorical propositions. If you do not know the difference between them, keep reading because it's unlikely to come up again. I will not need to give you an example here, now, because they are usually apparent, although sometimes I may have to point out that something either was or was not actually there; this might not always be possible because I'm not always able to confirm the author's veracity about these things. I'm worried this might complicate things later on in the story.

Ali seems to be as typical as anyone else. It is true that, because Ali is an amalgam, the author keeps changing a lot of accidental properties, things like Ali's biological sex, which is annoying; nevertheless, Ali is quite unremarkable. The author seems smitten with Ali at times, especially when Ali is female, but not when Ali is male; the reason for that is, "because." That was the explanation I got, when I asked the author why he wasn't smitten with the male Ali. The author simply said, "because." You can't really argue with that.

As previously mentioned, Ali has a problem, of which he is ignorant at the beginning. When we pick up, you will see what his initial problem is, which is apparent when you read the second sentence of the story, "Somewhere along the way, while he was trying to not concentrate on anything, his badge fell off and was lost forever; gone to that place where those things go." I will hold off on explaining more about the story because the author has begun to "create characters that we must endure." Oh, here he goes:

Our protagonist, Ali, has been working at the same Company for nearly twenty years. He has not been in the same department the entire time, mind you, he has moved an average of every two years or so; however, he has always been with the same Company. Since he started, he has "risen through the ranks" as the saying goes, but that is not the correct way of understanding how the Company works. There are no "ranks" like a military structure; however, the military mentality of a definitive and objective structure which is permanently present in some way, even when the rank itself isn't present, was present. If, dear reader, you are a veteran, that makes complete and total sense; if not, feel free to imagine any company, perhaps even the company that employs you. To my unemployed and/or unemployable reader, imagine the awfulness and horror of actually having a job. At the time of this story, Ali is a typical middle manager in a typical middle manager job, that is to say, he has responsibility, but no authority.

I am pained to do this, but the author has spent an incredible amount of time explaining to me the government system which Ali and the other Bunker Dwellers have developed. I cannot imagine how any of it has anything to do with Ali or this story in the least, especially given that I am not listening to the author's insistence that this takes place in an underground bunker; however, I think I can summarize it enough that I can satisfy the author's desire to get it in and yet spare you some of the legalese I was given. In keeping with Kant's definition of anarchy, that it is "Law and freedom without violence," the Philosopher Rulers, Kings being an unnecessary masculine anachronism, have instituted a policy that any person who does not commit him/herself to the public good on an action-by-action basis, must stand in a public pillory.

While standing in the pillory, the violator of the public good must announce all the social media commentary regarding his/her deeds. This apparently serves several functions: first, you cannot hide from anything while standing in a public pillory; second, the people are able to voice their grievances directly to the guilty and are able to have their voices heard; third, the shame of being in the pillory, and of having to read what your fellow dwellers think of you, is as effective a deterrent as you could imagine; far more effective than the death penalty because the law works very fast in the bunkers. If you're curious, it's "guilty!" and then immediately after the verdict, it's however long it takes that person to go to the bathroom and then walk to the pillory. There have been attempted stalls during this bathroom break, but eventually the guilty have to come out. The pillory sentence is over when people stop commenting about it for more than a week. The author has yet to explain how to enforce either the "public good on an action-by-action basis" or voluntary pillory shaming without the threat of violence; after all, a contract only works if it can be enforced and how do you do that while maintaining the peace on all sides? In other words, you cannot have a legal system without the threat of violence.

Of all the things about the Company, be they marvelous or malignant, forever or forgotten, one thing brings everyone together and that is the Company game of Cheepee. Cheepee is a Company activity which, upper management likes to stress, "is not a mandatory activity and is strictly voluntary." Upper management has stressed many times that Cheepee is not a requisite for employment with the Company. Ali himself is the co-cover for the Olives; however, there is a rumor circulating that he may be reassigned to the Gingers. Ali's teammates are Q, the team's box, Naomi, the team's other co-cover, and Fetch, the team's groove.

Q was born and raised in Guatemala. She said she talked to herself in Spanish and that her dreams were also in Spanish. She said her nightmares were never in her native tongue; rather, they were in a language she couldn't understand and that frightened her to hear. Q was a very sweet woman whom everyone liked; except the Uppers, because they hate all non-Uppers and most, if not all, other Uppers.

Naomi Houston was from Texas and "could prove it." For Naomi, "proof" was that she seemed to know every human being who: A. currently lived in Texas; B. had ever lived in Texas; C. might one day settle down in Texas; and D. had ever passed through Texas at some point in their lives. For Naomi, everything was about Texas; the history of the universe and all that had happened in it could be traced back to its true Texas origin. "The Star of Bethlehem" was actually "The Star of Waco" and Jesus was from "somewheres out 'n West Texas." The Pyramids of Egypt were actually found "'bout forty-mile southeast a' Odessa." Ponce de Leon was looking for the "Fountain of Texas" when he was killed in Florida. And the secret to bliss and the exact *telos* of all things can be located "down a hole in a holler 'bout two mile off a' Road D, right outside Memphis, TX, the birthplace a' President Elvis Presley! Yee-Haw!!" Whenever Naomi wanted to insult someone, she would say that person wasn't from Texas. If that someone happened to actually be from Texas, then that someone, "didn't have the Texas Spirit."

Fetch was a Southerner and had developed, what he called, Aggressive Southern Game, which, my friends, I should warn you the author will discuss later. Fetch was a good guy who seemed to be completely oblivious to the risks of life: he had been slapped in the face at least four-teen-thousand times; he smoked three packs of cigarettes a day, two of tobacco and one of marijuana; he drank one glass of water per ten drinks of alcohol and drank at least four glasses of water a day; and he had tried every drug that was reasonable to get and a disturbing number of drugs it was unreasonable to get. Be that as it may, he took it all with aplomb.

CHAPTER 2

WHERE THE AUTHOR BEGINS THE STORY PROPER, A BRIEF INTRODUCTION TO THE COMPANY, TO INCLUDE THE GROUNDS, AND THE MAIN CHARACTER CONSIDERS SOME THINGS; ALL THIS WHILE MOST OF US TRY TO UNDERSTAND THE BUNKER SITUATION.

As ALI WAS RUNNING down the road, he was trying not to think about anything. Somewhere along the way, while he was trying to not concentrate on anything, his badge fell off and was lost forever; gone to that place where those things go. The irony, Ali thought much later, was that had he not been trying to practice Zen at the moment he was running then he probably would have noticed his badge fall off in the first place. At the moment though, he was wondering how not to think about anything at all. He had overheard two Snails talking, and one of them said, "You have to release your mind of all thoughts and let yourself be free."

"But how do I do that, sensei?" the other Snail had asked.

"One must never hold on to a thought; one must accept that thoughts will enter the mind."

"But if thoughts will enter, oh honorable sensei, how am I to free my mind? It is as though you ask me to pay no attention to the guests in my home, even though my home is wide open and they will enter of their own accord."

The Snail called Sensei chuckled and said, "Ah little friend, you are young and you still speak silly words. You should seek a better way of understanding the problem, for when you encounter a puzzle, you rush into the maze and see only the walls. First, one must seek the destination, and that will give rise to the way. If one has that, one cannot help to be happy and never lost. Let us begin anew, with the destination. Where do you wish to go?"

"I do not understand, sensei."

"Then you have far to go to learn to free your mind." At this the Snails disappeared and Ali never got to hear anything further about how one should free the mind. He kept thinking about his destination. He was running towards the north junction, toward the Statue of Progress. Every time he thought about it, it would remind him to free his mind. This of course made the "clop, clop" of his shoes on the road a very persistent invitation to fill his mind with something other than clop, clop.

Running along Company Road, right before sunrise, was Ali's favorite time of day. It wasn't that everything went downhill from his morning run; it was just a nice relaxing time he could enjoy by himself, away from the hubbub of Company life. He needed to keep his endurance level high for the Cheepee quarterfinals as the Olives were the only group to utilize the 1-2-0-1 strategy and he didn't want to be out-covered by Naomi. Naomi was the Bureau of Actions' Non-Supervisory-Level Adjudicator, as well as an official Delegate of and Ambassador for Texas, which meant she was an Upper and he didn't need the hassle of an Upper on his case. Something else not to be ignored, he wasn't from Texas. It made absolutely no difference that he could not control that fact; it was as though he was a Hat-field, a Montague, or a plain old Catholic sinner. As stupid as it sounds, Naomi was a Texasist. Ali told her this, that she was a Texasist, to which Naomi had said, "and damned proud of it." I mentioned to the author that was true of most "ist" beliefs. I don't think he heard me because he kept telling me about the story.

The first rays of the sun began peaking over the horizon. If, dear readers, you have situated this in the Midwest, then it really needs to be slightly east of the Rockies; if you've situated yourself in the Pacific Northwest, then this needs to be slightly east of the Cascades; or for the brave, some say foolhardy, you could position this tale slightly east of the Olympics. As you can clearly see for yourself, this story cannot be in an underground bunker, despite the author's continued insistence on it. Friends, don't get me wrong, I like the author as well as you; the problem is, his insistence on certain points seems to be unreasonable at times, and now is a good time to show you how that is true. In the bunkers, which is not where this is happening, there is no system of money. This, of course, has been attempted, with more or less success, in countless fictional and historical examples: two cases being the movie *The Village* and the non-movie version of the actual Incan empire, respectively. The Bunker Dwellers did not observe the principle of ownership or property and instead based their lives on communal practices reinforced with principles of personal responsibility and reasonable self-reliance. As you can clearly see, that wasn't the unreasonable part.

There was a shaft coming from the surface to a chamber in the bunkers; keep in mind, it is unclear to me whether that shaft leads to its own bunker or a chamber somewhere in the bunkers; when I asked, the author said, "it makes no difference, that isn't the point." I find his lack of an answer disconcerting. This light somehow illuminates the entire chamber and then exits the chamber at the same time each day. During that time the ray of light illuminates a wall which contains a mosaic that is a picture of "our dear leader." The author will not tell me who this person is, even though I said I really needed to know. He replied, "No, you don't." His terse response was unsettling. This mural is down a long tunnel or hallway and the light shines perfectly on the mosaic for ten minutes every morning. This Abu Simbel event is witnessed by everyone in the bunker as a type of morning worship or something very similar, in both function and actualization. See, that is completely unreasonable because how does that happen every day at the same time? Personally, I think the author has confused the way the Earth moves through space with something completely different; what that is, I haven't the slightest idea.

As Ali was running and the sun was rising, he caught a glimpse of light, like the flashing of a mirror, from the top of Ditch Peak. Ditch Peak was a "mountain" that was not part of the Rockies/Cascades/Olympics proper; rather, it was situated as a type of sentinel mountain, like Kafka's Keepers of the Law, standing vigil over the plains before the earth was folded up and the mountains were made. Ditch Peak was situated behind the main Company grounds and was theoretically ascendable. There was a road that led to the peak, but there was a guard-shack and the guard gave Ali a gorilla-like gaze of such ferocity that merely turning in that direction might mean trouble.

The Statue of Progress was a good destination for his run because it was at the end of a long, flat road. His turn-around spot sat at a three-way T-intersection. To the left was the guard shack and the road to the summit of Ditch Peak. To the right was a road that led off into the distance, but that too was always closed. The road itself seemed to be completely intact and navigable but there was a "road closed" sign chained across two Jersey barriers that blocked off the road to car traffic. From behind the Jersey barriers the road led off into the expanse of the grounds to the northeast. The road wasn't marked on any map Ali had ever seen of the grounds.

Ali stopped at the turnaround and took a drink of water, stretching his right quad, which he hoped was just tight and not going to cause him any problems. As he stood there, stretching and drinking, he looked up at the summit to see if he could recognize what had caused the flash. The gleam had lasted a brief moment, like a lighthouse that made one revolution and then went dark. Whatever it had been was too far away to see, if it had come from the peak itself. Ali didn't know how high the mountain was exactly, but he knew he wouldn't have been able to run to the top. He walked across the road, closer to the guard shack, all the while still looking up toward the summit.

"Get back, asshole!" Ali jumped backwards. He was standing in the middle of the road, in between the white shoulder line and the double-yellow line. The guard from the guard shack was screaming at the top of his lungs. Ali watched as the guard ran towards him. "I said get back, asshole." Ali looked around, he wasn't sure where he was supposed to get back to, there was only the empty road.

Ali thought it was comical that the guard was so fervent in his duty. Ali had never once seen a car this far out on Company Road; traffic only ever went to the Multi. The Multi was on Company Road, Ali passed it every time he ran, but it was several miles behind him. There was nothing for any employee to use this stretch of road for; there was nothing out here worth coming to see. Ali thought that this would be a good time to practice Zen again.

Then he got very scared. The guard, who was only about

two-hundred feet away, had stopped. He said, "I have the authorization to kill you where you stand, should I feel you are a threat to me or if you violate the rules on the sign." The guard had his hand on his holstered gun and he had thumbed off the safety strap. From the look of it, he was fully prepared to draw and fire. He looked like he was fifteen-years-old and a master FPS player.

Ali didn't want to mince words or point out that there wasn't a sign anywhere. He also didn't want to admit that he didn't know the rules the guard was referencing. His eyes were still bouncing back and forth between the gun and the guard's eyes. Ali instinctually raised his hands and said, "I'm sorry. Please don't shoot me. I'm backing up. I'm no threat to you, officer." When Ali reached the far shoulder, the guard turned around and went back to the shack without saying another word. As he walked back, Ali saw him thumb the strap back down over the pistol.

Ali turned and began to run back toward the Multi. He was shaking like a leaf; he didn't know what was on the peak but it wasn't worth getting shot for, that was certain. His adrenaline carried him easily to the Multi, which towered up on his right, catching the sun's early morning light and shining like a sigil of technology and engineering. The Multi was where every Company event was held, from management seminars to Cheepee matches. The Colossus of Rhodes would have bowed before the Multi; the Hanging Gardens of Babylon would have wilted at its magnificence. I would describe the Multi to you, my dear friends, but it would be pointless. I asked the author to tell me about the actual building itself, so I could describe it to you and enrich your life; however, his explanation of it was not all that helpful. "Imagine the majesty of the Rose Window," he said to me. "Now imagine the beauty of the Taj Mahal. Now picture the sheer magnitude of the Grand Canyon." "Okay, I've got that all in mind." "It is all rubbish compared to the Multi; the Multi is better than those things. There, I've described it." See, to me, that is not helpful in the least.

Whenever anything happened which might be even remotely considered entertainment by members of the Company, it happened at the Multi. As Ali ran past it, he thought about the email that had reminded everyone that, "Upper management reminds all employees that use of the Multi is a privilege, and not a right. No employee's career will be held in ransom for non-use of the Multi. Membership is strictly voluntary."

Ali headed back home, which was on Company grounds. Dear reader, this, I admit, is a tricky position for me. If I explain where Ali lives, then I have to take you under the Earth and into the bunkers. There are several dilemmas here: the place Ali lives is, according to the author, below ground in the bunkers. However, later on, in this same story, you will read this: "As he was watering his lawn, Ali saw…" Don't worry about who and what and why, which is all appropriate stuff you should be asking if you focus on the two words after the comma; however, the real action, right now, is the bit before the comma. If Ali lives in an underground bunker, then what is he using to water the lawn? You ought not squander your potable water on lawn maintenance if you live underground, that seems irresponsible. Also, why are there lawns at all in the bunkers?

Lastly, there are parts, again, in this same story, that clearly take place where Ali lives and also, at the same time, clearly outside. It is a bit of a spoiler, and hopefully you will forgive me, my friends, but after the Olives win the quarterfinals, the team is having a BBQ at Ali's house and are driven inside by "a sudden and unexpected, yet delightful and spritely, afternoon shower. The joyful occasion, coupled with an air of esprit de corps shared by those people who win things, was too felt by every heart to let dump dampen their happiness; yet inside they went." In a bunker-style, doomsday scenario, wouldn't the "sprightly, afternoon shower" actually be a burst pipe in the ceiling that needed to be immediately fixed? I mention these things because the author said, Ali finished his run and found the secret spot to his bunker entrance, which he de-armed, unlocked, and then slipped into, as silent and stealthy as the extinct jungle cat of legend, the leopard. Before he disappeared from the surface, he considered his world.

There are those lot that never step foot on the Company grounds proper. These horrific abominations, who dwell in the actual-empty wastes outside Company grounds, are told tales of wonder, of trash-free streets, safe alleys in both the day and night, and food for all, even the poor. Their leprous young are told stories of the Company grounds, which these illiterate fools call "orporatio," the forbidden place. These tales offer them hope, anything to divert their feeble minds to something other than their own sad lot. This group calls themselves the Paddi'u, the unlucky ones, the heavy-clothed. They are never referred to as anything positive by anyone else; they never even speak of themselves as anything positive. They are a cursed lot, their fates their own, without even gods to help them. This sad lot will not burden us here, the author says, for the Paddi'u are a lost bunch, as no one will remember them, not even long enough to forget to grieve for them.

Those who work for the Company but do not inhabit the Company bunkers are the Snails. Snails are often seen but one never ventures to engage one of these vile things in any type of conversation. They dwell in the mostly-empty wastes between the actual-empty wastes and the Company grounds and are only allowed entry into buildings after medical examination and after being injected with a poison that kills them after twenty-four hours. The antidote is stored somewhere off Company grounds and the Snails are only given the location fifty-nine minutes before the twenty-four-hour period is over. People who have to speak to these grotesqueries have often repeated "Snail Tales" that are surely the work of the imagination; some of these things cannot be true. The Snails were as indistinguishable as strawberry and cherry jelly beans in a bell jar. One never had to fear the Snails; but there was much to fear from the Paddi'u.

Now you see what I mean. I am at a loss as to how to reconcile what just happened. The Paddi'u and the Snails, two of whom we have already read about, make a slight amount of sense in the non-bunker scenario. However, you would be hard pressed to explain them in the bunker version because, well, you read it. What am I supposed to do with the antidote idea? This all disappears if the author had said, "Ali finished his run and went inside his house to take a shower."

It was getting late and Ali needed to get to work. He got ready, grabbed breakfast, and then got in a maggot to go to work. While in the maggot, Ali plugged his phone into the wall and listened to Company news, Company weather, and Company music. Before they had installed the phone jacks, in an effort to give the riders a more "immersive experience," the maggot, as it travelled between bunkers, very much like a subway system, made a sloppy, squishy noise, like it was crawling along a tunnel. This was done as both a punishment and a reminder of what the people had done to destroy the surface, making it necessary to live in the bunkers. As further punishment you had to enter the front and exit the back of the maggot. The author said at a meeting of the council of Philosopher Rulers some lunatic had suggested, in an attempt to demonstrate further contrition, that to accompany the squish of the maggot's crawl, a fine spray of non-potable water and honey should mist out over everyone riding in the maggot. The Philosopher Rulers said "no" to this idea without hesitation or elucidation. The Z-Ruler gave a firm and resolute shake of the head.

Topside, Ali got off the Company tram, having ridden it since the Company outlawed personal vehicles. This was a wise strategy overall since it reduced carbon emissions, despite it tending to foster corporate colonialism. The tram did not look like the inside of a maggot, nor were the riders sprayed with something surely lethal, as was suggested by some lunatic. Ali got off the tram, thanked the driver and walked toward the security gate. Before him, on the left, was the massive Bureau of Action building; to its right was the equally massive Bureau of Information building. Behind both of them stood the small, diminutive Boss Shack, where the CEO was rumored to work. Ali walked up to the gate and reached into his pocket. He realized that he didn't have his badge.

CHAPTER 3

READERS ARE INTRODUCED TO THE MASSIVE BUREAU OF AC-
TION BUILDING; A FIRE BREAKS OUT IN THE BUNKERS; THE
AUTHOR PRESENTS A MODERN ETHICAL DILEMMA AND RESORTS
TO VIOLENCE INSTEAD OF REASON; AND ALI'S OFFICE-SPOUSE
COMES TO THE RESCUE.

FEW THINGS IN THE world rival the beauty of a bureaucratic building. The rectangleness is geometric preci-
sion; the dumpiness is a monument to all things squatty.
The Bureau of Action building, also known as Building 40,
was the squattiest of dumpy rectangles; the building probably knew this and was always somewhat slightly squattier
on sunny days and somewhat dumpier on rainy days. Indeed, employees, in their own odd way of using vocabulary, would often speak of the weather as though it were
Building 40, sometime called the "temible cubo confuso;"
many a family picnic being upset by dumpy weather. Often as not, a family found itself going to the shore, it being
a surprisingly squatty weekend.

The temible cubo confuso, also known as the Squat, was actually a near perfect cube. When the building had been commissioned in 1982, the Company had spared no expense and hired the eccentric and brilliant architect, Bruce McMilMcMitch. Mr. McMilMcMitch, being an eccentric genius, had proven his worth when he designed some other company's building. That building is a marvel of engineering. It is, in essence, a self-contained eco-bubble. Parts of the building move when the people are moving, which puts you in mind of a hamster-wheel. This is of course all done behind the scenes and the employees were rewarded for walking. This also helped them generate their own heat within the building. The water system was all recycled; the trash was all reused, everything that was compostable was made into fertilizer. This was done, incidentally, in the bunkers as well. The reasoning was different, as were some of the mechanics, but pragmatics are what they are.

Two notable differences between the other company's self-contained eco-bubble and the bunkers were: first, the other company's eco-bubble was designed by Bruce McMilMcMitch and the bunkers' eco-bubble was designed by Peter Klaus, the Head of Technocracy and whom you will meet later. Second, the other building had an array of Snails to keep the place clean; whereas, in the bunkers, the effects of misuse were felt immediately and punishment was more in keeping with what Ea told Enlil after the Flood.

The other company's building was a testament to environmental responsibility. That company held the patent to all the environmental designs and the features and mechanisms that made that building something to be treasured by all humankind. McMilMcMitch had given full ownership of his design to that company and was prepared to make an even more pronounced statement with his next building, the Squat, sometimes referred to as the M4 Project. With this, McMilMcMitch promised cutting edge science and "constantly improving aesthetic qualities that will cause one's teeth to weep and gnash."

The other company owned the patents to all of McMilMcMitch's inventions and therefore they could not be utilized by others without copyright infringement. Even though these patents could have helped people and could have saved the planet and prevented people from having to live in the bunkers, they did not share them. It doesn't matter though; a select few were made wealthier while the rest suffered. The wealthy provided bread and games and only destroyed things a little at a time; the wealthy had fresh food and clean water, so like I said, it doesn't matter.

Bruce McMilMcMitch was driving home one night, his new design complete and sealed in his dossier. The night being heavy with the dump, McMilMcMitch was killed when his car ran off the road. The Company was devastated, not the least reason was that they wanted a better building than the other company. While cleaning McMilMcMitch's office, a young protégée found a folder labelled, "BoA, 40." The protégée, being a protégée of both McMilMcMitch and the Company, rushed the plans to his boss. Inside the folder was a rough sketch of a blank cube. The Company wanted its money's worth so they set about building what they touted as, "Bruce McMilMcMitch's final building. A building which, according to the legend and architect himself, 'will cause one's teeth to weep and gnash.'"

The other company's building was a marvel. The M4 Project, also known as the BoA, was not a marvel; it was a giant cube. It was not a tesseract, as the author has claimed at times; nor is there a room within the building that contains a locked door that has a sign over the door that says, "Abandon Hope." It was not built in any coherent fashion, which, from an aesthetic standpoint, made the building very interesting. The first thing the Company did was build a giant cube. That was it. If you have ever seen the building that NASA used to house the upright STS, then that was a fair approximation.

For six months the Company had simply stayed with this design. For six months people who worked in the BoA, at this time called "the Box," were simply working in a giant, one floor aircraft hangar. It had no electricity, no HVAC, no plumbing; it had two doors, in the middle of opposite walls. Someone suggested that adding another floor to the one floor might have its advantages and that idea stuck. Very slowly, the building was built, a floor at a time. On average, it took roughly seven months for someone to comment that, "another floor would be nice," or something to that effect. Eventually, all the horizontal and vertical space was occupied but after another six months someone commented, "wouldn't lights be nice," and then other niceties kept cropping up, like plumbing, and HVAC, and an elevator. All of this happened independently on each floor. The effect was that each lower floor was always less technologically advanced than the floor above it and the elevators did not go from floor to floor, just one floor at a time; a trip to the fifth floor could take an almost infinite number of elevator rides after the first floor because most elevators only went up or down, not up and down.

The author informed me that the bunkers were facing this problem because "they too were following the same sorry road humanity has always taken and is likely to always take." He said that the bunkers were following an expansionist view of population migration and were mostly working their way laterally, that is, more or less at the same distance under the Earth. Geologically this is because the deeper you go the harder it is to get through the rock. This is true generally speaking; however, for the precise reader, it varies from place to place because of the material you are having to displace and what you intend to do with the displaced material. For my more fanciful reader, if you were a creature of the earth from folklore, like a dwarf or an earth elemental, then you would have a distinct advantage in probably every possible way.

Politically, the bunkers were spreading because of competition in resources and the non-social idea of the individual right to procreate at your own discretion. At first the bunkers existed in a state of equilibrium; however, once the inhabitants were given freedoms, like Glasnost, there was no restricting those freedoms in any meaningful way. There were six main political factions, the seppuku rule having been easily sidestepped years earlier, and the tension and electricity was in the bunker air about a fusion between factions. A fire started, gutting whole parts of the bunker. After the blaze was contained, three children lay dead and much of the potable water had been contaminated by the smoke and debris.

An investigation commenced and six suspects were arrested; it was discovered that all six were each a member of all six parties. Each had been given the mission to start the fire and make it look like another, or all the other, political parties had started it. The Philosopher Rulers were unsure how to handle the punishment for these six. The K-Ruler said they deserve what the freedom and logic of their actions dictate they receive, in this case that meant death. The U-Ruler said they should be punished in accord to that which would generate the overall most positive good in the bunker, in this case that meant death. The NL-Ruler said they should be met with the will of the members of the bunker, in this case that meant death. The Z-Ruler said nothing. The F-Ruler said that the guilt of the actions would serve as a punishment in and of itself and that additional punishment was unnecessary; the F-Ruler said that death was unnecessary, not excessive. The other Rulers listened; three children were composted; the pillory stood empty.

The main floor of "the Box," which they had renamed "Cube Town," was dedicated to the office of administration and paperwork for the Bureau of Action. The demagogue of this floor was Betty Cust, a mean and nasty tempered woman who was also the Indigo groove. She was a very good groove because she was extremely surly and caustic. She lorded over information like it was antidote for the Snails. You simply could not get to the second floor without passing her desk. She was a human Cerberus who guarded the staircase and First Elevator, the only elevator to go from the first to fifth floor, with all the patience of Job. Rumor had it that her mother was an actual nurse shark and she didn't require sleep, only constant motion to keep herself wound up, like some weird, angry perpetual motion machine. Because it was the bottom floor, and thus the first built, it seemed to never get an intelligent update in technology or décor.

Floor two was where one found the office of Roberto Piso, the Decision Directorate. Roberto was a fine man, with a school boy charm and an enormous head, which provided a great deal of padding for his school boy brain. As the Decision Directorate he was very passionate, some might say zealous. There was no whim Roberto was not willing to attempt, should an Upper suggest it. Roberto had been known to request volunteers to "shoe" other company VIPs. Anyone who volunteered was given one day of paid vacation; the only thing the volunteer was required to do was to tend to the foot needs of any of the VIPs, should anything happen where a "shoe" was needed. "Shoe" became a very popular term in the Deep, reaching such epic proportions of use that it, for a while, supplanted the F-bomb. Many a shout of "Shoe you, you stupid shoeing muthershoer," and "Well, shoe my life," and once, "Shoe me harder, I'm a naughty thing," were heard. Most people dreaded the sight of Roberto because there was almost no telling what "opportunity to shine" he was about to unload on you. Roberto was also the Yellow support.

Floor three was where Naomi Houston's office was and it was generally a very decent place to go; if you liked Texas. Naomi had the governor of Texas establish her whole floor as an official part of Texas. Walking into her actual office was like walking into a Texas Roadhouse restaurant, peanut shells littered the floor. Naomi would sit at her desk, leaning back in a chair with her cowgirl boots on the desk, suck at peanut shells, and spit them out onto the floor. She did this with unbelievable grace and sexuality; man or woman, to watch her made you hope that when you died you would come back as one of her peanuts.

Directly above Naomi was the floor of Beard Plott, the Supervisor-Level Adjudicator. Beard was a measly little man who had more power within the Company than anyone understood. Officially, Beard was the spokesman for all Company employees who supervised someone. Beard had restructured the Company in such a way that everyone supervised someone, especially since Beard had argued that "everyone is someone, and someone has to be in charge of them; therefore, I'm in charge of them." What this meant in reality was that Beard was somehow able to be involved in matters which he should not have had any say in at all. He was constantly competing with Naomi, who was vastly more popular. Given the restructuring that Beard had managed, he was attempting to have Naomi's job phased out, since there were no non-supervisors; as Beard put it to Naomi, "there are no non-someone's; therefore, you are a no one." Beard was co-groove of the Yellows, they and the Gingers being the most aggressive of the Cheepee teams.

The last accessible floor was where the Ginger co-groove, Booster Matthis, worked. Booster was the Underminister of Action, and therefore the second most powerful person in the BoA. His floor was a palace and was so technologically advanced that it seemed to be a magical kingdom. Booster himself was never known to have left the building. One of Ali's fellow Deeplings told him she once saw a map that showed a tunnel from the BoA to the Multi. Many people believed that Booster was able to become a semi-corporeal mist-like being that only ever went from his office to the Multi. He had a tiny bathroom in his office that had been designed for him to defecate while standing up, allowing him to discharge his duties of correcting employee rating reports while discharging his doodies. The only thing Booster ever seemed to be doing, indeed the only thing anyone had ever seen him doing, was editing and reviewing employee rating reports. Roberto Piso had once accidently left the wrong folder on Booster's desk. The folder was of a recently executed employee, Burt Deitas, and Booster, being the machine of bureaucratic efficiency that he was, had promoted Burt to the head of R&D. Two weeks went by before anyone realized Burt was both dead and in charge of R&D. When someone else was named head of R&D, morale within the entire department plummeted. One employee was overheard to say, "Mr. Deitas was the best boss I ever had. These last two weeks were our most productive."

Ali had been in the BoA on only one occasion, although he had been working with the Company for nearly twenty years. The one occasion had been when he was first hired and was told he needed to go meet with all the Uppers. He had met Betty Cust, who was pacing around her desk. Ali had walked meekly up to the desk and asked if Betty could help him. Betty looked at Ali and said, "What?" Betty snarled and poisonous acid dripped from her mouth and onto the desk.

"My name is Ali. I'm new and I…"

"Deepling?"

"Excuse me?"

"Where do you work?" Betty demanded.

"Over in the building in the hill."

"I'm actually in charge around here, and I know everything." Betty offered this to Ali, despite his not even asking. How thoughtful.

"Okay. I need to set appointments with the people on this list," Ali said as he handed her the new-employee orientation list.

Betty looked at the list. She handed Ali a pen and said, "write 'n/a' beside every name except mine. You don't need to see them, it's formality anyway. You will meet them all later." Ali did as Betty said and had left. The encounter was so long ago that Ali couldn't remember it very well.

The author told me that Betty had violated a bunker rule about not having more than six players on your bar trivia team. She had some friends from another bunker visit her in her bunker. They had penetrated the actual-empty wastes and escaped the clutches of the cursed and doomed Paddi'u, the cannibal tribes of the scorched grounds, as the French call them. During trivia, where the answer sheet clearly says, "No more than six people per team," she and her seven friends formed a team. They won first prize and were complemented by the trivia host for getting twenty out of twenty correct. This caused a tremendous amount of tension in the bunker. The author said that many of the Bunker Dwellers were stockpiling weapons and getting ready for the "coming trivia apocalypse" and many people were seeing the images of saints in the cracks of the bunker walls; especially in hard-to-reach places, like in the bunker bathrooms, behind the toilet seat in the second stall. The author said it could have been a saint, but it was hard to tell given the angle you had to be in to even see it.

Most of the blame fell on the bunker trivia host, the former Keith O'Der, who went missing one night while out checking something in one of the bunker outbuildings, however that works. Keith was found with eight of his fingers broken, six knives having been driven into his heart. A trivia answer sheet with "No more than six people per team" highlighted was superglued to his face. The author said the real ethical dilemma was this: given there is a social norm in place amongst the regulars/locals in the bar, that norm being to have fewer than seven people per team, then what should you do about newbies/non-locals who come in and either through ignorance or through something else upset the balance of the people who do follow the rules? You cannot chastise the newbies/non-locals because you need the new business for the bar; however, you need the loyalty of locals to provide a solid base for the bar. After much debate amongst the Philosopher Rulers, it was decided that the new trivia host would also reiterate that teams may not be more than six, as the trivia answer sheet clearly says.

The new trivia host, Keith O'Ter, has seen many of the regulars highlighting the rule, "No more than six people per team," and commenting what a shame it was that Keith O'Der was found missing all his internal organs. That was true and only the killers knew that fact. And the media. And anyone the media told. Except it was a leak of false true information concocted by the bunker media; except the media didn't name the source, it only said, "sources said only the killers know that Keith O'Der was found with all his organs missing." So, no one knew what the killers knew and did not know; nor did the media know what they knew or did not know. Everyone knew the girl with blue hair killed Keith, but no one knew who did what with the organs. That was the weirdest part of all that.

Ali felt around for his badge. People were streaming into the security grotto for processing and screening. The guard had been looking at Ali since he had stopped short of the grotto. Ali looked down; he was standing with his toes on the red line. The red line was accompanied by a sign that said, "All persons stepping past this line are subject to and subjects of the Company. Stepping across the red line demonstrates that said stepper rescinds the right to the principle of forfeiture. Have a great day!"

"What's wrong love? Are you about to get yourself into trouble?" Ali took a step back and looked around. Her office-spouse, Maggie, the Company Future Accident Negation Officer, and the Red box, was walking toward her. Ali and Maggie had been office married for six or seven years; neither really knew the exact date. Maggie was a stunner; she was tall and had the smoking-hot body of a salutatorian. Her fire auburn hair and eyebrows were like a sunset. Ali knew it made her gay, but she wanted to have sex with Maggie very, very badly.

Dear reader, I'm sure you caught that switch that was

pulled on you. It, as you have probably now guessed, since I mentioned it, was, in fact, the author and not me. I stood my ground and, ladies and gentlemen, you should have seen and heard me having a discussion with the author about this; we were both up in arms. At one point I read the entirety of Chapter Two back to him! A few minutes later, the author picked up an epee and nearly ran me through. Luckily, I always take notes with pen and paper and used my pen in a swift and deft riposte, ha-ha, I will not be foiled. The author had sharpened his epee like a bastard sword on one side and that was ridiculously unfair. First, he sharpened it because there has been a thief in the bunkers and people practice non-Christian virtues there; you're allowed to kill whomever has offended you so long as two neighbors agree and assist in the killing. It isn't because they don't believe people have value, you can believe in that without reference to the Almighty or by practicing non-religious values, you can think love gives things intrinsic value, for example; or, that life is intrinsically valuable without need to reference its origin.

Second, the author believes in fighting honorably. The first rule to fighting honorably is to never, ever fight fairly. If there is a contradiction there, everyone is guilty.

Third, the author is not above fighting unfairly either. At one point in the battle the author must have tied the epee to something, like a prehensile tail. It wasn't really an epee anymore, either; it was, to be honest, like a giant razor whip, the author having bought an XX-long epee from somewhere "over the great desert," (he never told me which one) and he was swinging it like a freakin' weeping willow tree branch using a strong, titan overhand swing. Like I said, he must have tied it to something because at one point I was dodging the epee and he was swinging both of his hands at me. I had to take the slapping from his left hand, which was cold and limp and when it hit me it felt like I was being slapped with a dead fish. Not a big fish, like a trout, but more like a panfish from the local pond, something little Billy can catch and throw back and feel proud.

This all started because I asked, "Isn't Ali a guy?"

CHAPTER 4

COVERS.

Few positions in the game of Cheepee offer the thrill, the excitement, and the all-encompassing beauty of the cover. If a team has a good cover, then that team must be taken seriously. The cover is considered, by many, to be the playmaker on the Cheepee field; however, there are those who adamantly defend the groove as the playmaker. Dear readers, the author and I are in total agreement about this, as are all the other covers in the Company, as well as the ones who would be covers if they did not live in the bunkers, where Cheepee isn't so much "played" as it is a strategy to survive and thus "lived."

We are also in total agreement that Carey Gugglo, Maroons '02 – '04, is without a doubt the greatest cover to ever play the game. Even after the prohibition against live ammo in the game, Carey still wore full tactical body armor, an unnecessary seventy-eight pounds of inflexible metal. When explosions were banned after the first and only intentional explosion in a Cheepee match, Carey still wore blast padding, ninety-seven extra pounds. Carey was considered completely insane on a Cheepee field. She would follow every rule in the topside rulebook. She was rumored to have memorized the entire 1,969-page section on when and how and where and why someone is allowed to call a time-out. Incredible!

Her genius, nay, her madness, came from the fact that she, among all Cheepee covers to ever play for more than twelve months, had not once been fined by the Company during or after the game or been sent to wrestle the otters in the snake den during the match; wrestling otters in a snake den being the standard penalty for all Cheepee rule infractions during the '02 season.

As I have said, Carey was without a contested doubt the best cover to play the game. Everyone agrees on it. What no one agrees about is whether Carey was a real "Company woman." Some fiercely regard her as a traitor because she worked for the Company; others called her a hypocrite because she was the Company "lateral thinking organizer and head" and was in charge of creating innovative and "out-of-the-box" solutions to problems. There were more rules in that department than anyone could hope to know; still others called her a maverick who was working "from within." As a cover she once jumped two running emus; that is a noumenal demonstration of her brilliance.

The reason her character was debated was because Pauline Anderson published an article in the Company newsletter that was lauded "a masterpiece for the common employee" and something about Pauline being the true voice of the workers. Pauline's article said something to this effect: the workers were given all the necessary information regarding the construction of a more social transportation system (e.g., mass transit). In the bunkers this was jokingly called, "breeding the maggots." In order to pay for this, the Company was going to tax the workers who owned cars, this being before cars were outlawed in an effort to foster corporate colonialism. The algorithm used to calculate the taxes necessary to pay for this did not make a lot of sense, and the company hired to write the algorithm even said it was a work in progress, TBD, and the details would be given after the vote. The workers voted "yes" to the tax.

Then the tax man cometh and everyone's good will was extinguished when the workers saw how much good will actually costs them. A roar went up over the misunderstanding and the Company said the company was bad! The company said all the necessary info was there, it just was not conveniently laid out or easy to find, especially when you are either busy working and/or you do not pay attention to the thing for which you are voting. The Company said the company was bad!

Pauline's article said that, after all the money was collected from this new tax, a meager 63.16 would be transferred from point A to point B. To quiet the collective groanings of the workers, it was announced that the Company would give some of this 63.16 back to the workers, but not a lot, maybe something like 0.00000001% each. This was to satisfy the workers who were complaining about the new tax. The Company actually surprised everyone and gave them back 0.0000001%, which made everyone happy because of the unexpected windfall.

Carey, on the other hand, was not that kind of worker and did not vote for the tax increase because the initial figure was very, very large (not 63.16 large but about 20.15, which is still large when you consider that those numbers are in millions of dollars) and money does not work like subatomic particles or Naomi defending the Alamo, i.e., it has to come from somewhere.

Carey's position was that the Company's solution was to hire another company to fix the problem. Carey said that this "fix" would add a level of bureaucracy to a system that was already suffering from the burdens of bureaucracy. This, Carey said, was evidenced by the fact that the workers needed the Company to hire the company to fix what the workers wanted and had asked for in the first place. The Company said the company did not present the information to the workers as it would directly impact an individual worker, and the fact that the information was not conveniently located within a thumb scroll of the Cheepee scores or your Friends Unified Collective account, was blamed.

Carey's bravery and audacity as a cover was rewarded with her becoming a groove. Unfortunately, Carey was only an average groove, and she faded into obscurity.

There is a secret organization within the bunker complex, known simply as "the Prynne," which claim Carey was a demi-god and that she had been given the gift of prophesy but had suffered Cassandra's ironic fate. Their doctrines are said to be simplicity themselves; however, in order to join you must make a demanding and horrifying sacrifice. No one will say what the sacrifice is: those who have made the sacrifice suffer the shame of their courage; those who could not make it suffer the shame of their cowardice. Each of the members bear a strange, identical mark on the body.

The author says that the Prynne are not as organized as people believe. The most common thing they do is sit around and produce signs that say "Wake Up" and "Think." I tend to agree with the author because he is a member of the Prynne and he has the key to the storehouse they use. It's a small building but it is crammed to over-spilling with crafting supplies. There was also an incredible number of "Wake Up" and "Think" signs. There were enough slogans for action that every Bunker Dweller could be given 3.18 signs.

The problem with the Prynne, said the author, was that they did not have a "starter;" someone who could actually "get the ball rolling." Instead of doing anything productive they mainly occupied their time by meeting every Saturday from 1pm – 3pm in the bunker sub-basement under the library and making signs. Sometimes someone would bring cake or cookies; most often not though. The actual meeting places where they discuss "action" are a secret to the non-Prynne. The author inadvertently let it slip that there has actually never been an "action meeting" although it is occasionally mentioned; most often not though.

I asked the author if they were like Freemasons and he said no. He said the Freemasons were an organization that had famous members in the past; whereas the Prynne had an unclever literary name and no one seemed to care at all about them. The sacrifice thing, although true (I know this because the author said, "I can't tell you, I'm too ashamed of my courage," whatever the hell that means) is lame. It turns out the sexy part of the organization is in not knowing much about it; once you're in, it was a big let-down. They had good sign-makers though, so there is a positive in all this. Art matters.

One thing that made the Prynne so popular amongst the bunker youth was that they created illicit art. Dear readers, I think I can handle this:

"How does the activity of making signs create 'illicit art?' Seriously, what the hell does illicit art even mean?"

"Come on now, don't be daft, art can be illegal."

"Sure, some 'art' could be illegal; for example, pornography or sexually explicit art could be illegal if it involved someone without the capacity to consent. Child pornography would fall into this category, but only if you counted that as art, which I don't think qualifies, categorically."

"There you have it," the author said with a completely unjustified yet smug sense of satisfaction.

"There I have what?"

"An example of illicit art."

"Wait a minute, the Prynne aren't engaged in child pornography, they are making signs. How is a sign illicit?"

"Because in the bunkers the Philosopher Rulers have banned all art," the author said, somewhat perturbed.

"Oh, this is happening in the bunkers?"

"Of course, the whole story takes place in the bunkers."

My dear friends, I walked right into that. I was only half paying attention anyway and I thought we were still topside. Apparently, the Philosopher Rulers have banned art in the bunkers for a very bizarre reason, see if you follow any of this:

The P-Ruler said that art was three levels removed from the real source of the art, which was apparently either a guy named Art or some weird personification and/or objectivization of the concept, thus Art proper. There are Bunker Dwellers who actually have small personal shrines to both Art the guy and Art the universal concept. Both types of shrine are contraband material in the bunkers.

This episode of the Philosopher Ruler's discussion was absolutely crazy to watch happen. All of their discussions were open forum and completely transparent. When they had disagreements, which happened with far more regularity than you'd think, it could be a very entertaining spectacle. Most of the time they were blathering on about the most complicated and inane topics which meant, pretty much, absolutely nothing to the Bunker Dwellers, either personally or collectively. However, when they had a disagreement on an actual bunker policy, or got into arguments about basic matters of principle, the show was on; the author seems eager to get to it!

The P-Ruler said that producing things that are both wrong and stupid was a terrible idea and thus art was forbidden in the bunkers. The VE-Ruler said, "What on earth are you talking about?" The Z-Ruler raised his eyebrows. The U-Ruler said, "How does that work?" The other Philosopher Rulers muttered in a more or less collective way.

The P-Ruler went on to explain that it is wrong to pretend you know what you are talking about. Everyone seemed to kind of agree but there were a bunch of mumbles. The P-Ruler continued, saying that knowledge of things not concrete was not eternal and therefore anything that keeps getting further from the original, unmolested thing is wrong, from both a moral and epistemic position.

The H-Ruler drew a huge guffaw when he said, "knowledge of concrete is eternal." No other Ruler took the H-Ruler seriously, and to be honest, it was kind of hard to take him seriously; that being said, he was an absolute God in the Deep Bunkers, where the other Others and the bat-like things live.

The VE-Ruler said that the P-Ruler had made things a whole lot more complicated than they really needed to be and that appealing to nonsense in the sky didn't help anything. The scribblings were taking notes, and when they set down their tablets unwatched for even a second, a group of sub-scribblings would steal those and make notes based on the scribbling's notes, each sub-scribbling claiming to be closest to the primary source. It was a weird thing to watch the scribbling interactions, they were so busy taking notes they didn't seem to notice the sub-scribblings stealing their notes. The sub-scribblings would write even more complicated notes, stealing and/or borrowing notes back and forth between themselves. This created a very complicated system when the notes reached the horseradish-fleshed Paddi'u; they would pick individual pages of sub-scribbling notes and go to work on setting up entire ideologies based on it.

The VE-Ruler went on to say that if you attempt to remove the Bunker Dwellers' outlet for creative expression and thus deny their ability to reach catharsis, they will actually start doing those things in real life. There was a great deal of pushing and shoving in the crowd and someone said one of the Philosopher Rulers muscled-up on another but they were separated and cooler heads prevailed. A few of them still walked around with "Imaginary Lat Syndrome" pretending to be big, but that was peacocking.

The actual surprise during this was when the NL-Ruler, whom everyone thought was besties with the VE-Ruler, said that the P-Ruler was correct. The VE-Ruler looked devastated in a "my son has shamed me" kind of way.

The NL-Ruler said that the P-Ruler was right but not about Art. He was right if he applied his argument to gratuitous advertisement. Everyone agreed that there was no art in advertisement. The Z-Ruler did this weird yes/no nod with his head, kind of like he was bobbing. This bobbing sent his scribblings into an uproar. The author related a horrifying history about the ongoing sub-scribbling wars in the actual-empty wastes of the ham-fisted Paddi'u that I think he invented in his own imagination, this being one of those formal versus objective times I warned you about because no one would be stupid enough to actually go to war because they thought they had the Truth and others did not.

The NL-Ruler concluded that it was against the collective good will to promote advertisement on a gratuitous scale but that art that was not aimed at selling anything should be allowed. The W-Ruler chimed in that the P-Ruler's epistemic argument did not apply to abstract expressionism; no one knew what he was talking about at all.

"And there you have it," the author said again.

"There I have what?"

"Illicit art."

"You mean advertisements are 'illicit art.'"

"Yes."

"Why did they ban art then, if art and advertisements are different categories?"

The P-Ruler said that time had borne out that the VE-Ruler was wrong, that it had been demonstrated that the P-Ruler's argument was correct, that certain things should not be allowed in the interests of the collective good.

The P-Ruler said failed artists become ad-agency employees and art should be banned for that very reason. He also said because the ad-agencies had an unlimited supply of money, the gratuitous advertisements they produced were supplanting an actual education. He went on to say that gratuitous advertisements instead of an actual education was catastrophically and irreparably damaging. Every Ruler agreed that this was damaging, but they weren't sure how or where the damage was being done. For the next four months the only dialogue between the Philosopher Rulers was about what exactly was being damaged by gratuitous advertisements instead of an actual education, and that was a boring four months! The scribblings' notes during this period were incredibly dull; the sub-scribblings' notes were either unreadable or incomprehensible.

The VE-Ruler said, "But to your original point, how is it demonstrable that certain things should not be allowed for the collective good? This isn't another appeal to some lofty notion in the sky, is it?"

The P-Ruler replied, "No, I do not need to appeal to anything other than empirical evidence. It is demonstrable because people become inured to violence, they become islands of narcissistic individuality and the universal foci of their own vanity. When given the means to show their true selves they set about on one another like savage animals; they end up either not caring or not thinking. In the end, they wind up destroying themselves."

"That is all conjecture."

The P-Ruler said, "Where are we standing and why are we here?"

The VE-Ruler ceded the point, and thus no art or gratuitous advertisements in the bunkers.

Chapter 5

WHERE THE AUTHOR TRIES TO USE THE DEEP AS PROOF THIS
ALL TAKES PLACE UNDERGROUND; AN EPEE FIGHT "EXPLAINED"
TO ABSOLUTELY NO ONE'S SATISFACTION; A QUEST BEGINS, AND
WE MEET PEOPLE WE DON'T APPARENTLY MEET AGAIN.

ALI AND MAGGIE BEGAN walking toward the Deep, the massive Bureau of Action building and equally massive Bureau of Information building to their left. They began climbing the stairs leading to the top of the hill.

"Where's your badge?"

"I don't know. I think it fell off when I was contemplating nothing this morning."

"When you were what?"

"Doesn't matter. Do you know anything about the road past the Multi?"

"What do you mean?"

"Have you ever been past the Multi, to the Statue of Progress intersection? It turns into a T. If you go left you presumably go up Ditch Peak; if you go right the road leads off in the distance. Do you know where that road goes?"

"No, I've not been out there since they had the parade when they decided the Statue would be out there. You know you'll have to get a new badge, right? That goes in your employee report, I'd be careful if I were you. I hear it isn't as bad if you can find your old badge. You should look for it."

"Not tonight, it's the quarterfinals."

"I didn't mean tonight. Everyone will be at the Multi tonight. But you really should look for it tomorrow." They were nearing the crest of the hill and about to enter the Deep.

Dear readers, this will more than likely be confusing because it will seem like this story is taking place inside the bunkers and that I have been lying to you. Allow me to explain:

The Company Uppers worked in either the massive Bureau of Action building or the equally massive Bureau of Information building. The CEO in the Boss Shack was not an Upper; the CEO was something else entirely. If you were not a Snail or an accursed Paddi'u then you worked in the Deep. The Deep could refer to one of two things: the building itself or the hill in which the building was situated. Two histories exist on why the building was not *on* the hill, but rather *in* the hill. The Upper version is that the building was built and then the hill was created around and over the building in an effort to be both greener and to protect the building from the elements. This was the official version and when on a tour of the Company grounds, it is completely plausible. This is the surface history of the Deep.

The Deeplings themselves believe that the Uppers put the Deep in the hill so they wouldn't have to look at them. No Upper ever contradicts this so no one is sure whether there is any legitimacy to it. A persistent rumor in the Deep is that the outer walls are bare earth and that to get to an earth-wall you had to go through a locked door that only the Snails used. No one really wanted to look in there. In the bunkers they used the advantage of the steady temperature and redistributed the heat evenly through the bunkers. Individual units were heated according to the energy use of that individual bunker unit. Any misuse was immediately felt because the heat was recycled within that individual bunker and there was no way to dissipate it other than natural air cooling. There was no "out of sight, out of mind" in the bunkers. No one in the Deep Bunkers, where the other Others and the bat-like things live, thought there was an "outside" and life was brutal and there was no hope.

The acoustics of the Deep made the entire place echo like the inside of a mammoth cavern. There was not one single window looking outside in the whole place. There were so many rumors about tunnels and secret rooms and all kinds of madness that determining the truth of any of them was pointless. From the Snail Tales you would think the place was a nexus point for all types of strange inter- and extra-dimensional interactions. Almighty only knows what fables the Paddi'u cooked up when information was filtered to those wretches.

Because there were no windows, one never knew what was going on outside while in the building; in that way it was like a casino, but without the hope of "winning big on loose slots." Because the building was located inside a hill meant it always smelled of damp earth. Because the Deep was in a hill the author insists it is proof that there are bunkers in this story, which there are not. As you entered the Deep, which was only possible from the top of the building, you had to walk what seemed like an endless number of corridors to get anywhere. The place was not laid out with any theory of convenience or efficiency in mind. Coupled by the fact that the Uppers changed both the office occupants and the Deep organization chart at unpredictable intervals, meant that you were always getting lost in the building, no matter how long you had worked there; it also meant you were never 100% sure where anyone's office was from day-to-day, including your own.

Maggie was walking in front of Ali. "Do you think you all have a chance tonight?" Maggie asked, the din getting louder as they descended the maze of stairs to their respective offices somewhere in the building. "The Blues run a 0-1-2-1. That might be hard to counter with a 1-2-0-1 like you all use."

"We have a very good shot, I think." Ali said; she was

staring at Maggie's shapely behind wishing she could "get all up into that." I suppose we should address it and now seems as good a time as any, especially since the author made an unnecessary and pandering sexual comment. Apparently, Ali is a female when Maggie is involved because, as the author says, "there should be a sense of the sensual in the relationship and only a woman can be sensual; therefore, two women can achieve a higher level of sensuality than can a male and a female. Given this and my artistic endeavors, Ali is a girl with Maggie."

I countered with, "Doesn't that mean there can be no sensuality in a gay relationship, since it lacks females?"

"It does; however, that isn't to say that gay relationships are inferior, they just lack sensuality."

I asked, "Is there a corollary to female sensuality in a gay relationship?"

The author seemed to consider this question and finally said, "I'm not sure. I suppose you could say 'intensity,' that men reach an intensity that women seem to lack." The author insisted I emphasize that 'sensual' and 'intense' are not ethical terms and, if they denote any objective value at all, it would be an aesthetic value.

That was well and fine, no one had any real questions about any of that, almost everyone had already figured all that out; what I wanted to ask, but wasn't able to in this chapter, was why he initiated the epee fight. The only thing that ended the epee fight, by the way, was a bunker alarm that turned out to be nothing.

"Stop staring at my butt." Maggie didn't turn around. "I can feel you staring, you hussy." Maggie moved like a fluid in a glass, sort of sliding side to side, a perfect example of erotic ambulation.

Ali got closer to her and whispered, "We still need to consummate our marriage, you tease." Maggie nudged her gently in the breast with her elbow and playfully swatted at her. Ali backed up and continued, "Do you have any hope against the Gingers? They run a 0-1-1-2; it only goes one higher, the famed 0-0-2-2."

"I know, and probably not. We have a solid 1-1-1-1 but I think it might be outdated. I think my office is this way. I'll see you later."

"Bye." Ali winked at Maggie and watched as she walked away, going off to see if her office was where it had been yesterday. Ali knew the Gingers were going to slaughter the Reds in their match tonight; fortunately, the Philosopher Rulers have indefinitely suspended killing your opponents during a match as a strategy for winning the game. This was a wise decision after last year's semifinals, where there was no one left alive to participate in the finals. The trophy is still in the case as a tribute to them all, so there's that. Even though you aren't allowed to kill your opponents during the match, the Philosopher Rulers have not clarified if you are allowed to use that strategy before the match begins. The presumed answer is "no," but some of the "accidents" seem like foul play. Ali was mostly sure they would see each other again.

Ali was walking toward what should be his office when he heard, "¡*Hola! Coma estas*? Where's your badge?" Q smiled but wasn't really smiling.

"I lost it."

"¡*Ay*! Bummer, that'll go in your file."

"I know. You still running for endurance?"

"*Si*. Why?"

"Have you ever run past the Multi, out to the Statue of Progress?"

"No. Why?"

"There's a road out there and I'm curious as to where it goes. You look sad, what's wrong?" Even though Q smiled at Ali when she saw him, it wasn't the real Q smile, which was warm; the smile she gave Ali was wan.

"*Pesadilla*. A nightmare last night."

"I'm sorry. Do you want to talk about it?"

Q began in her Spanglish to explain her nightmare, and what she described truly was a nightmare of epic proportion. "I was walking in a wood, very dark and very damp. A pervading sense of pressure enveloped the place, almost as though the air was physically thicker, making it harder to breathe and creating a pressing feeling against my skin, like being in *agua*. I was on a path that was very narrow and rocky; I didn't dare step off for there seemed to be no ground, only deep blackness, *solo vacío*. The trees seemed to rise out of an *hondura*-like mist, it seemed to shiver like a living thing."

Q and Ali had stopped in the break room. Ali was pouring himself a cup of coffee. As Q described her dream, other Deeplings entered. When they heard her, they would stop and listen, the words coming out of Q's mouth and the imagery they conjured both transfixing and immobilizing those listening.

"Ahead there was a *brillante* light, what looked like a clearing bathed in sunlight. The path began to narrow and the rocks began to move, causing me to stumble. I hurried along the shrinking path to the light. Behind me I could hear the sound of rushing air and the faint sound of wings flapping. The air smelled rank with evil. I dared not turn around. I could feel something breathing and getting closer.

"My back began to get warmer, with damp, hot air moistening my neck and causing me to scream. From in front of me, where the light shone, the sound of children could be heard. The light seemed to offer salvation and comfort. I stumbled ahead, near terrified to tears. I reached the clearing as I felt a hand touch my back. The hand must have belonged to a *coloso*, for one of its fingers touched the top of my head and the thumb brushed my left thigh. I fell out of the woods and onto green grass.

"I lay there on my hands and knees panting, like a dog after a race. The ground was damp with morning dew. The air was cool but crisp; early morning air in autumn. The sun shone, but it was not quite ready to warm the earth. The sound of *niños* laughing and playing was soft and gentle on the air. I closed my eyes, steadied my breathing, and looked back at the wood. It was gone, replaced by fence with cross-hatched privacy slats; I couldn't see what was behind them. I heard a laugh and turned toward the center of the clearing.

"When my *abuela* passed, I cried very hard. When I saw what was in the middle of the playground, I cried the same tears, only many, many more. Before me was a swing-set. Instead of swings, skinless hands held two creatures; the hands extended up, eventually becoming blood vessel and vein links holding the hands in place. In those hands sat two *demonios*. The one on the left had a *jirafa's* head and neck, only the face was maligned with viciousness. Its eyes were dead but seeing. Instead of a *jirafa's* body, it looked like a little boy, maybe two- or three-years-old. It was wearing baby coveralls, like a little farmer. In its lap it was choking a baby koala, the face having gone dark blue, its purple-black tongue hanging limp from its mouth. Instead of feet, little tongues protruded from the bottom of his pants. They occasionally licked the hems.

"The one on the right was in a little girl's bright green Easter dress. Instead of feet, the bottom of her legs terminated in a set of little hands. Her leg-hands would sometimes grab things off the ground and hand it up to its arm-hands. It would bring the object, often a rock or piece of trash, up to its face. The head contained a massive eye; it took up most of the thing's face; it had no nose or ears or mouth, just a giant eye. When it blinked, honey-like sap oozed out, spilling onto the dress and creating a sticky mess around the neck."

Q began to cry again, little sniffles punctuating the horror she was describing. Most of the listeners were visibly ill. Ali was filling his overflowing cup; the coffee was pouring on the floor. One coworker simply left and walked into the mighty, mighty Pacific Ocean; which, depending on where you think this story is taking place, is a pretty long walk. Ali was seriously hoping Q had woken up at this point, or that he would at this point, or that someone would at some point. It didn't matter to him too much what needed to happen to make Q stop.

"The swing-hands were suspended under a dress, like two swaying *bolas*." At the word '*bolas*,' an intern fell dead on the spot, collapsing like a ninety-five-pound sack of potatoes dropped from a roof. Trevor Furt went through her pockets because he did things like that. Everyone in the bunkers suspects Trevor is the thief. "Instead of swing-set poles, two chicken feet protruded from under the dress and clutched and scratched at the ground.

"Wearing the dress," Q continued, her vision gone misty like she was seeing it; and if she was, Almighty help her, "was the trunk of a body. At the top of the trunk, where the neck should be, was instead an enormous top-hat; the hat must have been over one-hundred feet tall. The dress was a hip skirt, once bright red but now dingy and ancient maroon. It had two harpy breasts; bare, wrinkled, and sagging with age. Instead of *pezones*," Q indicated her own *pezones* with the thrust of two thumbs, "it had the lidless eyes of a *garza*." No one knew what '*garza*' meant in Spanish so the effect was absolutely, soul-crushingly awful; you had to insert what you thought '*garza*' meant and in this context, none of the listeners imagined something nice or pleasing.

No one said anything for an interminably long time. Q dabbed at her eyes and sniffled quietly; the coffee pot and cup shook and drooped in Ali's hands; Trevor Furt put something that was in the intern's pocket into his own pocket; and that one coworker disappeared into the mighty, mighty Pacific Ocean.

The silence was broken when Doug Watson, the Deep Non-Supervisory Advisor, walked into the breakroom and saw Ali. Doug said, "the boss wants to see you," he stood in the door and stared, disdain shooting out of his eyes. The man had contempt for everyone; everyone except Beard Plott. Since Ali was solidly in the category of people who were not Beard Plott, Doug had a certain amount of anticipated loathing for Ali as par for the course; however, Ali had been the lucky winner of extra contempt because he was completely unawed by Doug. Whereas others either had a genuine awe of the man, or a much-practiced feigned awe of the man, Ali found the latter difficult without snickering and the former simply impossible. It was hard for him to take Doug seriously. He reminded Ali of a crane: the author said you can take your pick between the device that lifts heavy objects or the bird; but he says it is hard for him to endorse the bird imagery because they are pretty creatures and Doug was neither a bird nor a pretty creature.

"The boss wants to see you. He's been waiting and he's getting impatient." Doug grabbed a handful of confetti from his pocket and threw it into the air. It glistened down over his head and shoulders. "He told me to tell you to get to his office, pranto." Dear readers, I feel I must be honest with you, as is my style. That is not a typo, please do not become critical here. I told the author I thought he meant "pronto." He said, "I had to endure this conversation so I am quite certain of both what he said and what he meant. They were not the same words."

"How long has the boss been waiting?" Ali asked.

"For a while. Like I said, he wants you in his office, pranto." See, my friends, he said it again just like before so I'm thinking Doug either really said it, or the author is consistently lying about this. Doug walked away towards his office, muttering under his breath and throwing more confetti in the air.

People in the breakroom were rushing out to call their families and tell them they loved them, Q's story sending a primal need to be cared for into the hearts of all that heard her. Ali began walking towards Silas' office. On the way Ali passed by Mildrew's office. On Mildrew's desk was a steaming cup of coffee. The steam indicated that Mildrew was somewhere in the building, or at least had been before his coffee had gotten cold. In all actuality it meant next to nothing. Mildrew was the Deep Routine Manager and also the Ginger shift; however, no one had actually seen him in over one-hundred years. There were pictures of Mildrew at every Company function and he had won Employee of the Year twenty-three times in the last thirty years; but not one single person had ever actually seen him at work. Even the people who had their pictures with Mildrew didn't actually remember seeing him.

Ali went to Silas' office and saw Vernon. "What are you doing here?"

"It'll cost you." Vernon was playing penny hockey on the desk. Vernon Roberts was the Deep Life Support Engineer, which is to say he was in charge of the Deep's finances. Vernon related everything to money. He was also the Blue co-shift.

"This was Silas' office two days ago. Did they move him?" Ali dreaded talking to Vernon. He wanted out of the office, pranto.

"He's cashed out of this office. Can't say for sure where they deposited him."

Ali didn't know if Vernon was aware that he spoke in "capitalism;" some of the things could have easily been non-capital remarks, but with Vernon's pecuniary vocabulary, it seemed unlikely that it was a mistake.

"Did your badge take a dive?" Vernon asked. He scored with his penny and picked it up. He licked it and then put it in his shirt pocket. "Looks like you're in the red."

"Lost it this morning."

"You should have secured it. The Uppers always put a lot of interest in these things."

"Where was your old office?" Ali thought maybe Silas

was there. Sometimes when the Uppers were lazy, they would switch people's offices directly; sometimes they moved everyone at once. If it was the latter, Ali might not be able to even find Silas today.

"It was beside the ATM."

"Thanks." Ali left and went to the office by the snack bar. Vernon called everything that had to do with cash the ATM, in this case it was the snack bar lockbox. He looked in Vernon's old office and there was Silas. He knocked and said, "You wanted to see me?" Silas Gough was looking at his screen. Silas was Co-Deep Head, the other being Helen Hendersen. Why there were Co-Deep Heads no one could figure out; between the two of them there was enough work to keep someone busy for maybe thirty minutes the entire day. Either despite of their lack of anything productive to do, or because of it, they usually requested the craziest tasks from the other Deeplings. Silas was not as bad as Helen, whose requests for things could reach mythical proportions.

"Grab a chair and close the door." He said it is such a way that Ali knew pretending to be a monkey and jumping on him was not in the cards so he closed the door.

As Ali was closing the door and walking to a chair, he asked, "Have you heard about Q's dream?"

"No. How bad is it?" Q's dreams were so devastating that people often did not make it to the end of the descriptions before succumbing to the icy grip of the Grim Reaper.

"Do you know what a '*garza*' is?"

"Waiter?'" Ali thought about putting two waiters inside the breasts of the swing-set creature's *pezones*.

"I hope not." Ali sat down. "What's up?"

"I've got bad news and worse news. Which do you want?"

"If I only have to pick one, I'll take the bad and leave you to it."

"Very funny."

"Uh, well, I guess things usually go from bad to worse, so let's keep that tradition alive."

"I know Maggie had to sign you in and I can see you have a temporary badge. That has to go in your employee file. My hands are tied, I'm sorry. Do you know what happened to your badge? If you can find your old one, it isn't so bad for you." Ali looked at the badge on his shirt. Instead of a picture of a nice clean Ali, smiling dopily into the camera, there was an enormous "T," telling the world Ali was terrible.

"I think it fell when I was running this morning. What's the worse news?"

"The boss wants to see you." Ali's soul held its breath. Silas was Ali's boss and that was the only 'boss' he ever had to deal with; above Silas was Quetzalcoatl, the Aztec God of blah and learning. That of course wasn't true, but still, it might as well be. All of Silas' bosses were Uppers, the rumor was that he and Helen had nine-hundred Upper bosses in total, all of which had 1,000,000 life points each and could regenerate lost appendages. The part about them having nine-hundred bosses was false; however, all of Silas' bosses did have over 1,000,000 life points each; no one could confirm the regeneration thing, it was probably whimsy.

"What do you mean? Who wants to see me?"

"I got a call on the interswitch and you need to go see the boss. I don't know why. How do you think you'll do in the quarters? The Blues run a good 0-1-2-1."

"We have a good shot, I think. Must be nice to have a bye and already be in the next round. Gingers or Reds?

"Gingers. You need a new badge. Get the paperwork from Henri Racheal Michelle."

"I will. Have you been out to the Statue of Progress lately?"

"Not since the ceremony commemorating the pedestal. Why?"

"There's a road out there and I wondered where it went."

"No clue, never noticed it. You need to go to Cube Town and see what they want."

"You don't know?"

"Like I said, the interswitch said you were needed by the boss."

"What did it say, exactly."

"'Send Ali Kim over.'"

"That's all it said? Where am I supposed to go?"

"I don't know, go over there."

"And see whom?"

"I don't know, someone should be able to tell you over there. I guarantee you that the information you are wanting isn't in here and I have work to do. Go get your new badge paperwork and then come back here before you leave to sign your employee report."

"What report?"

"The one that says you lost your badge."

"Oh. Alright, I'll take care of it." Ali got up and opened the door to Silas' office.

He looked at his T-badge, what amounted to a big mark of shame. Ali headed toward Henri Racheal Michelle's office to get his new badge paperwork. This, *mon ami*, is when I started to think that the author might actually be a little crazy; I mean, "medication crazy," and not "kind of quirky." Henri Racheal Michelle is, as is pretty obvious, the paperworker. Or rather, are the paperworkers. Henri, Racheal, and Michelle are the paperworkers in the Deep. These three completely interchangeable characters were always referred to as one person, although there were three people. Each of the three were married and had two kids, one dog, one cat, one 20XX BMW, one 20XX Kia, a 2813 sq^2 house, and all of them were having an affair with someone named Pat. Their spouses' names were Racheal Michelle, Henri, and Henri. The six kids, three dogs, and three cats were all named Alex. All three of them played the shift position for the Reds, which was allowed because they were completely interchangeable in every possible way.

Henri Racheal Michelle was arguably the most important person in the Deep. They alone had the one printer in the entire building that worked. Statistically, every office had 2.6 printers; however, none of those 2.6 ever worked. There was forever something wrong with the Deep printers: no toner, paper jam, missing tray, no paper, no plug-in, no power cord, and in one strange instance, no power chord. Because no printer in the Deep worked, every piece of paper printed in the Deep was printed in Henri Racheal Michelle's office.

This kept them very busy. The printer ran nonstop, like a Gatling gun. The paper had to be loaded constantly. The Company had sentenced a Snail to feed paper into the printer but Henri Racheal Michelle had knocked into it, some say on purpose, but I don't know. The Snail fell into the paper feeder and got sucked into the printer. The printer, because it never stopped running, spat out 8.5" x 11" sheets of Snail paper for a little while. It's morbid, but in the Deep Bunkers, where the other Others and the bat-like things live, these "Snail sheets" are very valuable.

All Henri Racheal Michelle ever seemed to do was put paper in the printer, take paper off the printer, and help other Deeplings look for "that thing that I just printed and need ASAP!" There was always a massive line outside the office door, it moved like an airport security line at Thanksgiving. If you weren't waiting for something off the printer you didn't have to wait in line; one intrepid intern decided to fake a non-print job and cut in front of everyone else. When the people waiting in line found out what "that little bastard" had done they formed a two-column gauntlet. That "son-of-a-bitch" had to pass through the gauntlet on his way out of the office. The "asshole" made it through six people before being bludgeoned to death.

In the bunkers they had instituted a system where when a print-job came into Henri Racheal Michelle's office, then Henri Racheal Michelle would announce the subject line and that person would come get their paperwork. That went like this:

Message #1. Henri Racheal Michelle said over the bunker interswitch, "Bunker compost schedule: modules 1 – 3 is waiting." Maggie came and got her message.

Message #2. Henri Racheal Michelle said over the bunker interswitch, "History of the Unmentionables – the truth they don't want you to know is waiting." Doug Watson ran into the office and out again in a hurry, throwing confetti the entire time.

Message #3. Henri Racheal Michelle said over the bunker interswitch, "A hard shoe is waiting." Every single person in both the Deep and the bunkers was lined up. Somebody said they even saw the VE-Ruler in line. Needless to say, Message #3 shut that little experiment down.

Ali was hoping to make this a very brief visit. Since there were a possible twelve things that could be called Alex in a conversation with Henri Racheal Michelle, the combinations brought about truly remarkable misunderstandings. Once, Ali had thought that either Henri or Racheal or Michelle was going to have one of the kids checked for worms and possibly euthanized. He had gone immediately to Silas, asking if he needed to call security or an emergency veterinarian. Silas had explained the situation but Ali could never keep up when "Alex" was mentioned. Most cases were pretty easy, band recital meant an "Alex-person" and vet appointment meant "Alex-pet." But "giving Alex a bath" and "snuggling Alex all night" were less clear.

It reached an unbearable level during the epic bunker heat wave of '14, when someone thought that Alex was going to give birth and that Alex was suspected of being the father. Alex had overheard Alex threaten to neuter Alex if any of the offspring looked like Alex. Alex thought that Alex was pregnant and that Alex was suspected of being the sire. Alex had overheard Alex threaten to castrate Alex if any of the litter looked like Alex. See what I mean?

As Ali passed people in the printer queue, their eyes became those of a bird of prey, watching Ali's every move. If that "piece of shit" made a move like he was cutting line the whole group was ready to turn loose on him, talons and beaks going in for the kill. Ali had heard about the intern's bludgeoning so he knew what was at stake here. He made sure he spoke in a loud voice so others knew he didn't need anything off the printer.

"Good morning, Henri Racheal Michelle, how's it going? I don't have anything to pick up off the printer." When he said this, he turned forty-five degrees to the right so the first three people in the queue could hear him. He was hoping the grapevine would send out the message that Ali was a friendly, not a "good for nothing" line cutter who deserved to die.

"Hey Ali. Oh, it's fine, Alex has the measles and Alex has a kidney infection. It could be worse, Alex told me that Alex has been diagnosed with some kind of disease that starts with "dis.""

"I'm sorry." Ali was already confused. He knew measles was a human thing but the kidney infection could go either way. He would have to wait on the "dis" disease because there are a lot of them, some were people diseases and some were animal diseases; there were a few that could be either. He wanted to get in and out so he got straight to it. "I need paperwork for a new badge." When Ali had said, "I need paperwork," he felt a brief spiritual presence over his shoulder, which inexplicably disappeared when he finished the sentence. One of the birds of prey in the queue must have additional powers. Ali was as sure as a prophet that if he had said, "I need paperwork off the printer," then the presence would have immediately relieved Ali of all the atoms in his body.

"Sure." Henri Racheal Michelle looked at Ali's T-badge, a testament to his incompetence. "Here you go. You need to have everyone on the list sign it and bring it back."

Ali looked at the paperwork. Listed were most of the Deepling offices, most of which Ali "supervised." As a middle-manager Ali was in charge of people when they were in trouble, but at that point whatever happened was "out of his hands." If his "supervisees" were not in trouble, then "whatever happened was out of his hands." The only real authority Ali seemed to have was signing employee rating reports and approving their vacation after it was approved on the master schedule. The disposition of any unplanned vacation was, you guessed it, "out of his hands."

"Thank you, Henri Racheal Michelle." As Ali walked out, he held up the paperwork and yelled back, "Thanks for giving me my new badge paperwork." This was simply to hedge his bets in case the game of telephone, which had started out as "I don't have anything to pick up off the printer," had somehow morphed into "the printer is down," which would have caused a Deep riot, or immediately worse for Ali, "that fucker cut in line and the paper in his bastard hands came off the printer. Kill him!!"

Ali realized he was in a terrible position. He had to go see the Uppers but he had a T-badge, a beacon of ineptitude. It was impossible to get a new badge in less than a month. Maybe his old badge would show up soon.

As Ali looked over the paperwork, he thought it was odd that he wasn't on it, even though he supervised almost everyone who was. He headed towards the Technocracy and Peter Klaus' office. Peter was the Blue cover. Maybe he could tell Ali who wanted to see him.

As Ali walked into Peter's office all his hair stood on end. There were so many computers in Peter's office and so many electronic doodads running that you could actually see little flashes of lightning between devices. These were accompanied by faint cracks of thunder, like someone popping gum. Ali liked Peter, but he did not like Peter's office. He was also supposed to play against the Blues tonight in the Cheepee quarterfinals, so he was hoping there wasn't going to be the usual pre-game tensions.

The Snails believed Peter's office was haunted by a poltergeist, and that was entirely possible in the Deep Bunkers, where the other Others and the bat-like things live, because all manner of things trounced about in that place. In the bunkers the Philosopher Rulers had banned superstition along with art and gratuitous advertisements so the poltergeists weren't allowed. This banning had no impact on the poltergeists' ontology, they simply weren't allowed. When all three censors went into effect word has it the H-Philosopher lost its omnisexual mind and pitched a fit that scared the daylights out of some of the others.

"Hey Peter." The fillings in Ali's mouth started to hurt, like he had bitten into aluminum. "Dude, I hate your office. Can we go out into the hall?"

"No. I need to fix these." Peter was restarting all the computers in the office.

"What are you doing?"

"Fixing these computers."

"Is that all you have to do, restart them?"

"Mostly. What's up?"

"How can I find out who called from the Squat or the Blah?"

"You can't. It's impossible. I've tried."

"Why not?"

"The switch connections in the Deep are easy to figure out, the schematics are all very straightforward; however, there's no rhyme or reason what happens after they leave the Deep. The lines themselves could be going anywhere."

"What about the schematics for the other two buildings?"

"The schematics show all of it as a black line that goes out, it isn't color-coded at all; even if I could get to the junction box, I couldn't figure it out."

"Where's the junction box?"

"Nobody knows. The schematics don't say where it is." As he was saying this a ball of electricity rose from behind a bank of computers and floated around the room. Ali watched mesmerized; Peter didn't seem to notice, he kept restarting computers. The little ball circled around and then went back behind another rack filled with discarded a/v equipment.

"Did you see that?"

"What?"

"There was a ball of lightning that came out from behind the a/v equipment, flew around the room like it was checking it out, and then went back to a different spot behind the a/v equipment."

"Oh, yeah, that's ball lightning, it does that. Don't piss it off, I think it's surly."

"Good heavens, isn't that dangerous?"

"It can be. It killed three Snails last week. I had to get rid of them. Smelled like hair for two days."

"I need you to sign this paperwork." Peter looked up and saw Ali's T-badge, his shame.

"That goes in your employee record."

"I know. Sign this." Ali handed Peter the paperwork. Peter signed it and handed it back.

"If you can find your old one it isn't so bad."

"I've been told." Ali took his paperwork. "See you at the game."

"Yeah, I'll see you out there."

Ali looked at the other names on the paperwork. He looked at his watch. He needed to go home and get ready for the game. He would have to go to Building 40 tomorrow wearing a T-badge.

Chapter 6

Cheepee quarterfinals.

Ali and the other Olives were sitting in Ali's backyard, taking in the beautiful yet drab outdoor weather and their victory against the Blues. Fetch was manning the grill; Q was sitting on the grass.

"That ref was not from Texas!" Naomi said, she had her shirt sleeve raised and was giving herself nicks in the bicep with a single-edged razorblade.

"*¿Que?*" Q asked.

"The ref, that sum-a-bitch was not a Texan. There ain't no way we only won by fifty. That ain't a Texas win an' that sum-a-bitch did it on purpose." Even if they had won by one billion points, which in the arcade version of Cheepee is totally possible, but not in the game "More Cheepee," which is a crappy game, the win would not have been "Texas enough" for Naomi. Nothing was ever "Texas enough."

"Not everyone can be from Texas, man. Other people

come from other places and that there are other non-Texas places and non-Texans in the world make the world a rich and diverse place," Fetch said while turning the food on the grill.

"There's plenty a diversity in Texas!" Naomi had finished nicking her arms and was opening a bottle of beer with a Texas-Army knife, the Swiss not knowing how to make a blade like the good people of Corpus Christi.

"What about people from Guatemala? Don't you like knowing me?" asked Q. That seemed a reasonable enough question to the others.

"A course, I like knowing ya. I like knowing all ya'll barbarians. Why, just here the other day I was thinking to myself, 'I sure wish Q was from Texas.' All the big towns in Texas have a Hispanic section, can't ya just be from there? An' Ali, wherever yer from, yer welcome in Texas. You too, Fetch; hell, we got plenty a skanks in Texas for ya to spread 'round."

"Naomi, you called us barbarians. How is that 'liking us?'" Ali asked. "And for the record, I grew up in Anthony, NM."

"So? That ain't Texas."

"I grew up on the corner of Livesay St and Charles Ave, which is approximately ninety feet from the Texas state line."

"Still ain't Texas."

"Naomi, I went to high school in Texas. I went to college in Texas."

"You ain't *from* Texas, yer *from* New Mexico. I'm glad ya had the good sense to get yer learning in Texas, probably why I don't mind being 'round yer kind."

"What kind?" Ali asked.

"¡¿*Si, que mierda, tu veux dire chienne*?!" Q demanded. Two things that no one on the team wanted out of Q was to hear her dreams, which were in Spanglish and which most of them could understand relatively well, and to see her get angry, when she spoke Spench, a combo of Spanish and French which none of them could follow because none of them knew French. When Q got mad, she turned into a Spench speaking Guatemalan Devil, like the Tasmanian Devil of cartoon lore only when Q did her version it was neither an impression nor an impersonation; it was also very much not funny.

There, of course, is a reason for this, my dear friends, and it only seems right that you know about it as it will impassion your very soul. Q was born in Guatemala to a young Guatemalan peasant girl and a French Legionnaire. They brought her to the US as a young child, hoping for a better life for themselves and young Q. Q said she had very little memory of any of this; rather, most of what she knew had come from her mother.

Her parents arrived in the bunkers two days later. Because they were outsiders it was feared they were disgraceful Paddi-u. They were given the choice between something called the Trials of Horus or losing an eye. Q's *mamá* chose losing an eye; her father, in a moment of sheer lunacy, chose Horus. Q never saw her father again; some claim his ghost haunts the bunkers at night, seeking the last piece of Horus' dark puzzle, at which point he can again gain corporality and exist among the living. His ghost still updates his blog so Q said she doesn't even really miss him. The Philosopher Rulers allow his presence because he didn't engage in any poltergeist nonsense.

"You know, the non-Texas kind. At least ya'll have the Texas Spirit, otherwise there'd be no handling any of ya."

"What's 'the Texas Spirit?'" Fetch asked, still manning the BBQ.

"It's a deep sense a belonging to som'in bigger 'an yourself; that you, a little, can be part of som'in big. It's a feeling in yer heart that swells wit' pride at the sight of yer brothers an' sisters; that no matter what yer differences, no matter what yer socio-economic status, no matter how down-on-yer-luck you might be, that you belong." At this point Naomi stood up and shouted, "It gets me out a bed in the morning wit' a hoot an' a holler!" Naomi climbed on top of her chair and screamed, "I thank Texas for my daily bread and may the Almighty bless Texas! HOT DAMN!!"

This speech was broadcast into the bunkers where everyone stood and applauded. Old men began weeping and holding each other; rival gangs sang and danced with one another, a young boy volunteered to clean the inside and outside of the maggots. In the Deep Bunkers, where the other Others and the bat-like things live, it had the opposite effect and there was a riot, where Deep Bunker Fetch kidnapped the mayor's children and threatened to drop them into a hole that went, no shit, directly to the center of the Earth, unless he was given a way out of the Deep Bunkers. Whole clans of Paddi'u beset upon other clans of Paddi'u and cannibalized them. This had nothing to do with the Texas speech, they did that because they were dreadful.

"Does anyone want to hear about my dream?" Q asked.

"No," was the triple answer.

"*Innombrable mangeurs*," Q whispered under her breath. She was picking at the grass and throwing it like a little kid who was pouting.

"What's got ya missing Texas, hun?" Naomi asked; in non-Texan this meant, "why are you sad?"

"I'm not from Texas and *rien n'est mauvais*." Q was still mumbling in Spench, which was a bad thing, because it meant she was stewing, like gumbo. Q was the only person to have an astral connection between her topside self and her bunker equivalent. Bunker Q lived in the French Quarter, which meant she spoke French as a primary language and was dirt poor. Q's Spanglish worked like normal Spanglish; however, Q's Spench was nowhere near normal. Bunker Q spoke French in honor of her father. When any version of Q got mad, the astral connection between her topside self and her bunker self opened up full bore, thus giving Q access to English, Spanish, Spanglish, French, and Spench.

What made it one level worse was that the astral connection went all the way down to Deep Bunker Q, who was the second most powerful voodoo priestess in the solar system. She and Deep Bunker Fetch are playing a very dangerous game of cat and mouse. There is a rumor she has access to voodoo incantations capable of reaching topside, it's fucking madness, I know!! There are so many rumors about Deep Bunker Q that her legend extends throughout every level of the earth; mentioning her name to a Snail would turn it into a block of salt. She spoke Haitian Creole, giving Q access to another language.

"I think I'm gonna write the governor. Tell 'im about our win," said Naomi, grinning with pride, bleeding from the many nicks on her arm, and still standing on her chair. "I think he'll be tickled to know that Texas won the quarterfinals."

Q's brooding was getting more serious, she had picked a spot of Ali's lawn completely bare like a hungry nanny goat. Everyone noticed this, especially Ali, who was a finalist for bunker Lawn of the Year.

"Are you sure you're okay Q?" Ali asked her. He wanted her to stop picking at his grass. "You seem awful grumpy."

"*Mwen pa vle pale sou li*," she said. Everyone looked back and forth at one another because no one knew what any of that meant or even what language it was.

"¿Que?" Fetch asked.

"I said I don't want to talk about it." My fellow readers, I know you are wondering if that is what she said or if I'm messing with you; I will explain in a couple of paragraphs.

"You don't seem okay, hun; you look like Galveston after a storm." Naomi had jumped off her chair and onto the picnic table where they were supposed to eat. "Why, I bet it'd take two Texas cowboys to get ya going. Almighty-damned shame too, if ya ask me; after this match, they'll be singing our praises from El Paso to Texarkana." Naomi stood on top of the open jar of pickles and let out a Texas holler that was heard by every reprehensible Paddi'u within fifty miles. Those loathsome degenerates carried news of the sound to the Paddi'u king, who sacrificed the messenger to a dark and utterly made-up demon-god that, for reasons left to your imagination, had a gigantic penis.

Then it happened, Q turned into that thing I warned you about, the Spench speaking Guatemalan Devil! She stood up and said, "*Tais-toi stupide idiot.* My *mamá* is sick, *ella tiene cáncer.* You know why? Because she had to work in the bunker air and filtration *departamento,* cleaning *la pisse et la merde,* fuck! You know why she had to take that job? *Mon père* might be "of *posib* Paddi'u *orijin.*

"So, she gets cancer and they tell her she's going to die. She asked, "*¿Hay una cura?*" They said, "*sí*". She asked, "Can I have it?" They said, "no, you are too poor." Can you believe that?! *Yon madichon sou ou ak licker chen pitit ou yo.* They tell her she needs a last will and testament. She goes to a law office. They tell her it's a $200 fee just to talk. She doesn't have that kind of money. She goes to register with the Bunker Future Death and Compost Department.

If she does not pay them $1000, she will be composted into pet food. My *mamá* deserves to be fertilizer in *un jardín*."

Q wasn't finished, she looked at Naomi and continued, "It's pointless to claim locational superiority over another location. Just because you are from Texas doesn't mean anything. No one asked to be born in Texas; if you were from Ohio or Denmark or Istanbul, you'd spout the same *merde*. If Texas is so great and friendly, why are there gangs and people killing each other and stealing from each other and rivalries between schools over their *sportifs idiotes*? Are you saying that no one in Texas ever disagrees with one another? People from Texas don't get along with each other. If you don't believe me, ask an East Texan about a West Texan. You are spouting the same *merde* people from other countries spout in order to stroke their egos. The way you tell it being from Texas gives you special status when all it gets you is a chip on your shoulder the size of Jupiter. *Sacrebleu, la puta!*"

Everyone waited to see if Q was done speaking. They still had no idea what she was saying or what languages she was using. They had followed the English and the Spanish and the Spanglish; when she switched to whatever else was in there, then it was every person for him/herself. The breeze caught the aroma of the BBQ and reminded everyone they were supposed to be eating and enjoying their victory.

Q sighed. "I'm sorry you all, I'm worried about my *mamá*. I'll be okay, thanks for supporting me."

Ali went and gave her a hug, strategically moving her away from his prize rose bushes, lest she pick those clean too. "It'll be okay, she won't be kibble."

Q gave him a squeeze back. "*Gracias*, Ali."

"You know what, I'm tired of all this talk, let's play cards." Q said.

"Yeah, plus the food is ready," Fetch announced.

"What should we play?" Ali asked.

"Hold 'em." Naomi said, finally jumping down from the pickles.

A shadow passed over the sun and a cloud burst forth a sudden and unexpected, yet delightful and spritely, afternoon shower. The joyful occasion, coupled with an air of esprit de corps shared by those people who win things, was too felt by every heart to let dump dampen their happiness; yet inside they went.

CHEEPEE SCOREBOARD

Gingers 500 Reds 2

Olives 55 Blues 5

WHERE THE MAIN CHARACTER BEGINS HIS SEARCH FOR THE BOSS AND THE ANTI-VIRTUES ARE ENCOUNTERED IN THEIR NATURAL ELEMENTS.

THE QUARTERFINALS WERE OVER and the Olives were moving ahead. It was good to win, Ali thought. He felt bad for the Reds, the Gingers had crushed them. He also felt bad for Q's *mamá*.

As Ali was running and nearing the guard shack, he noticed a new sign; rather, he noticed the back of a sign. It was facing away from Ali so he couldn't see what it said. There didn't appear to be a corresponding sign facing Ali. He would read it when he reached the turnaround.

Ali stopped at the Statue of Progress and stretched for a minute. He noticed that there was a red line going across the road in front of the guard shack that hadn't been there when he last ran to this spot. He could see in the early morning sunrise that the paint was still tacky; obviously the red line was recently painted. It reminded Ali of the red line in front of the security grotto. He made sure that he stayed on the other side of the line. He had his T-badge, but he didn't want to risk this being an area where a badge that showed you were pathetic would get you killed.

He walked over to the sign, staying well to the left of the line. He approached the sign; it said, "No Standing." As Ali stood there, he heard feet running toward him from the guard shack. The kid-cop was running and screaming. The blah was blowing away from Ali and he couldn't hear what the guard was saying.

As the kid guard approached, Ali got scared again. This time the gun was out and in the guard's hand. "Do not move, asshole!" Ali froze in place and raised his hands into the sky, trying to show the guard he was not a threat.

"I mean you no harm, officer." Ali felt ridiculous calling this kid "officer," but guns make people safe and obedient. The bunkers had outlawed guns completely. No one was happy about this because topside, before they were driven underground, was replete with guns. There was no problem topside with the guns so the Bunker Dwellers thought they should have them too. The Philosopher Rulers wouldn't even budge on this; even the Z-Ruler shook his head no.

In the Deep Bunkers, where the other Others and the bat-like things live, there was basically whatever you needed for whatever you needed it for, no questions asked. Since you could get nearly anything you wanted, the Deep Bunkers were very safe. There was an 80% chance of being "safe" in the Deep Bunkers and the "safe" rate for fifteen-to twenty-five-year-old males was 95%; if someone used a gun on you in order to make themselves safe, then it was your own damned fault for not being in a position to be safe too. Or so the argument went.

"The sign says no standing, asshole!"

"I'm not standing officer, I'm stopped. I was reading the sign."

"It is Company policy to obey all posted signs, asshole. I am authorized to use deathly force on you if you cross the red line." Ali looked down; he was at least fifteen feet from the line. "Your badge does not authorize you to cross the red line, asshole!"

Ali looked down at his T-badge, hoping it didn't look like a target. "Yes sir, I apologize. I'm not crossing the line. I'm going to run back home. Is that okay?"

"Don't let me see you breaking the rules again, asshole!" The kid guard started walking back to the guard shack. He was still holding the gun. Ali began running back home. As he was jogging, he saw the lighthouse beacon of one flash on Ditch Peak. He squinted at the spot but there was no telling what it was. He ran home.

After his shower, Ali took the tram to work. He said goodbye to the driver and headed toward the massive Bureau of Action building. Ali walked up to the security grotto and waited. His T-badge didn't allow him access through the grotto even though it allowed him access to everything once passed it. Ali waited for Maggie, who should be on the next tram.

"Hey lover." Maggie said to Ali. "You look lovely."

"Thanks. Sorry about the match yesterday. I know it wasn't really a surprise. Was it Rachael or Henry that got electrocuted?"

"I think it was Rachael, but it's hard to tell, they are completely interchangeable. I mean, even though they all have different races, ethnicities, religions, ages, and skin color, you can't tell them apart."

"I know what you mean." Maggie signed Ali in and headed toward the Deep. She noticed that Ali wasn't following her. "You coming?"

"No, I have to go see the boss in the massive Bureau of Action building."

"Which boss? Quetzalcoatl?"

"I don't know. Silas said 'the boss wants to see you.' He didn't say which one."

"Why?" Maggie asked.

"I don't know, he didn't say."

"Didn't you ask?"

"He said he didn't know," Ali replied.

"Are you nervous?"

"Should I be?" Ali was nervous, she didn't know why she was needed in the massive Bureau of Action building.

"I'd be worried."

"I'm a big girl, I can handle myself," Ali said without inner conviction.

"Okay. Let me know how it goes. Bye."

"Bye." Ali watched Maggie glide off, her sock line visible through her pants. She was so intelligent it made Ali's breasts tingle and her girl area go "yeah!"

"Stop staring at my butt," Maggie said without turning around. She gave Ali a wave and headed off toward the hill to go to the Deep.

Ali walked to the massive Bureau of Action building and entered the first floor. The air was thick and blue with cigarette smoke. Ali wasn't a smoker so he had a hard time breathing. As Ali walked toward Betty Cust's desk, he noticed several oddities. First, no one was using a computer; everyone had typewriters. On each desk, which was a block of wood, was a typewriter, two stacks of papers in boxes marked "IN" and "OUT," an overflowing ashtray, and a single-bulb lamp.

A Snail pushing a cart was collecting the papers in the OUT boxes. The cart looked perilously close to tipping over. The Snail pushing the cart was leaving a Snail trail wherever it went. The papers had a glisten to them.

The Snail went from desk to desk, collecting papers. When it stopped at a desk that was unoccupied, it sifted through the ashtray looking for cigarettes that were still smokable. It would put the butts in its pockets and move to the next desk. The desks with occupants ignored the Snail; no one wants to interact with these critters unless necessary. As the Snail moved along an occasional lit cigarette was flicked at it by someone who thought that would be entertaining.

The second oddity was that it was stifling hot. Ali could

hear fans running; however, it was hard to say where they were. He certainly couldn't feel a breeze, just heat and mugginess. The air was getting warmer, causing the place to feel like a swamp where all the reptiles chain-smoked. The click-click sounds of typewriters was nerve-wracking.

The floor had glass-walled offices on the periphery, affording no privacy for the occupants. The middle of the floor was all desks with typewriters. As Ali walked along, he noticed the paper-Snail heading to an office where people were folding pieces of paper; from the fold it looked like they were going to be placed into envelopes. The Snail dropped off the unfolded paper in the cart and collected an equally large stack of folded papers from the office. In the adjacent office, people were putting the folded paper into envelopes.

The Snail dropped off the folded paper and collected the envelopes. It carried the envelopes to the next adjacent office where people were licking the envelopes and sealing them. The tongues of the envelope lickers were bloated and crisscrossed with paper cuts. The Snail continued its rounds and dropped off the unlicked envelopes and collected the sealed envelopes. From there it carted the pile out and began delivering them to the typewriter people in the middle of the floor. Ali arrived at Betty's desk as he saw the Snail begin the process over again.

"Hello," Ali said to Betty. She was walking around the desk watching the Snail. She turned to Ali and an acrid smile crossed her face, venom from her teeth dripped onto the floor. She looked at Ali's T-badge and a cloud of disgust crossed her eyes.

"What!?" she hissed.

"Silas told me I was needed by the boss." Ali was trying to be pleasant. He didn't want Betty mad; she might have only been the sovereign of the first floor, but she was an Upper, and any Upper could cause serious problems for anyone. As he was standing there, a typewriter person came up and stood close to Betty's desk, a folded piece of paper and a bloody envelope in her hand.

"What!?" Betty hissed.

"Ms. Cust, I was told you wanted to QC my work." The poor thing was trembling. Betty was a vicious sovereign. Deep Bunker Betty was a street art master. Although her talent would have easily surpassed Picasso, she only ever painted images of torture and violence. Since she did it for enjoyment and not to make a point, she was never going to be famous for her *Guernica*.

Betty snatched the page from the trembling girl, who looked near comatose with fear. Ali watched as Betty began scanning the paper.

"One, two, three, four, five, six." She stopped counting and looked up. "Six errors in the first sentence. You disgust me." Ali thought that was a weird thing to cause disgust. He also wondered how someone could make six errors in the first sentence. "Report to the licking room." The girl began quietly sobbing, fat tears streamed down her face, leaving trails of mascara. She turned and ran to the room with the other envelope lickers; she took a seat and began her punishment.

Betty looked back at Ali. "What!?"

"Uh, like I said, Silas told me I was needed by the boss."

Betty walked over to her desk and examined her desk calendar. She moved back and forth the entire time; while Maggie's walk was a sexy glide, Betty's movements were a snake's sway. If she had looked up and spat venom directly into his eyes, it wouldn't have surprised Ali too much.

Betty noticed Ali looking. "Do you mind? This is personal information and it is none of your business. Keep your eyes off my things."

"Sorry, I was just…"

"Oh, shut up. Who did you need to see?"

"Silas didn't tell me. He said come over here because the boss wanted to see me." On Betty's desk was an old rotary dial phone. The dial seemed extra-large, almost like a joke phone.

"I don't see that you have an appointment. Go back to the Deep."

"But Silas said I was supposed to come see someone."

"You don't even know who you're here for. I know everything that happens here, I'm in charge of this whole place. Ask anyone. They know. I know you don't have an appointment because I would know. Since I don't know, you don't have an appointment. Go back to the Deep."

"Can't you call someone? Silas told me to come here."

"I know everything and I don't know that Silas said that

so I doubt he told you. Silas does not know anything. Go back to the Deep."

"Would you mind calling someone? I don't want to tell Silas I didn't see the boss."

"How could you even dare consider seeing anyone in this building when you're an imbecile."

"Excuse me?" Ali knew that Uppers could do what they wanted and had blanket immunity from Company law, but he didn't like being called names.

Betty pointed at the T-badge. "Only an imbecile would wear a T-badge and ask to see the boss. You must think you're something. We know all about you Deeplings and your disgusting existence." Betty was still moving back and forth. Ali tried not to look into her eyes, he didn't what to be hypnotized and eaten while still alive.

"Oh, I'm getting a new badge."

"Where's your old one?" Ali thought it funny she didn't know. He wanted to ask her why she didn't know, but he knew better.

"I lost it while…"

"Deeplings, disgusting waste," Betty muttered. "You don't have an appointment. Go back to the Deep."

"You can't call upstairs and ask?" Betty reached into her desk and removed a mouse by the tail. She stared at it and it went limp. She unhinged her jaw and dropped it down her throat. She gulped and Ali thought he heard a tiny squeak when it hit her stomach acid.

"I know everything." The telephone on Betty's desk

rang. "Who is it?" she said into the receiver. For someone who knew everything, Betty sure had a lot of holes in her epistemic matrix. Betty listened as the person spoke into the other end. "In a minute, an idiot Deepling with a T-badge is bothering me. What? What? What? Okay, but not on the First Elevator. What? No." Betty slammed the receiver down so hard it broke the cradle in half, destroying it. She glared at Ali with a crazed look. She quickly flicked out her tongue as if she were smelling the air. "Piso wants to see you. He has a task for you to do." Betty pulled out a pack of cigarettes and lit one. She blew the smoke directly into Ali's face.

"Thank you." Ali began walking toward the First Elevator. He was about to push the call button when Betty flung herself between him and the button.

"What do you think you're doing?"

"I was going to the second floor."

"Not on this elevator you aren't."

"Why not, I need to go see Mr. Piso."

"The First Elevator is for employees only."

"What are you talking about? I am an employee."

"You are a Deepling."

"Yes ma'am, who is employed by this Company."

"This elevator is for select employees only. Find another elevator or go back to the Deep." Betty was looking at Ali with complete contempt. Her cigarette dangled from her lips; when she exhaled through her nose, she somehow managed to blow the smoke directly into Ali's face.

"Okay, I'll go find another elevator." Ali walked away, trying to push himself through the fog of smoke that enveloped the first floor. If a fire broke out, you'd never even know it.

Ali walked past the licking room and saw the girl whom Betty had condemned. She was still silently crying, her tongue was bleeding and swollen, fat in her mouth. Ali made eye contact and gave her a pitying smile. The young girl yelled something at Ali, but with her triple-normal sized tongue it could have been almost anything. It was certainly derogatory, whatever she had yelled.

Ali watched another Snail heading towards a hole in the wall. It looked like an old dumbwaiter. The Snail climbed in and shut the wooden door. A few minutes later there was a crash that sounded like the dumbwaiter had fallen from the second floor. The dumbwaiter opened; the Snail was gone but its mucous trail was still clinging to the inside.

"No way," Ali thought. He was having serious trouble breathing because of the smoke. He had already spent a long time looking for another way to the second floor, but every elevator he encountered didn't go up for some reason. He needed air but he really didn't want to take the dumbwaiter.

"Get upstairs, Piso is waiting for you!" Betty was slithering over to him and pointing at the dumbwaiter.

"You want me to ride in that?! It's covered in Snail mucous."

Betty lit another cigarette and finished the whole thing in one drag. "Get off my floor you worthless, T-badged Deepling." Smoke poured from her mouth, nostrils, and ears; somehow all of it went directly into Ali's face. Ali was absolutely convinced if he didn't get in the dumbwaiter, Betty was going to breathe fire and immolate him, like a crazy and angry dragon.

Ali jumped into the dumbwaiter and Betty slammed down the door. "I hope you die in there!" he heard her scream. Seconds later he heard, "You too!" That was no doubt directed at the swollen-tongue girl. Betty was an outrageously mean-spirited person.

There were no buttons in the cramped space, just a rope that was covered in slime. Ali began pulling himself up to the second floor, trying not to vomit.

Ali kept pulling on the rope, the task becoming increasingly difficult as he battled gravity. The dumbwaiter came to a stop, Ali pulled but there was something abutting the elevator from above. He must be on the second floor but he didn't know how to get out of the dumbwaiter. If he let go of the rope to open the door, he was going to plummet down to the first floor again; there seemed to be no way to secure the rope.

"How did the Snail get out?" Ali wondered. Maybe it hadn't. Ali began kicking on the door. "Hello? Can anyone hear me?" Ali called out. The rope was slowly slipping through his hands, the slime making it difficult to hold. "Help! Anyone?"

The wooden doors opened and Roberto Piso, the Decision Directorate, was standing in front of him. "What are you doing?" Piso asked, his massive head sitting precariously on his body like a boulder about to topple down a hill during the next strong gust of wind.

"Trying to get out of this elevator." Ali said. He was hoping that was enough to cue Roberto into helping him.

"That's a Snail Box." Roberto didn't seem to be cued in at all; he was standing there looking at Ali. "Where's your badge? It's so stupid for you to be in here with what amounts to a sign that declares your incompetence."

"I lost it when I…."

"Shut up. I have an opportunity for you to shine. We have some other company VIPs coming in and I need someone to tag along with them in case there are any accidents. What do you say?"

Ali thought the only accident Piso should be worried about was the one about to happen, the one which involved Ali and the dumbwaiter dropping down an entire building floor. "Well, Mr. Piso, it sounds interesting, but at the moment, I have two more pressing concerns. First, I'd like to get out of this death trap; second, I need to go see the boss."

"Which boss? I don't know anything about an appointment with a boss. I need to check my calendar." Piso began walking away.

"Mr. Piso, sir, can you give me a hand here?" Ali hated asking Uppers for anything, it normally meant you "owed" them.

"With what?"

"Getting out of this dumbwaiter."

"It's a Snail Box. You shouldn't even be in it."

"Sir, I would be delighted to get out of it, I'm not sure how. How do Snails get out?"

"Who cares how they do it? Just be brave and get yourself out; come to my office when you've gathered your courage." Ali thought he heard Roberto say "cowardly Deepling" as he walked away.

Ali mustered enough strength to throw his legs out and let them dangle outside the Snail Box. He slowly slid out, using the Snail trail as a foul slip-and-slide to help him. He slowly moved his hands down the rope, the box lowering the whole time. Ali came to the terrifying realization that he was, for all intent and purposes, basically inside a guillotine; if he released the rope whatever was inside the box, which at the moment constituted his upper body, would easily and painfully be separated from whatever was outside the box.

When he made it completely out, he released the rope and the dumbwaiter plummeted to the first floor. "No wonder no one comes here," Ali said to himself. He wiped as much Snail off him as possible and headed towards Piso's office.

The second floor was not nearly as smoky as the first; however, it was still very bad. The office desks were not basic blocks of wood as they had been on the first floor; these were metal desks with drawers and an area where your legs could fit under them. The typewriters were electric but the clicking of the keys was still interminable. The main difference was whenever someone was done with a line of type, it was accompanied by an automatic sliding of the carriage instead of the manual sliding he had seen on the first floor. No one seemed to have a telephone at his/her desk.

"Are you here to volunteer?" Piso asked as Ali walked into the office. Roberto's office was like a shrine to himself. Pictures of Roberto in military uniform with incredible weapons of war hung all over the place. He had trophies and medals and certificates extolling his accomplishments, some of which were: being an honorary firefighter for having rescued children in a burning building; having smothered a live grenade and saving his platoon; single-handedly foiling a bank robbery by disarming all six thieves; and finally, having lifted a car off a pregnant woman.

"No sir. Silas told me to come see the boss."

"Which one?"

"I don't know, he said 'the boss wants to see you.'"

"Did you ask Betty?"

"Yes sir. Ms. Cust said she didn't know what I was talking about."

"She knows everything."

"Yes sir." Ali wanted to say, "it doesn't appear so in this instance," but he knew that would have been fatal. "Be that as it may, I still need to see the boss."

"Let me tell you how you can shine for the Company." Ali was about to take a seat when Roberto stopped him.

"Don't sit down you ridiculous Deepling. You're covered in Snail waste." Ali shuddered at the word 'waste.'

"Sorry sir."

"You probably don't know this because you're a Deepling and you are only marginally better than the gunk covering you, but we have some very important VIPs coming next week and that gives you an opportunity to be better than you are."

"Yes sir, you mentioned it while I was…."

"The very important VIPs will get here on Monday." Piso apparently didn't need any more details about Ali's escape from the death trap dumbwaiter. He also seemed unaware of what VIP was an acronym for, unless the Company were hosting very important very important people. "Because they are VIP people, we want to avoid any accidents that may occur." Perhaps they were hosting very important very important people people.

"What kind of accidents…."

"If we can, we should try to eliminate any accidents before they occur; however, if one should occur, that would need to be handled. What do you say, shall I put you on for Monday thru Wednesday or just Monday and Tuesday?"

"I should probably check with Silas first, before…."

"Why?" Piso had a look of complete bewilderment on his face.

"He's my boss and he probably…."

"He's a Deepling, he doesn't get to decide anything. Besides, these are VIP important people and just getting to talk about them should fill you with such a sense of wonder and awe that seeing the rings of Saturn from your own space yacht would be unimpressive in comparison."

"Yes sir, I understand it's a great opportunity. I just don't want…."

"No one cares what you want, Deepling. Should I sign you up for Monday thru Wednesday or just Monday and Tuesday?"

"I suppose I'll take Monday…."

"Great, Monday thru Wednesday it is. Are you free Thursday thru Saturday?"

"No sir, I don't…."

"Good, I'll put you down tentatively for Thursday thru Saturday too." Roberto began typing on his typewriter, ignoring Ali. He was looking at a book of famous heroes throughout history. He seemed to be transcribing the information on the page in the book onto the sheet of paper in the typewriter.

He finished typing and removed the paper. He checked it against the book and smiled. He removed a frame from his desk and placed the sheet inside the frame, which he then hung up on the wall next to dozens of similar frames. Ali glanced at the frames and saw that Piso had been awarded the Congressional Gold Medal, the National Intelligence Medal of Valor, and the Department of Commerce Gold Medal. His latest "award" was the NOAA Corps Meritorious Service Medal. One of the medals hanging on the wall had accidently been turned over. The medal was blue with a gray stripe in the center; Ali could see a price sticker on it.

"Sir, if I may say, you seem to be an exceptional person. I've never seen such accolades. What is your secret, how do you…?"

"There is no secret. It doesn't surprise me that a mere Deepling isn't aware of the concept of bravery."

"Excuse me? What concept…?"

"See, you're too dumb to even know what bravery is. Bravery is knowing what is worth being afraid of in the first place. I have no fear because nothing is truly worth being afraid of in the first place."

"And you earned all these for being brave? That is…."

"The awards and tributes are nothing to me; knowing I am a brave man is enough." Ali guessed the many, many monuments to himself were Piso's way of staying humble.

"Sir, for this accident duty, is there anything…?"

"Oh, about that, you will need to buy all the supplies yourself. Here is a list." Roberto handed Ali the list. Ali scanned it; toilet paper, flushable wet-wipes, napkins, paper towels, rags, clean underwear of various sizes, and stain remover.

"Sir, these accidents, are they…." Piso's telephone began to ring. Piso answered and ignored Ali.

"Hello? Yes sir, I have the courage. Yes sir, I can muster the pluck to complete that. No sir, it does not present any danger to me whatsoever. No sir, I am not afraid." As Piso talked into the phone, Ali went to look at the medal.

He spun it around to see the face. It said, "Department of State Heroism." Piso hung up the phone, his eyes filled with tears, his hands shook.

"Sir, are you…?"

"I command you to action, Deepling."

"What?" Ali had never been commanded to act before.

"There is a mouse in one of the bathrooms and I need you to go kill it."

"Sir, I need to go find out who wants to talk to me. Can't you…?"

Piso stood up and flung his chair back, sending it crashing into a wall. He screamed, "I'm a brave person! Mice do not scare me. It is below my dignity to…to…to…." And then he burst into tears. He rushed to his wall of bravery and began kissing the frames, muttering, "I'm a brave man," the entire time.

Ali slowly backed out of his office. Before he turned to leave, between sobs Piso said, "Don't forget about accident duty on Monday. Don't forget, and don't be a coward. Now go kill the mouse." Ali left Roberto standing by his self-generated wall of honor, a proud man with a remarkably long list of paper achievements.

Having relocated the fearsome mouse, Ali luckily found an elevator. He was not going through every office looking for "the boss;" he would head back to the Deep and ask Silas what to do. He pushed the only button in the elevator and the doors closed. Ali waited for the elevator to start moving down but it didn't; it headed up, towards Naomi's office on the third floor.

"Maybe Naomi wanted to see me," Ali thought as the elevator climbed. The doors opened and the Texas heat was crushing. There wasn't a cloud in the sky. Northwest, towards Lubbock, Ali could see that Texas Tech University and Angelo State University were locked in trench warfare. The odds were stacked against TTU because ASU was being reinforced by the B-1s at Dyess AFB and Goodfellow AFB's entire Intel school.

To the West, everyone in Dallas and Fort Worth were engaged in an epic game of freeze tag. In the bunkers, hide-and-seek is the official pastime; Mildrew, who has remained hidden for eighty-seven years, is winning by a wider and wider margin. No one can find him. The DFW-region game of freeze tag seemed to have been concocted by people into BDSM because to "unfreeze" someone, a player had to slide between the person's legs. This slide was accompanied by a solid jab to the crotch. No one seemed terribly upset by being frozen or unfrozen; they all seemed to play on with glee!

To the South everyone was arguing about walls. There seemed to be only two sections of wall, one was old and rickety and the other was a state-of-the-art weapon, complete with arms, cameras, and what looked to be a flamethrower. People were on either side of the wall yelling back and forth; the din was so cacophonic Ali couldn't make out any words other than "hate," and "*odio.*"

"Tornado!" Ali heard someone scream. He looked up and a funnel cloud was headed to the floor. Mammoth sized "personal" computers were flying through the air. Keyboards the size of windshields came zipping past Ali. Three eight-inch floppy disks hurled past and stuck into the side of the saloon. Ali ran inside the building, hoping it would protect him from the twister.

"Don't mess wit' Texas." Ali heard a mechanical noise. He turned around, Naomi was holding a Winchester Model 1892, the gun held in her right hand and coolly resting by her waist, her index finger on the trigger. She wasn't aiming at Ali, but he knew she didn't need to aim to hit him.

"No ma'am. I wouldn't dare mess with Texas." Naomi relaxed and tossed the Winchester on her desk. When it landed it went off and shot a Snail right in the heart; it had been innocently sweeping the floor. Naomi didn't even seem to notice or care. She sat down, kicked her booted feet onto her desk, leaned back and began sucking on peanut shells. Ali took a couple of steps forward and realized he was crushing shells into the floor. The floor itself was hardwood covered in a layer of dirt.

Naomi's face indicated she had been in either a fight or an accident. Her lower lip was twice its normal size, her left eye was black and still partly swollen closed. Ali had noticed her wince when she sat down in her chair.

"Ms. Houston, are you okay?"

"Why? Don't I look okay?"

"Well ma'am, when you left my house last night, you didn't have any bruises. You didn't get that from the match, did you?"

"Ya know, Deepling, ya got a lot of damn gall coming inta my State and askin' me questions. Why, the Texas governor hisself is considering passing a law that allows residents a Texas to defend themselves against non-Texans wit' lethal force. An' the Company is fixin' ta consider the same law wit' Uppers an' Deeplings, 'specially crap Deeplings wit' a T-badge." She spat out a peanut shell hull and started sucking on another one.

"Yes ma'am, I lost my badge…."

"Ah, shut the hell up. What do ya want?"

"Silas told me the boss wanted to see me and I was trying to find out whom I am supposed to see. You didn't need to see me, did you?"

"No, I didn't want to see ya; no Upper wants to see a Deepling." Naomi was nicking herself in the arm with her razor.

"Yes ma'am. Do you mind if I ride out the storm in here?"

"Yea, I do mind, now get the hell out a my State." Naomi pulled out a fresh ribeye steak from her desk and put it over her black eye and lip.

"Ms. Houston, I hate to ask again, but are you okay? I didn't hear about any accidents last night."

"Listen, these here scratches ain't nothin' but a reminder a how wonderful Texas is." Naomi never removed the ribeye from her face; she talked through it. "After the game last night, I visited me a professional Texas dominatrix. I told 'er I wanted the "Fifty Shades" treatment. That girl lowered a Texas boom on me I will not soon forget; my ass must be fifty-five shades a red. At one point that chick was digging fer oil. She got it too! Ya know, I didn't know I could do that. Hell, it figures, Texas is always gushing up oil, so might as well let a cowgirl too! Yee-haw!"

Naomi's "Yee-haw" was so explosive that her desk split in half, the entire inside of the building shook, and everyone in every Texas heard it. It shattered glass and buckled aluminum cans. No one in the Deep Bunkers, where the other Others and the bat-like things live, were affected by this at all. They were used to people screaming or lamenting in general.

Ali looked outside; the tornado was gone but so was Amarillo. "Ma'am, do you know how to get to the fourth floor?"

"Head over to'rds Texarkana. Ya ain't abandoning Texas, are ya?"

"No ma'am, I'm trying to find out who wants to talk to me. Ms. Cust and Mr. Piso said it wasn't them, and I know it isn't you, so it has to be someone on the fourth or fifth floor."

"Well good luck son, ya keep Texas in yer heart and it'll be okay."

"Thank you, ma'am." Ali left Naomi's Roadhouse and went looking for a way out of Texas, still clueless as to who wanted to speak to him.

Chapter 8

Grooves.

A groove is an absolute necessity in the game of Cheepee. It is of necessity because a groove is the only position in the game that can score any points. This is being reviewed by the Uppers, and everyone is waiting in the balance to see if they allow anyone else to score; even people in the bunkers are interested in the decision, which the Philosopher Rulers don't understand since Cheepee isn't a game in the bunkers, but a technique you need in order to survive. The groove is considered, by many, to be the playmaker on the Cheepee field; however, there are those who adamantly defend the support as the playmaker. Many years earlier, before the groove was allowed to use his or her feet on the rolling jum-jum ball, the par excellence of the groove position was Rusty Matthews, Teals, '92 – '94, Teals '96 – '99. Before the accident of '94, Rusty was considered unstoppable in the position. He scored so many points in one match that he killed three rolling jum-jum balls. On the Cheepee field he would turn into a bull elk in the rut, an elephant musth; and like his bestial cousins, he was hell bent on scoring.

Before the accident and off the Cheepee field, Rusty was a great guy, a beacon of the community and an inspiration to his fellow employees. In addition to always having excellent employee reports, he worked in a soup kitchen, volunteered helping illiterate adults learn to read, often visited the infirm and non-ambulatory, and he dressed up and played Santa for the kids. After the accident Rusty did none of these activities. In fact, the Company saw a different Rusty; he was overheard, at the Multi, explaining to his interlocuters, what he called, "The Problem with Poor People."

The people who complain about the rights of the poor and start causes to help the poor, are not themselves sufficiently poor to be complaining on behalf of the poor or starting causes for the poor. Because they themselves are not in the correct category of poor, meaning they are not "*poor enough*" to receive the benefits they want the *poor enough* to receive, they cannot know what they are talking about because they are not, themselves, in that category; that is to say, they are not in the category of being *poor enough*. People who are not *poor enough* can effectively be ignored because they only speak out of ignorance, again, not being in the category of which they themselves are speaking; Rusty's unstated premise has to assume that the only trustworthy source of information about the conditions in that category necessarily comes from someone within that category. If you are not in the category, you can only speak from ignorance about it.

Being educated and well-spoken are two necessary categories for the "*not poor enough*;" this is because they have to be informed of the issues and must be able to speak on those same issues. Being *poor enough* and being educated are mutually exclusive categories. Being *poor enough* and being well-spoken are mutually exclusive categories. In order to be a champion of the *poor enough* one must be educated and well-spoken in order to be listened to and taken seriously.

Because the *poor enough* cannot be in either the educated or well-spoken categories, one should never listen to them because they are stupid and they don't know how to communicate their own problems. In addition to this, even though they are in those categories, they themselves never complain, because no one ever hears them complaining. The only people anyone ever hears complaining about the quality of life for the *poor enough* are the *not poor enough*. As the *poor enough* are not educated, they can be dismissed as ignorant; as the *poor enough* are not well-spoken, their words are idiocy; as the *not poor enough* are not in the *poor enough* category by default, they too can be ignored. That is the problem with the poor. QED.

After the author and I said our goodbyes the author went back, he says, into the bunkers and had a conversation with Ali about the Rusty Condition, as he had taken to calling it.

As he was watering his lawn, Ali saw the author coming up to him.

"Hey amigo, what are you doing tonight?" asked Ali.

"*As-salamu alaykum.* That guy who's ghost-writing our story and I just got back from the Multi. I think I might have picked the wrong guy, he's not very thorough."

"Why do you say that?"

"He doesn't seem to be paying attention to the whole story. I snuck a peak at his notes while he was in a shiteasy and there are several points in his notes that seem very unusual."

"Do you have an example?"

"Yeah. He keeps mentioning something called 'The Statue of Progress.' I don't know what he's talking about. Do you? What's wrong?"

Ali was looking at the author, the hose in his hand no longer moving; a small puddle of water was forming on the lawn. He seemed transfixed by what the author had said. "What did he say about it?"

"Only where it was and that it was a turn-around point for your morning run. Why?"

"Where did he say it was?" Ali was firing off the questions like he had been sitting on them for a while. He eagerly listened to the answers.

"At the end of a long flat road past the Multi. He said it was at a T-intersection."

"He didn't say where it is now?"

"What do you mean, 'now?'"

"Don't worry about it." Ali went back to watering the lawn, looking disapprovingly at the puddle he had created.

"You're weird. Hey, do you remember Rusty Matthews? The Teal groove?"

"Yeah of course, he was the best groove to play before the accident. Why, what about him?"

"Well, I overheard him say he knew what the problem was with poor people."

"What did he say the problem was?" Ali went to turn off the hose. The bunkers have very strict water rationing rules that, if broken, can lead to very regrettable situations like having to use non-potable water for potable uses because the effects of any one person's actions are visited upon that person, not other people. The Bunker Dwellers took the lessons from the Flood very seriously. We are probably talking about the same Flood, but probably not the same book.

"In essence, he said that poor people are not the ones who are complaining, it was the better off poor who were complaining on the poor's behalf."

"But poor people do complain about the conditions of being poor. And what the hell is 'better off' poor?"

"That's what I thought too, but Rusty was saying that only the well-to-do poor, I think he called them the '*not poor enough*,' complain and we shouldn't listen to them because the conditions of which they are complaining do not actually affect them."

"Wait a minute, you have to be affected by a problem to complain about it?"

"He didn't actually say that but he has to believe it, right?"

The author and Ali both considered this. A bat zipped past in the night air. There was a rumor that in the Deep Bunkers, where the other Others and the bat-like things live, the bat-like things are also called "The Unmentionable."

Ali scrunched up his nose like he was thinking. He had a habit of that, puckering his lips and twisting his mouth to the left. "Isn't Rusty offering advice about a category to which he doesn't belong?"

"How's that?" the author asked.

"Rusty was explaining why we shouldn't listen to the *not poor enough*, right?"

"Yeah."

"One condition was that being *poor enough* was mutually exclusive with the condition of being either educated or well-spoken. Rusty is at least in one of those categories because otherwise you wouldn't have understood him; whether he's educated is another matter. Therefore, we know he isn't *poor enough*. Since he is saying what the problem is with poor people, he is saying what is wrong about a category he himself is not in, by definition, because he too isn't *poor enough*. Therefore, can't we as easily ignore Rusty by his own argument?"

"Well yeah, the logic is there, but he was the best groove in the game," the author reminded Ali.

"Yeah, but that was before the accident; still, I guess

we are supposed to at least listen to him because he was a groove."

"Well, the good news is I doubt the world agrees with Rusty Matthews anymore. They probably remember the good Rusty."

"I wouldn't be so sure."

"Why not?"

"That argument is a cookie cutter argument." Ali said.

"What's that?"

"You should be able to cookie cut categories into the argument. The real trouble starts when you start switching out categories, then you get odd combinations."

"I don't understand." The author always seems perplexed by arguments that require imagination, which is odd in a way because the stories he writes frequently require a complete suspension of disbelief, maybe even a complete abandonment or outright disregard of disbelief.

"Okay, take 'the poor' out and replace it with 'the Jews' or 'the Blacks' or 'Women' or any other historically disenfranchised group. Anyone with this argument can simply swap out categories and say someone isn't 'Jewish enough' or that they aren't the right kind of 'black person.' When you start categorizing further, then you eventually get to where you shouldn't listen because the person speaking isn't a real 'poor, black, Jewish woman.' You cannot get out of these categories, either. It is a kind of fallacy. This is evident by the fact that Rusty, I bet, always falls into a better category than the one he is deriding and also conveniently in the category of being correct."

"What makes you think Rusty thinks he is right?"

Ali seemed incredulous at the question. "Seriously? When was the last time you presented an argument that you believed to be wrong? And I don't mean when was the last time you presented a bad argument; I mean an argument you believed to be wrong."

"Well, what if Rusty was playing devil's advocate?"

"I can say with certainty that the devil does not need an advocate. What Rusty ought to do is play the advocate of a reasonable person for a change. Or better, perhaps he can turn his superhuman wisdom on identifying a solution to the mess we are all in instead of saying what's wrong with someone else."

"He was the best groove in the game."

"Yeah, there's always that."

CHAPTER 9

READERS ARE INTRODUCED TO THE MASSIVE BUREAU OF INFORMATION BUILDING; SOMEONE IN THE DEEP BUNKERS, WHERE THE OTHER OTHERS AND THE BAT-LIKE THINGS LIVE, DISCOVERS IMPORTANT INFORMATION; A PHILOSOPHICAL DOCTRINE IS PUT FORWARD; AND AN ARGUMENT FOR JUSTICE IS PRESENTED.

IF FEW THINGS IN the world rival the beauty of a bureaucratic building, then fewer things still can rival the one standing beside it. The grayness is aesthetic sublimity; the drabness of it a testament to all things blah. The Bureau of Information building, also known as Building 16, was the drabbest of the gray blahs; the building definitely knew this and was always somewhat more blah on windy days, and drabber on cloudy days. Indeed, Company employees, clever devils with a lexicon all their own, would often speak of the weather as though it were Building 16, sometimes called the *"ridículamente aterrador cuadrado,"* many people complaining about the blah weather. Or often as not, many people taking their own lives for granted on drab days.

The *ridículamente aterrador cuadrado*, also known as the Blah, was actually an irregular polygon. When the building had been commissioned in 1983, the Company had skimped massively and hired the crazed and institutionalized architect, Axe Ponohonopolowitz. Mr. Ponohonopolowitz, being a criminally insane architect, had only designed one building before he went mad and was institutionalized. In all actuality, Mr. Ponohonopolowitz went criminally insane two weeks after his first building was commissioned; no one knew about his insanity until after the building was opened, at which point no one doubted that he was bonkers and a danger to others. It is, in essence, a nightmare deathtrap of such epic proportion it's akin to trying to solve a Rubik's Cube from inside the Cube. The front door is a spring-loaded trap that immediately slams shut when you walk through it. The door is indistinguishable from the non-door beside it because the entire inner diameter looks like the same door.

It seems easy, "stand by the door you came through." That section of wall/door isn't the next one that opens. The next "door" could be doors away. There was no pattern to it. Someone new would by chance walk into the building and the people inside, some of whom had been trapped for years, would beset the newcomer with demands and questions like: "what is happening in the outside world?" and "how did you get in here?!"

In the Deep Bunkers, where the other Others and the bat-like things live, it was also a chance occurrence that made Deep Bunker Fetch realize there was something above him. One day, while he was disposing of another conquest in that hole that went, no shit, directly to the center of the Earth, Deep Bunker Fetch had heard a scream. Two remarkable things about this were that first, this was coming from above; and second, there shouldn't have been a scream at all. From above him a body zipped past. Upon realizing there were people above him and therefore a way out of the Deep Bunkers, he began making plans regarding escape and the mayor's kids.

Axe Ponohonopolowitz's first building was objectively dangerous because the inside was a fascinating and ever-changing, near living, work of art and/or craft. Mr. Ponohonopolowitz, in a move that either demonstrated his absolute brilliance or took him to the next, worst level of psychopathy, had hired Slugs in addition to Snails. The Snails were there to do what Snails do, which is of course whatever they do. Slugs on the other hand, are vastly different than Snails.

All Slugs are master artisans or craftspeople, the disjunct being very important here; no Slug is both an artist and a craftsperson. The confusion is of course easily mitigated by referring to them as either A-Slugs or C-Slugs. The main difference between the two, as you probably know, is that art has no practical value and crafts have no artistic worth. A beautiful set of stairs that don't lead anywhere is useless as a set of stairs; ugly stairs, even though so well-crafted a dinosaur could use them, are so visually abhorrent that no one wants to use them. A beautiful set of stairs that both lead somewhere and could support a dinosaur are just a set of stairs.

It was this fact that made Axe's first building doubly-objectively dangerous. First, anything beautiful in the building was utterly unusable for its intended purpose: beautiful vases would not hold water; flat surfaces could not bear any weight; vertical surfaces were not safe to be near; jewelry had an immediately lethal effect on the wearer; writing with nice penmanship was a death sentence.

Anything crafty was a revulsion to the senses, and the better the crafter the more senses that could be offended at once. Desks that could support the weight of a bus looked like they wanted you, personally dear reader, to die. The main floors were a nightmare to have to behold because they always appeared to be moving; old-timers know to never, ever look down. Employees over forty were rare creatures, like albino eagles.

What made the double in "doubly-objective" is that certain A-Slugs and C-Slugs would actually work together to create beautiful and useful things that would kill you in the most bizarre ways. Exotic leather scissors would make you pierce your heart; sleek kitchen appliances would empty your brain. These groups would have elaborate contests to see which teams could do the most damage to the most people, utilitarianism's evil twin brother, ineptitism. The trompe-l'oeil traps were an ineptian's movie franchise wet-dream.

Mr. Ponohonopolowitz was commissioned to design the Blah, now known as the "WDC," while institutionalized. He was far gone at this point, but the ineptitists delight in keeping this stuff going. Axe decided that efficiency cannot happen with privacy and that secrets are a bane to trust; therefore the "WDC" is his life's perfection, a building of absolute trust and efficiency.

The outside of the "WDC," now called the BoI, 16, was a normal looking building. The only way to enter was a door that led down an escalator. While descending, everyone was continuously scanned in multiple ways: visually, thermally, infra-red, and X-ray. The displays of those scans were broadcast on the screens that lined the walls. Everyone could see everything about you and there was no hiding it from the screens. Many employees learned of their health conditions simply by going to work.

Eventually, this became a serious burden and the "no pockets" policy came into being. Once inside the question of trust and efficiency became immediately apparent. The entire inside of the building was see-thru. Only two places allotted any modicum of privacy: floor six, which was Erin Russell's office, and the one bathroom on each floor. This was not a full-privacy bathroom, the room was only slightly opaque. There was only one stall in each bathroom on every floor, which made using the restroom a matter of supreme efficiency. A lazy intern once took an extra-long number two and when she exited the bathroom, she was tormented by her fellow excreters in a truly demented way. Monkeys in zoos have more decorum and restraint than did the excreters.

The BoI, often called the See-Thru, was completely wireless, completely paperless, and completely open access; there were no user-IDs, no passwords; anyone could see what you were working on at any time. Wireless earbuds were not private; personal electronics were not permitted.

The main floor of the See-Thru, often as not called the Know-All, was the primary office of Hope Faith, the Keeper of Knowledge, a woman of unbounded kindness and unshakable religious fervor, a prophet of the Almighty. Dear reader, I know you are wondering which of the Almighties she was a religious fervent and prophet of and that is both fair and easy. Hope believed in the One Almighty. What she worshipped had no sects or divisions, no children, no spouse, no personality and it endorsed no religion. Hope must have read everything ever written; if you quoted something she would also quote from the same source, in the original language. No matter what, Hope would end every conversation with, "I will pray for you child."

Floor two found the offices of Tutor Carey, the Keeper of Wisdom. Tutor was extremely soft-spoken, very loquacious, and he must have done everything there was to do because he could always one-up someone, although never in a cocky way. Whenever someone talked about a book, Tutor had been to the place the book was about; if that place didn't exist or couldn't be gotten to, then Tutor had been to the closest best thing. Among the many, many places he had been included Devon Island, Mauna Kea, Pavilion Lake, Ellesmere Island, and even Antarctica. Whenever someone talked about a deed, Tutor had done something even more spectacular.

Floor three was the offices of Calliope Goff, the Keeper of Facts. Calliope was extremely formal and no one had ever seen her smile or laugh. She would relay facts like they were contextual islands, never seeming able to put them together in any useful way. She was also unable to understand the implications of the facts she had. "You have twenty-four hours to live" and "I like toast" were doled out with equal flatness and lack of affect. She would often simply relay facts about people straight to them; because her earbud was always active, she always heard everything people were saying, and by extension people could always hear her.

Floor four was where Fetch, the Subkeeper of Information and Ali's teammate, worked. The floor above Fetch belonged to Acrimony Taylor, Underkeeper of Information. Acrimony's bone marrow must have contained chunks of ice that never thawed because, according to her, she had not been warm in over two-hundred years; shaking her hand caused the shakee's hand to go numb and the arm to turn ice cold. She was always wearing a military-grade cold weather parka. It was one of those unfashionable but highly functional puffy ones with a fur-lining in the hood, some relic of the Cold War.

Her office was so hot that being summoned there was like being told to go to one of the lower circles of Hell. Acrimony wasn't the Devil, the Devil has a personality, something Acrimony could not claim to possess, that piece of her being shattered like glass by the ice in her bones many years ago. She was devoid of expression and had never been heard to utter a warm word to anyone. The humidity in her office was like a Carolina swamp in August. Snails claimed it was infested by venomous snakes and poisonous toads. They collectively refused to enter.

There was of course a collective mentality in the bunkers. This collectivist idea brought up a very interesting ethical dilemma in the bunkers, one which the Philosopher Rulers are still debating. There was no police force in the bunkers, the Bunker Dwellers had to establish their own safety and security; however, one intrepid dweller began putting flyers in the bunkers with the faces and names of the people who did not commit themselves to the public good on an action-by-action basis.

While the pillory was used as punishment for those guilty of neglecting the public good, this posting of the offender's picture before being pronounced guilty presented a solution with a new problem; the other Bunker Dwellers found that a swift stomping of the offender was both faster and more of a deterrent than the pillory. This was great for immediacy but it wasn't always accurate. Whereas with the pillory the offender could defend his/her actions before the Philosopher Rulers, with a horde of

Bunker Dwellers there was no reasoning. The Philosopher Rulers were flummoxed because the posting of the flyers had both tempting pros and dangerous cons.

While this did cut down on the number of offenders even making it to the Philosopher Rulers, it also increased the propensity to incite vigilantism or worse, mobs would form to seek "good old-fashioned justice." This was unquestionably shorthand for *lex talionis*; however, *lex talionis* cannot be visited upon the innocent. Mobs, being reasonless by definition, are incapable of determining innocence or guilt, they can only satisfy vengeance; this is perfect when vengeance and justice are synonymous, but it is categorically wrong if they are not.

Mildrew wrote a "Bunker News" op/ed explaining that when in public, no one had any expectation of privacy and therefore any act they did in the public forum was available for review and subject to collective judgment, public opinion being one of two ways to enforce the Bunker Social Contract. He added that any person or persons acting in opposition to the Bunker Social Contract was subject to either, or both, of these tools of enforcement. In the Deep Bunkers, where the other Others and the bat-like things live, there was no contract to follow, that place having more of a solipsistic ideation.

Mildrew rebutted the argument that posting the faces and names of the offenders was wrong. He said the offenders acted against the Bunker collective in public, making them doubly guilty. He concluded by saying that the vigilante mindset was a good thing because it made people act like they were part of a collective and not individuals that did not need to consider their actions and the consequences of those actions on the public good. The posting of the offender's picture was a harmonious idea because while people get to partake in the public good, they also must bear the responsibilities of doing the public bad. Justice, he said, was not to be found only with the Philosopher Rulers; justice was everyone's responsibility.

As Mildrew wrote, "Justice belongs to the individual whereas the law belongs to everyone. When the Philosopher Rulers say, 'justice,' they mean 'law' or 'legal.' Thus, any violator of the Bunker contract is being unjust as well as breaking the law. If the Philosopher Rulers get to invoke the latter; any individual can invoke the former."

The dreadful Paddi'u adopted this stratagem as well; however, they based their concepts of justice and law on accidental properties. This made both justice and the law very easy to mete out; all they had to do was see a Paddi'u that didn't look or think exactly like them and that troglodytic Paddi'u was both guilty and wrong and therefore must be consigned to the flames, making Hume happy, in a way.

The author told me that there were no examples of this kind of Paddi'u mentality topside, before people were forced into the bunkers. I told him I thought he might be wrong about that.

CHAPTER 10

ALI ENCOUNTERS A TYRANT AND STANDS HIS GROUND; A SNAIL
SECRET IS REVEALED; COMPANY DISCIPLINE IS METED OUT; A
RIDE TO BE FORGOTTEN; AND WE MEET A REAL COMPANY MAN.

Ali made it to Texarkana and found an elevator that looked like an abandoned mine shaft. Two Snails were digging for diamonds near the elevator doors and took off when Ali approached. They left a fresh trail behind them around which Ali had to navigate.

The door to the elevator was slightly ajar, the elevator itself sat five feet below the door. Ali barely squeezed in; he had contemplated greasing himself in the slime to lubricate himself into the opening, the mucus from his ride in the Snail Box having gone hard and crusty, like peanut brittle. When he landed on the floor the car groaned like it had almost had enough. He pressed the button, hoping this took him to Beard's floor and not to the bunkers or worse still, the Deep Bunkers, where the other Others and the bat-like things live.

When the elevator stopped and the doors opened it was again five feet from the floor. As he wiggled out of the elevator, Ali was scared to death it was going to give up the ghost and deftly cut off his legs.

Ali wished he could see Beard's floor from the top because he was looking at a maze. The entire floor was a cubicle city; everyone was isolated from everyone else. The whole place looked like hallways and doors. Snails shuffled between the offices, doing the things Snails do.

As he walked along the hall, he passed an open office. A soulless flesh automaton sat in front of a sleek laptop computer. The person-like thing sat and typed without ever moving its eyes from the screen.

"Excuse me. I'm looking for Mr. Plott's office. Can you tell me where it is?"

Automatic Jay stopped typing and looked at Ali. He saw Jay look at his T-badge. "Deepling?" it asked, its voice a mechanical drone.

"I work in the Deep, yes. I was…."

"You are a disgusting creature with a disgusting T-badge." Ali knew the thing was half-correct.

"I lost my badge while…."

"I don't care. Go back to the Deep." Auto-Jay began typing again, staring at Ali the whole time. It manipulated the mouse and pressed a button. From within The Box, Ali heard, "you've got mail" sound out from what must have been every office on the floor. This was accompanied by the slamming of multiple cubical doors.

"Can you tell me how to get to Mr. Plott's office? I'm supposed to…."

"Go back to the Deep." Auto-Jay began typing again, its face alit by the glow of the laptop screen. Ali was about to walk away when Auto-Jay said, "Close my door, before more of you get in here."

Ali closed the door and headed down the hallway. All the doors seemed to be closed. As he walked along, he overheard someone in an office talking on a phone.

"I don't think I can, we are on lockdown." Pause. "I'm not sure, we got an email warning us to lockdown." Pause. "The email said there was a disgusting creature roaming the halls and it would be best to shelter in place until the danger passed." Pause. "I don't know if it's a drill."

Ali had never caused a lockdown before; he was both ashamed and proud of himself. Despite the closed doors, Snails still went to and fro. There was a long line of them outside an office door, the only open door on the entire floor.

Ali took his place in the line; he knew that really good employees did two things: asked no questions and stood in line. Ali said hello to the rear Snail but it began shaking and trembling so violently that he left it alone. It began speaking Snail to the one next to it; a weird gooey language that Ali had never heard before. It made his ears cry to hear it.

The Snails in line would enter the office at the sound of, "Report!" As the Snails entered Ali heard muffled conversation. The non-Snail said, "Have you seen it?" "Gurgle gooey goo," was the response; apparently the non-Snail could communicate with them in their native tongue. He heard a chair scrape across the floor and Beard Plott, the Supervisory-Level Adjudicator, was standing in the door frame. Upon feeling his presence, the Snails dropped to their knees like supplicants before the Pope.

"You!" Ali looked around. He was the only one on his feet so he thought that Beard must have been talking to him.

"Yes sir?"

"Get in here and report to me." Beard disappeared into the office. Ali walked around the supplicant Snails and tried not to slip in their collective slime, which was puddling underneath them.

Ali walked into the office. Beard's office was a mockery of standard office convention. He must have had thirty computer screens, all of them displaying information about various people. The room was covered in plaques testifying to Beard's awesomeness. Motivational posters covered the few sections of wall that were bare of the Beard iconography. Ali noticed two of the posters as he entered, "Teamwork: a chance for me to shine" and "Perseverance: the way I make it to the finish."

"What do you want Deepling? You have caused undo trouble as it is. I could have you fired for not having a badge." Beard was a short man, maybe five-foot-four and a stocky but not obese one-hundred-sixty pounds. He had eyes that shone with a dedication to himself.

"Yes sir. I lost it…."

"Shut up. Why haven't you reported to me yet?"

"I beg your pardon?"

"You Deeplings are little better than the undignified and unemployable Paddi'u. Heaven only knows what you do over there in the hill. You are little better than unnecessary and broken cogs in a broken and obsolete wheel." At this one of Beard's computers beeped and Ali noticed Q's face and name. Beard noticed Ali noticing Q and screamed at him, "Stop invading my privacy! I could have you killed at my whim you crap dog." Ali knew the rumors but he had never even seen a crap dog, let alone been called one.

"Report!" Beard shouted out into the hall. A Snail entered and reported to Beard. Ali watched in complete disbelief as the Snail lowered itself to its belly and inchwormed over to Beard's feet, where it began kissing his shoes and gooeying on the ground. "Rise." The Snail stood up but kept its head in a deep bow.

"What it this?!" Beard was pointing at the screen with Q's image. The Snail began saying something to Beard which Ali didn't even know was speech until it was done. Ali thought it had been trying to get the taste of Beard's shoe out of its mouth, the words sounded phlegmatic.

"Keep a watch on her. She should not know Haitian Creole." The Snail prostrated itself and kissed Beard's shoe goodbye. It gooped out of the office like a quadruped.

Beard looked at Ali and shouted, "I said report!"

"Mr. Plott, I came to see if you had asked to see me. Silas told me to come see the boss and that's what I am doing here. There, I've reported."

"You call that a report?"

"Yes, I do."

"What!?!"

"Sorry. Yes sir, I do."

Beard was seething with anger and fury. Had he been a toaster, he would have burnt the living shit out of your bread my friends. How his internal organs withstood the temperature and pressure was unimaginable and certainly not natural.

"Okay Mr. Kim, I see how it is." Beard was still seething, but it was the kind you see on cartoons where they are depicting people like a pressure cooker. Beard hit a button and on every screen was everything an Upper needed to know about Ali.

"You may leave Mr. Kim. You will need to go see Booster Mathis on the fifth floor."

"Is he the one who wanted to see me?"

"I have no idea."

"Then why did you say I needed to go see him?"

"Goodbye, Mr. Kim. I have paperwork to complete."

"Okay. Thank you." Beard didn't acknowledge Ali; he began using his laptop. As every screen was the same, Ali could see what he was doing. Beard seemed to be fully aware of it as well. He pressed a series of keys and a form appeared over the image of Ali and his Company records. Ali saw the heading of the form: EMPLOYEE DISCIPLINE

Report. Ali had enough time to see the form before Beard pressed a button and all the screens went blank, a scrolling text pronouncing: "This computer belongs to Beard Plott!" As Ali was walking out, he caught one final poster, "Success: what I have and you never will."

Ali needed to get to the fifth floor in a hurry. He knew Beard was writing him up for disrespect, a term the Uppers used to pronounce judgement in the same subtle way the Spanish Inquisition once converted non-believers and brought apostates back into the fold of the Lamb. Ali had been written up once for disrespect; the incident had happened the way the report said, but it wasn't Ali who was either the disrespected or the one doing the disrespecting. The incident happened eight years before Ali was even born; it couldn't be corrected because once the term "disrespect" enters your record, it doesn't go away.

If Ali could make it to Booster's office before Beard completed the report, he might be able to mitigate the damage. He knew there was no stopping it, but it could be softened. *If* he could get off Beard's floor. He didn't even have a ball of string, there was no way he could navigate this labyrinth and find an elevator that went up at the same time. Accomplishing one of them could take a week.

There is a labyrinth in the bunkers that the Philosopher Rulers use as part of the voting system to determine the "Bunker Dweller Speaker." This position is open to all dwellers over the age of twenty-one. In order to qualify, you only need one vote and you can vote for yourself.

Multiple votes do not matter; a twenty-one-year-old candidate with one vote was as qualified as a ninety-year-old with five-hundred-thousand votes, not that there were that many voters left in the bunkers.

Once the nominees have secured the single vote needed, they are all placed alone in a room within the labyrinth with no means of contacting the outside world. They are given a test that changes every year; this test covers many, many subjects. These tests are graded by a computer and their score determines how long the nominee has to escape the labyrinth. If anyone escapes the labyrinth, that person is in charge until the next year, where they are given the chance to "run for office" again.

Several years see no one exiting at all. The author said he wasn't sure if they ended up in the Deep Bunkers, where the other Others and the bat-like things live, or out in the actual-empty wastes with the garbage Paddi'u. He said they simply aren't seen or heard of again. You would think, of all people, he would know what happens to them. Years also find multiple people coming out of the labyrinth; the people who exit the labyrinth after the "winner" are simply congratulated and given a medal and food, like when you finish a marathon.

The Bunker Dweller Speaker is the mouthpiece of the other Bunker Dwellers; however, the Speaker is largely ignored. The real fun, it seems, is in the contest of who will be the Speaker. The Philosopher Rulers are unquestionably in charge and can shut the Speaker up by asking, what they call "a fairly basic question" that always perplexes the living bejesus out of everyone. The author said at the last debate, when the Speaker asked about the conspiracy that the Philosopher Rulers had access to the Light and were oppressing the people by not giving it to them, the W-Ruler said, "Well, the fact that you are even considering a conspiracy is proof you do not have what you are after; which is free, by the way."

The Speaker turned to the crowd and stretched out the arms wide, saying, "See?"

Ali heard a "psst!" He turned and looked around. All he saw were Snails.

"Psst!" The Snail who had reported to Beard's office was standing down the cubicle path. The Snail caught Ali's eye and motioned with its head for Ali to approach. Ali walked over.

"Fifth floor?" said the Snail, in remarkably good non-Snail language.

"Yeah, do you know how to get there? I need to go see Booster Mathis before Beard can finish his report."

"I know how *I* can get there; I don't know how you are supposed to get there," said the Snail; it continuously and anxiously looked around.

"I don't understand. What does that mean?"

"I know how *I* can get there."

"Oh." Ali realized the Snail meant the Snail Way to the fifth floor. In the Deep, Snails could move through the tunnels in the hill and they would often appear out of seemingly nowhere and disappear as soon as you took an eye off them. Ali didn't know how the Snail Way worked in an actual building.

Ali realized that he would probably never have this opportunity again and his curiosity was too much to not ask the question.

"Okay, can I go your way?"

"You're Snail-friendly, it's safe for you. Let's go." The Snail fast-walked down the maze of Cube Town, Ali following in tow, wondering what "safe for you" meant.

Ali was glad he was following the Snail, there was no way he could have navigated this by himself. He was lost as soon as they started. Everything was the same and there were no real references to help orient yourself. Turns in the hall happened with no intelligible pattern; it was like the Stanley Hotel and the impossible window on a much more grand and intentional scale.

Ali followed the Snail; he wasn't even trying to keep track anymore. The Snail stopped beside a water fountain and stood there. Ali stood beside the Snail and waited for a minute.

"What are we doing? I'm not thirsty, but thanks for stopping."

"Are you sure?"

"Am I sure I'm not thirsty? Yeah, I'm sure. Should I be?"

"No, are you ready to go my way to the fifth floor?" Ali looked around. There was no "way" he could see; there was the hall, several closed doors, and the water fountain.

"Yeah, but I don't see anything. What are we supposed to do?"

"Follow me, and stay relaxed. This is probably going to be…," the Snail seemed to be searching for the right word, which made Ali more uncomfortable the longer it took to find the right word, "weird for you."

"Okay." Ali watched as the Snail simply passed through the wall beside the fountain.

"No way." Ali couldn't believe it. He knew he had to go because he didn't have a chance of finding an exit from the floor before he starved to death.

Ali closed his eyes and stepped through the wall. "Weird for you" might have been correct. Ali was completely surrounded by something that was wet and sticky. Whatever it was pulsated like a small intestine. Ali began to move upwards, the innards he was in scooted him along. Ali was fighting a battle with a steroid-infused wave of nausea. He tried to think of nothing, which made him think of the Snail Sensei and then the Snail Way and then nausea was back with reinforcements.

And as easy as that, Ali was standing on the fifth floor beside another water fountain, fighting back vomit. The Snail was standing there, smiling apologetically. Ali noticed he had no evidence of slime on him, he was as clean as a whistle; the innards must have had a taste for peanut brittle.

"I told you it might be weird for you."

Ali didn't consider a ride in a building's ascending colon to be all that weird; there were a flood of other adjectives vying for utterance though.

"Don't mention it." Ali meant that on a multitude of levels. He certainly never planned on mentioning it, or hopefully even remembering it.

"Booster's office is over there." The Snail was pointing to an office at the end of the hall. "Thank you for always being kind to us," the Snail said.

"How's that?"

"You always say hello and thank you."

"Oh, okay. You're welcome." Ali thought about it for a second. "Hey, can I ask you something?"

"Yes, but be quick. I have to go."

"What was that crap with reporting to Beard?"

"He demands it of us."

"But why do it?"

"If it wasn't us, it would be Ants or Crickets. I have to go." The Snail disappeared into the wall again and was digested down to wherever, Ali didn't want to think about it.

Ali was amazed at the technology the Uppers on the fifth floor were using. Everyone had on wireless headsets; attached to these headsets were what looked like small horse-blinders. On these were projected information like a heads-up-display. Everyone seemed to be talking to themselves but they were in fact talking to the Company server and the information they were requesting was displayed on their little screens.

Ali walked to Booster's door and knocked.

"Come in." Booster looked up. He was a comely looking man, he was well built and had dark, ebony skin. Booster's desk was covered in employee reports, not a trace of his desk visible under the papers. "What can I do for you?"

"Mr. Mathis, Silas told me the boss wanted to see me, but he didn't say whom exactly. I was wondering if he meant you."

"I do not think so. What is your name?" Booster looked disapprovingly at the T-Badge.

"Ali Kim, sir."

"Where is your badge, Mr. Kim?" Booster was not wearing horse-blinders, he had what looked like an LED light attached to his ear. Information was projected in front of him; no matter where he was looking. Booster said, "Ali Kim," into his headset and Ali saw his Company history begin flashing on the blank screen in front of Booster.

As Booster was reviewing Ali's records, Ali scanned the room. Booster was no doubt a Company man. Everything in his office was a testament to his commitment to the Company. Plaques, awards, trophies, all Company mementos for a "job well done." One poster said, "Teamwork: there is no I in Company."

As Booster was reading a chime went off in the room. "Read new mail." Ali watched as an email was opened in front of Booster. The subject line said, "Kim, Ali. Employee Discipline Report." Ali watched as Booster read.

"Mr. Kim, this is your second report for disrespect and you have a T-Badge. I should fire you right now."

Ali stood there. He didn't have anything to say, he could explain what happened with Beard, but he thought that it wouldn't make much difference; any match between an Upper and a Deepling always ended the same.

"Sir, my badge fell off while I was running. I have paperwork for a new one." Ali thought maybe that was good enough.

"Mr. Kim, please consider yourself on probation. Any negative reports on you for the next twelve months will result in your immediate termination. You may also be fired. Do you understand?"

"Yes, sir."

"You may leave."

"Thank you." Ali left as Booster began working on more employee reports. As Ali exited, he saw a sticker above Booster's light switch that said, "What have you done for the Company today?"

Chapter 11

Cheepee semifinals.

Ali and the other Olives were sitting in the winner's box in the Multi, their improbable victory against the Yellows catapulting them into "talk about" and "thumbs up" status. The Yellows, the disgusting losers they are, were being deloused and disinfected with scalding hot water in the Multi basement. The Indigos, who had lost to the Gingers, were also being deloused and disinfected with scalding hot water; however, not for the same reason. The Indigos were being scalded as punishment for losing the semifinal match. The Gingers had decided on scalding water because the Philosopher Rulers had instituted a rule in the bunkers that the winner of any Cheepee match could, "have a moment of fun to celebrate the win." The Gingers had interpreted this to mean they could torture the losers.

No one else agreed with that line of reasoning until Mildrew wrote another very compelling "Bunker News" op/ed explaining why torture was a primary good and an end-in-itself. He even went so far as to claim that being a torturer was a teleologically necessary condition for the torturer and to deny someone's *telos* was *de facto* immoral. After that it was impossible not to agree with him; people who gave logic the finger still disagreed, but they're ridiculous as a people. Now the Company pipes the screams of the disinfected through the Multi speaker system. It's a hoot when a torture-scream harmony kicks up.

The reason the Yellows were being disinfected and deloused by scalding hot water had nothing to do with the loss; it also had nothing to do with Mildrew's article because the bunkers do not exist. The reason the Yellows were being disinfected and deloused with scalding hot water was because they had asked for both a delousing and a disinfecting.

This, of course, was the most intelligent thing they could have possibly requested because Fetch had gone *au naturel* for the semifinal match. The fact that they were allowed to request this was because of a seldom-used rule called the Sleazy Transfer Invective. This is one of those rare times, my reader friends, where life in the bunkers and life topside are completely parallel with one another. It is one of those bizarre twist of fate things too because Cheepee is a game topside and more like something you need to do to survive in the bunkers. This similarity is sheer coincidence and should not be interpreted as meaningful in any possible way.

The aforementioned STI is in place topside because during the '12 season an obscure rule change allowed players to have sex during the game. Even if you did not want to have sex during the game, because it was part of the game, you might find yourself being sexed. It wasn't technically rape because everyone voluntarily played Cheepee. There was no validity to the topside rumor that you would be fired for not playing or the bunker rumor that you would either be killed, composted, flushed into the Deep Bunkers, where the other Others and the bat-like things live, forced into the mezzo-tunnels with "The Other Unmentionables" and the real Others, and/or sent out to die with the scum Paddi'u. That is all conjecture and no worth should be attached to it.

Everyone thought this rule change made the game fairer. However, it presented a problem because none of the grooves wanted to score Cheepee points, they just wanted to have sex with one another. While some of the best Cheepee matches ever recorded came out of this period and many young boys in bathrooms across the globe have watched and re-watched the more aggressive games, every match ended in a 0-0 tie.

In an effort to mitigate the problems caused by the original rule change, the STI was contracted. The STI stung a little but the rule said, "Sex is only allowed without a cover; if sex is allowed then the losers may request a disinfecting and/or delousing." Since sexual promiscuity and a collapsing gene pool were two of the things that drove people underground in the first place, no one would possibly violate this rule. It was a very wise decision.

At least, it was a wise decision at the time it was made, during the '12 season. The STI sat dormant for years, until a new outbreak of the rule occurred. Fetch had hit upon a very crafty way of exploiting the rules, one which, had it not been Fetch, would not have worked.

Dear readers I have to be fast, the author went outside, ostensibly to "check the weather" but that's code for having a smoke. Since he's not here, I can tell you a secret. I can tell you without fear he will find out because there is absolutely no chance he will read this. He's wrong about "sexual promiscuity and a collapsing gene pool" being "two of the things that drove people underground in the first place." It was a double whammy all the same, but different Whammies. First, it was the mistreatment of our water system via the draining of our aquifers for drought mitigation and the polluting of our fresh surface water. This, coupled with an innate drive to expand which we, as a species, misinterpret as a command to dominate and acquire everything around us, drove us there. Sadly, the bunkers are on the same fateful journey. He's back, don't tell him he's wrong or he'll sulk!

Fetch sat on a chair at the table in the winner's box, the other Olives sat on the cushioned bench, well away from him. Fetch was somewhat gloomy, which, given they would now be in the Cheepee finals, was a surprise to everyone.

"Ya'd think ya'd be happy as Texas, Fetch," Naomi said. "That was some brilliant thinkin'."

"Thanks, man." Fetch was looking at his phone. "It's all good, man."

"Why are you *melancólico*?" Q asked.

"Nah, man, it's all good. I'm jazzed we won and I'm super-jazzed I got to have sex. It's also real cool we're in the finals."

"Then what are you doing?" Ali asked. Everyone was quite happy where Fetch was sitting; none of them really wanted him to get too close. The harmonious screams of the Indigos and Yellows being broadcast throughout the Multi were a subtle reminder to not get yourself into a position where you needed a delousing and/or disinfecting.

"I'm checking on this app, man."

"Which app?"

"I'm checking Friends Unified Collective. The Master Edition is about to go online and I want to make sure everything is working the way it should. It's all good." There was little point in him telling his teammates what the conundrum was and why he wasn't enthralled with the victory and was instead looking at the Friend Unified Collective app. There is every point in me telling you though.

As mentioned way back in Chapter One, Fetch had developed, what he called, ASG. According to Fetch, ASG stood for "Aggressive Southern Game." There is a faction in the bunkers, led by Maggie, who think ASG means "Assertive Southern Game," despite the fact that the inventor of ASG calls it something else. Whether you believe it means aggressive or assertive depends on how you feel about the rest of this chapter.

A very popular phone application had been invented where you could communicate with other human beings. These human beings could use words to relay information between one another and would oftentimes send these words back and forth between phones. Someone who either couldn't read or was lazy and didn't want to read decided to use that same idea but instead of words, it worked on the same premise using pictures instead. So far, so good; this is all pretty normal.

Fetch developed a private upgrade for Friends Unified Collective, called the Master Edition. This allowed Fetch to have undetected and undetectable administrator rights to any account on the system. That was scary enough for Ali to delete his profile. Fetch used this information to target women with whom he wished to dwell in their ocean of carnal delight. That was scary enough for Q.

Fetch's ASG worked as follows:

(Scene: Any bar)

Fetch (approaching woman at table with pitcher of beer and two glasses): Hey you want to help me finish this beer? (sitting down)

Woman#1 (putting her phone away): No, my boyfriend is in the bathroom.

Fetch: Hey, man, that's all cool. Can I get your number or do you want to go out back real quick and make out?

Woman#1 (slaps Fetch across the face): Leave me alone you creep!

Fetch: Later, man. (Grabs pitcher and glasses. Goes to another table)

Fetch (approaching woman at table): Hey you want to help me finish this beer? (sitting down)

Woman#2 (putting her phone away): No thank you, I'm waiting for a friend.

Fetch: Cool, cool. Hey, any chance I can get your number and call you. We can watch TV and have sex.

Woman#2: What?

Fetch: Can I get your number?

Woman#2 (Slaps Fetch across the face): No, get out of here, jerk.

Fetch: Cool man. (Grabs pitcher and glasses. Goes to another table). Hey you want to help me finish this beer? (sitting down)

Woman#3 (putting her phone away): What is it?

Fetch: Just something they had on tap man. (pours out beer in each glass). Cheers!

Woman#3: Cheers! (they click glasses. Fetch takes a big drink, Woman#3 sets her glass down on the table without drinking).

Fetch: Whoa, man, you gotta take a drink.

Woman#3: What? Why?

Fetch: It's bad luck to toast without drinking.

Woman#3: Oh, I didn't know. (takes a sip)

My friends, things here are a little crazy and I will keep the details to a minimum, the reason is "because." This conversation happened exactly like this, both topside and in the Deep Bunkers. In the Deep Bunkers this part went crooked fast. Deep Bunker Fetch is a remorseless sociopath; he said he could easily have killed Jack the Ripper, Julius Caesar, and/or Jean Luc-Picard. He made his own rohypnol and had access to a hole that went, no shit, directly into the center of the Earth. In the Deep Bunkers Woman#3 was never seen again after that sip. It was sip, slump, and Fetch carried her out, telling the bartender he was going to take care of her. He was in the Deep Bunker Bar the next night, with more alcohol and Women#3's left ear in his back, right pocket.

Fetch: Yeah, it's a Viking thing, I think. Hey, can I get your number?

Woman#3: Why?

Fetch: You seem pretty cool, I thought we might be able to go watch some TV and make out.

Woman#3: Okay.

Fetch: Cool man.

With the Master Edition, Fetch didn't need to ask anyone for her number. As a secret admin account owner, he knew their names, numbers, email addresses, physical location, bank account numbers, routing numbers, shoe sizes, dress sizes, pant sizes, bra sizes, movie likes and dislikes, book likes and dislikes, schedules, contacts, and if their refrigerator were online, if they needed to stop and get milk on the way home. This was scary enough for Naomi to modify her account and a constant reminder to buy Texas milk.

Deep Bunker Fetch used this information in a very naughty way. He was part cyber-stalker, part actual stalker, and all Alpha-predator. He used information to his exclusive advantage and others' exclusive disadvantage. He informed the Friend Unified Collective parent company about the Master Edition and told them he was releasing it for $9.99. The parent company blocked the Master Edition with a patch fix; Deep Bunker Fetch had someone on the inside and both knew about, and anticipated, the patch; he worked with the parent company to develop Friend Unified Collective – Your Own Universe, which was free with ads; $29.99 upgrade to premium, which was seventy-five percent ad-free; $49.99 with only targeted ads tailored to you.

Fetch used the Master Edition to find girls with whom he could swim in the beauty of their ocean. He used information to woo and charm. He slept with everyone he dated; he had a firm rule about it too: you had to put out on the first date or there wouldn't be a second. Fetch said he did not believe in condoms and that all sex was safe if it was meaningful and/or enjoyable. Fetch's legendary status of having unprotected sex with everyone in the Company was tolerated; but he would sleep with Snails, and that was going too far.

Because Fetch would have unprotected Snail sex, when he showed up *au naturel* for the match, everyone was worried he might have a Snail trail on him. However, given the STI, people weren't too worried. Then it happened, what will go into the Cheepee annuls as pure strategic brilliance.

In the pre-match meeting, conference, and, as the Company has repeatedly said, non-mandatory merchandise collection period, Fetch asked the following, "What is the STI?" He was slapped in the face and a Cheepee referee said, "Sex is only allowed without a cover; if sex is allowed then the losers may request a disinfecting and/or delousing."

Fetch said, "The Yellows don't have a cover." Fetch was right, the Yellows were playing a 1-0-1-2, which means no one was playing the cover position and hence, no cover. This meant sex was allowed during the match; and, because there was sex during the match, the Yellows did request both a disinfecting and a delousing because Fetch had been *au naturel* and might have Snail slime on him. Fetch had simply scored a point and then had sex with the Yellow's two grooves. Since the Yellow grooves were being sexed, the Yellows couldn't score.

Now for the real question: was Fetch being aggressive or assertive?

CHEEPEE SCOREBOARD

Olives 1 Yellows 0

Gingers 800 Indigos 5

The author says Ali snuck out of the bunkers in the early morning to go for his run. He was in the Cheepee finals! He felt a profound sense of happiness as he passed the Multi. He had been tempted to ask for a delousing and disinfecting with scalding hot water too, because better safe than sorry. The main reason he hadn't was because he was trying to be more water conscious.

The bunkers used a clever system to keep their water clean. First, although they did have running water and in-bunker plumbing, they did not have indoor toilets. Water to each individual bunker collective was rationed on a weekly basis. This allowed the Bunker Dwellers to have water for the luxuries of life: a quick hand wash, a thirst-quenching glass of agua, brushing, etc. Laundry was done in a communal bath much like Ancient Rome, sans the slaves acting as weird human agitators. This was not particularly horrific as the Philosopher Rulers had established a system of uniforms in which everyone partook or went naked; it was about thirty/seventy, so says the author, but he's a reprobate, or so I'm told.

There were communal toilets which did offer a kind of privacy. I don't actually know what to think about this, I mean aesthetically, morally, and perhaps artistically. When outies went pee standing up, they peed into a giant hole that went, no shit, directly into the center of the Earth. There was no shame here because the Philosopher Rulers had allowed cosmetic prosthetics in the bunkers. The prosthetics ranged from obviously fake to "no way, you can feel that?" real. Penises and breasts were of course numbers one and two, respectively. Nudity wasn't that big of a deal because you were almost certainly not looking at an actual piece of flesh, merely a prosthetic.

Amber Dellio was critical of the fact that only outies could pee into the hole. In an attempt to stop what she called "piss hole inequality," she always peed into the hole while standing up like the outies. One day Amber was peeing next to Trevor Furt when she "fell" into the hole and plummeted down screaming, presumably into the center of the Earth. She still updates her blog so no one even really misses her. Many people think that Trevor pushed Amber, but there is no proof, just lots of speculation. Trevor almost certainly did push her because he did things like that.

When outies went poo, or were doing an outie lazy pee, and when inies went pee or poo, that Bunker Dweller went into the E-building, checked in with the front desk, went into a stall, sat on a gripping toilet and posed for two pictures. The first picture was of the toiletee's face from the front, like a driver's license. In fact, cars being impossible in the bunkers, the people who once worked in the DMV now had this job. The other picture was an overhead shot of the toiletee and the stall, which was a nice stall with plenty of space for those with a wide defecating stance; however, it did have a very low ceiling.

When the toiletee was finished, a button was pushed that said FLUSH and a second overhead shot was taken. If the toiletee had befouled the place, then the waste water from the next five toiletees was blasted directly into that stall with said befouler still in it. It dumped in like a cyclone so there was no getting away from it. The gripping toilet had you so you weren't moving. For those with umbrellas, the ceiling was far too low for that. Some of the best bunker engineers were in charge of this and they were shitting on you with math and science. Of course, if you had been a befouler, the post-befoulment picture was all over bunker social media.

Deep Bunker Maggie was the entity known as "The Flush" because she could befoul a stall, while locked in a death-grip toilet, and walk out as pretty as ever. The Flush had taken a running befoulment over the hole that went, no shit, directly into the center of the Earth. It was always crazy times in the Deep Bunkers!

Since the bunkers were on a water rationing system, your waste was immediately felt; there was no "out of sight, out of mind" mentality in the bunkers. In the Deep Bunkers there was a brackish-water market and Prohibition-era style "shiteasies" that offered unconditional toilet privacy, for a very steep fee.

I do not personally know what happens in a Deep Bunker shiteasy and here is why. The author and I were having coffee and arguing about the book you are reading. This dude next to us was not even trying to pretend not to be eavesdropping and the author asked him if he wanted to know. Dude said, "Yes." The author whispered something into the guy's ear and, I swear, that cat got up and tied himself to a train-track and waited for an oncoming train. The author didn't even say all that much so my dastardly curiosity was zapped all to pieces.

As Ali was running, he thought about how best to go about finding "the boss." He had seen all the Uppers in the massive BoA, and that had resulted in a reprimand, a near fight with someone who thought he was a god, a ride through the colon of a building, a tornado, and from his heavy breathing, most likely a case of emphysema. There seemed no plausible way he was supposed to see Antoinette Quilerby III. He would have to go to the massive Bureau of Information building and start anew.

Ali sped up slightly at the turn around because he didn't want kid-Rambo to come running and accuse him of "standing." He rounded the turn and noticed the guard was on his radio, his gun in his hand. Ali sped up instinctually and turned to face the road. He noticed the sign was different; it still said "No Standing" but under this it also said "No Stopping" and "No Waiting" and finally, "No Loitering." On top of the sign sat a monarch butterfly slowing opening and closing its wings.

He jogged along, heading back home. He waited for it; the flash on Ditch Peak. When he saw it, he kept his eye on the spot relative to several ground markers and ran what he felt was a safe distance from the guard shack. He looked up at the summit but it was too far away. He needed binoculars or something. He began running back home, took his shower, and headed to work.

As the tram was nearing the security grotto, Ali looked at the massive buildings and thought it would be funny to go tell Betty that he had an appointment with Antoinette. As Ali got off the tram, he was about to say goodbye to the driver when he noticed another butterfly, a western tiger swallowtail, on the side mirror of the tram. The Snail saw Ali looking at something and turned to see what it was. The Snail looked back and said, "Are you okay, sir?"

"What?" Ali looked at the Snail. "I'm sorry, excuse me, I didn't hear you."

"I asked if you were okay." The Snail was humbly smiling at Ali.

"Yes, sorry, I was looking at the butterfly."

The Snail turned back and looked out the window. Looking back at Ali, the Snail asked, "What butterfly?"

Ali looked; the butterfly was gone. "Hmm," Ali said to himself. "Never mind. Thanks, have a nice day." Ali got off the tram and waited for Maggie, still needing an escort through the security grotto.

"Hey baby, congrats on getting to the finals." Maggie walked up to Ali and pinched her butt. "I didn't think you'd pull it off, I thought Beard was trying to kill you; well, when Fetch wasn't sexing him."

"He was. That creep wrote me up for disrespect yesterday, can you believe it?"

"Yeah, of course I can." Maggie signed Ali in and they headed towards the Deep. "Did you ever find out which boss was looking for you?"

"No. I need to go ask Silas what to do. I still don't know whom I need to see and now, to make matters worse, I'm on probation."

"Did you see everyone?"

"Nearly everyone. I didn't see Antoinette, but it's crazy to think she needs to see me." Ali stopped as a cloudless Sulphur butterfly flew between them and landed on his left shoulder; it opened and closed its wings four times and then flew off toward the massive Bureau of Action building.

"What is with all these butterflies?!" Ali looked back at Maggie but she wasn't there. Maggie wasn't even walking towards the Deep, no one was. Ali was standing completely alone. The guards in the security grotto were gone as well.

"What is going on?" Ali said aloud. As he was dumb-foundedly looking around, a checkered white butterfly flew towards him and alit on his left shoe. "What do you want?" Ali asked the butterfly. It sat on his shoe and slowly opened and closed its wings four times.

As Ali watched the checkered white, another butterfly, a fiery skipper, flew in front of him and headed towards the massive Bureau of Action building; the checkered white and cloudless Sulphur flew off and joined it. Ali watched as they flew away; all three butterflies landed on the door handle to the building.

"Am I supposed to follow them?" Ali wondered aloud; there certainly wasn't anyone to speak to in the area. Aside from Ali and the butterflies, still sitting on the door handle, there wasn't another living thing around. Ali walked to the door, as he got there the butterflies took flight and circled his head. He opened the door and walked inside.

"What the hell is this?" Ali said. The entire floor was empty, there wasn't a single Upper or Snail on the floor. The smoke was gone, as was all the furniture; the floor was completely empty, it looked like no one had ever been in it.

"Hello?" Ali called out. He was getting seriously freaked out about this. This had the makings of one of Q's dreams, and he would rather be in the Deep Bunkers than in one of Q's dreams.

All the butterflies Ali had seen so far, the monarch on the sign, the western swallowtail on the tram, the cloudless Sulphur, the checkered white, and the fiery skipper were all flitting in the empty air.

As Ali watched the butterflies, he heard a ding, like the sound an elevator makes when it has reached the proper floor. All the butterflies zigzagged their way toward the sound, which, given that the floor was completely empty, was both remarkably loud and the source of which was easy to identify.

The butterflies led the way as Ali walked to Betty's desk; he hoped she too had vanished. Not only was Betty not there, neither was her desk. The First Elevator was there, wide open, the elevator car waiting. The butterflies all entered the elevator and landed in a little row on the inside banister. Ali walked in with them and stood on the opposite side, across from his five little friends.

Ali looked at the call buttons. Unlike the other elevators in the massive Bureau of Action building, this elevator seemed to be a normal elevator. First, unlike the other elevators he had been in, this one wasn't a death trap that he was frightened of; and second, this one had numbers that read one through six.

Ali looked away from the buttons and stared at the sitting butterflies, all of them rhythmically raising and lowering their wings; they did this in perfect timing, never once bumping each other even though their wings overlapped. As he stood watching them, a sixth butterfly, a Melissa Blue, entered the elevator and flew directly in front of Ali's face. It darted in front of him for a few seconds and then slowly descended. Ali carefully put out his hand and the Melissa Blue landed on his index finger.

"What do you want? What is happening?" Ali asked the butterfly. He felt stupid talking to this little creature.

The Melissa Blue took off and flew around the button for the sixth floor. "Is that what you want, to go to the sixth floor?" The butterfly flew to where the other five sentinels were and took its spot by the fiery skipper, falling perfectly into wing rhythm with the others. Ali pushed the button for floor six, the floor of the Minister of Action, Antoinette Quilerby III.

The elevator door opened. There were butterflies everywhere. It was a cavernous single room full of butterflies. Ali looked up and it seemed as though there was no roof; whether it was an optical effect or some kind of architectural feat, the butterflies seemed to have open access to the outside. As Ali looked around, he noticed Antoinette standing about thirty feet away, looking directly at him. He walked over, the butterflies moving out of his way.

"Hello." Ali said, he didn't know if he should shake her hand or not.

"What can I do for you Mr. Kim?" Antoinette said matter-of-factly.

"I have no idea what is happening right now. Where did everyone go?" Ali was too dumbfounded to obey etiquette and not simply ask, the situation was too weird.

"No one went anywhere."

"Well, ma'am, I hate to disagree, but Maggie disappeared from in front of me, as well as all the other people who were headed to work. I turned to watch a butterfly and I looked back and everyone was simply gone. If the butterflies hadn't led me here, I'd likely still be outside."

"I will explain this to you Mr. Kim, although you are likely to not understand it. This floor is the summation of the Bureau of Action, it is a place where all time is visible at once."

"What does that mean?"

"I told you that you were likely to not understand it. Mr. Kim, all time is visible in this place at once; this means the past, the present, and the future. Since all time is visible, all time is available, although not necessarily reachable. Causal connections exist the way they appear but that isn't to say that events in time don't and can't exist independently of those causal connections. The simple explanation is that we see the results of causal connections, the effects, without seeing the cause; however, that does not mean the causes are not there, simply unseen.

"Here, time is not linear and all the links are available, both the seen links, the unseen links, the possible links, and actual links. This applies to the effects as well. Here, there are causeless effects and causes without effect. This allows for possible arrangements of time. Does that help explain things?" All throughout Antoinette's talk, butterflies were flitting about; it made it very hard for Ali to concentrate.

"Not really. Can you at least tell me why I'm here?"

"This is one version of a possible series of events. Since time effects and causes can and do exist independent of one another, entire timeframes can be isolated from one another. This has caused the effect of making everyone seem to disappear."

"Why are there so many butterflies?"

"They are side-effects of these temporal isolations. Perhaps because they begin life as one thing and end as another. Call them the summation of action; the ability to metamorphize into something completely new."

"So why am I here right now?" Ali thought he would ask something with a more manageable answer, the last two 'answers' were mind-numbing.

"You were wanting to see me."

"I thought you wanted to see me," Ali said.

"Why on earth would I want that?"

"I don't know, Silas said that…."

"Yes, I know about that and your visit to the building. Silas did not mean me, he meant someone else."

"Do you know who I'm supposed to go see? I've seen everyone in this building and no one seemed to be the one who was looking for me."

"It must have been someone in the Bureau of Information."

"Oh, I thought it was someone here."

"It isn't." Antoinette said it flatly.

"Well, thank you for taking the time to…."

"I didn't take the time, I simply isolated one possible

occurrence; if I had taken my time then I wouldn't have needed to isolate this instance to explain these things."

"Are you saying this isn't happening now?"

"Don't be ridiculous; as you can see, this is happening, just not 'now,' as you call it."

"It sure seems to be happening now."

"Then where is everyone? If this were happening now, then others would be involved or at least seeing it. As you've mentioned, everyone is gone, 'disappeared' is the term you used. Therefore, this is not happening now."

"Then when is this happening?"

"As far as time goes, it isn't happening. When you leave here, which should be very shortly, you will return to where you were and everything will pick up as you left it."

"Will I have a memory of this?" Ali couldn't believe this explanation.

"Certainly, your timeline includes this. No one else's does."

"This is too crazy."

"That will be all, Mr. Kim. Please see yourself out."

"Yes ma'am. Thank you." Ali turned, went to the elevator, and left the BoA.

He walked to the security grotto and looked around. A dull firetip flew toward him and landed on his shoulder. It raised and lowered its wings four times and flew off.

"Hello, earth to Ali."

Ali turned around and nearly died of fright. Maggie was standing there. People were streaming in and out of the security grotto.

"What?" Ali looked around; it appeared as though nothing had happened at all, that the events with Antoinette were a fiction.

CHAPTER 13

ALI COMES BACK AND GETS A SCANNING; THE ROLE OF THE
BUNKER CENSUS IS MENTIONED; AN ENCOUNTER WITH RATIO-
NALISM AND EMPIRICISM; AND THE RULES TO DEEP BUNKER
GAMESHOWS ARE GIVEN.

ALI STARED. MAGGIE SEEMED to be completely unaware that Ali had disappeared into the butterfly dimen-
sion with Antoinette.

"I said, did you see everyone?" Maggie was looking at
Ali in a weird way, like she was worried.

"No, I think I need to go to the massive Bureau of Information building."

"Good luck."

Ali watched Maggie glide away, a peach of a girl, wondering if the world was going to stop again. It didn't. Everyone kept right along, going hither and tither. Ali looked
at his watch; the time was correct but there was no way to
account for the time spent with Antoinette. It was crazy
but it seemed like that event did not temporally happen at
all; that, or Ali was going insane.

Ali proceeded to the BoI and joined the line going down the escalator. Ali had never been in the BoI before; everyone said that the first time you went in, it was like that ubiquitous dream/nightmare we all have as kids. You know the one. No one would describe it to someone who hadn't been there; but not in a childish way, more like a "you have to see it with your own eyes first," respectful kind of way.

As Ali proceeded down the escalator he was inundated with visual, thermal, infra-red, and X-ray images on the walls. He was looking at his fellow escalator riders as they descended. No one seemed to be in awe of the images, those who worked in the building would make a quick scan every minute or so and continue on their way. At least, until Ali's images began showing. Everyone in front of him on the escalator turned and looked at him. Everyone could see, thanks to the X-ray, that he had $0.85, a pen, his wallet, and a set of keys in his pocket. People were staring at him and then looking at the screens. The thermal imagery could show his color change from embarrassment and perspiration. He could see his armpits getting slowly redder. All Ali could do was give an awkward smile as he was being examined.

As Ali left the escalator, he arrived at something that looked like a large glass tube. People filled the tube to capacity and were raised up as if on a platform, a whoosh noise accompanying their ascent. Except there was no platform there, it seemed to be open air.

"Never been in the air lift? You must be new." Ali turned to face the voice, which belonged to a very attractive woman. The woman noticed Ali's T-badge.

"No, ma'am, I work in the Deep." Ali said.

"We have a Deepling in the building," the woman said. She must have been talking into her earpiece because everyone turned and looked at him; he could feel their collective eyes on him. The woman took a step away from Ali, as though he had an infectious disease.

Ali heard a whoosh of air behind him and then heard the glass door open. All the people who filled the chamber kept away from him, even mushing against each other to avoid direct contact.

Ali heard another whoosh and he was rising in the air with the other occupants of the air lift. The lift carried the people to the first floor and opened.

When Ali exited the air lift and saw the full extent of the inside of the BoI, he was mesmerized. The entire inside was made of some type of plexiglass and he could see every person in the building from where he was standing. There was not a modicum of privacy at all, except one small room that had slightly opaque walls. While the opaqueness prohibited seeing any details, it was obvious the room was a toilet.

As Ali was standing there outside the air lift, the lights on the entire first floor, which had been giving off a soft white glow from see-thru sconces placed in the walls, turned a reddish tint. The floors above him remained in the cool glow of the soft white light; the first floor seemed to be the only floor that was glowing red.

Ali stood there not knowing where to go. While he could see everyone and everything in the building, he didn't know most of the people he saw. Ali scanned the floor looking for Hope Faith, the Keeper of Knowledge. In the bunkers everyone knew everyone else. This was keeping with a principle that the Philosopher Rulers had adopted early on in the history of the bunkers. When people were first driven underground by the collapsing gene pool, so says the author, the Philosopher Rulers gathered and agreed that to maintain any type of order, things would have to be more manageable. Since overpopulation is *de facto* unmanageable, some measure of population control needed to be introduced. While direct methods were considered, eventually they all managed to agree that this was not the best method.

One of the main concerns they had when selecting indirect methods of population control was the concept of individual, inalienable rights. It was debated whether these things exist at all and whether, if they did exist, they applied. Most of the really old Philosopher Rulers were confused by the concept of individual rights and dismissed it outright. The VE-Ruler couldn't stop laughing; when the Younger Rulers explained it wasn't a joke, it made him laugh harder.

Eventually the Philosopher Rulers decided that the rights of the bunker collective were sovereign to those of the individual. They conceded that this principle might not be universally true; however, it was particularly true in the bunkers. Anyone disagreeing was welcome to leave the bunkers and return topside, where they would be free to practice freedoms unbounded, so long as they didn't mind seeing how that worked out in the first place. The NL-Ruler suggested an alternative to both topside and the bunkers, but the H-Ruler hushed him up before he could explain.

In order to maintain the population, it was decided that an annual census would be taken in the bunkers and that, should the number of inhabitants exceed a pre-set limit, then a bunker resource consumption list was generated and people would be asked to leave by order of the families which used the most resources. Since there was a community mentality in the bunkers, and most resources were distributed directly to the residents instead of being available for consumption, anyone asked to leave could effectively be isolated from existence, should they refuse to go. A refusal to leave, as far as even the oldest residents could remember, never occurred.

Ali saw Hope waving at him from across the building. She had a smile on her face and when Ali caught her eye, she motioned for him to come to her. Ali thought that the most unnerving part of the BoI experience was having people walk directly over him on the second floor. Luckily no one was wearing a dress, because that would have been too awkward.

Ali began walking toward Hope's office. It was disorienting getting there because the walls were all plexiglass and Ali kept running into them. The first time Ali hadn't expected it and ran into the glass so hard he thought he broke his nose and he left a face-stain on the side of an office wall. The office occupant had a great guffaw at Ali's expense. When he stepped back a Snail was immediately beside him cleaning the plexiglass. The Snail scared the daylights out of Ali because he didn't know it was there. It seemed to show up out of nowhere. Ali looked at the laughing Upper and then back at the Snail. It was gone. Where it went and/or how it had gotten there was anyone's guess; Ali didn't even have it in him to try to understand, he kept rubbing his nose.

Eventually Ali made his way to Hope, after navigating the clear floor like some type of carnival funhouse maze. Ali had taken baby steps with his hand slightly out, that way he wouldn't smack into anything else. Everyone else in the BoI was zipping around without running into anything; even as they stared and openly mocked Ali, they never collided with anything.

"Almighty bless you child. I saw your struggle to get over here, I take it you are the reason for the red light?" Hope had a very calm and soothing voice. The tension from his journey slowly waned as she spoke.

"I don't understand what you mean. If you mean the red lights glowing on the walls, how could I be responsible for that?"

Hope looked at Ali's T-badge. "Deepling, right?"

"Yes ma'am, I work in the Deep. I lost my badge while I was running. I've looked for it, but it's gone."

"Shame. That counts against you." From memory Hope cited the exact verbiage of Company policy regarding badges. She was talking for quite a while. At first Ali thought she was simply repeating what was being said in her earpiece, which was possible given that the technology in the BoI allowed for this; however, Ali came to the conclusion that Hope simply knew all of the policy by heart because she kept elaborating on the policies and sub-policies.

"Yes ma'am, I'm sorry about losing it." Ali didn't think Hope was looking for an apology, she was so kind he couldn't help it. "Ma'am, you didn't by chance need or want to see me, did you?"

"Why in the Almighty's name would I want to see a Deepling? I'm not all that fond of the red lighting, it makes it harder to read. The sooner you leave the floor the sooner I can get back to work. Why would you think I needed to see you?"

"Well, Silas told me that the boss wanted to see me but he didn't say which one."

"It could have been someone in the BoA," Hope said, a warm smile on her face.

"No, I was there all day yesterday and I may or may not have been there this morning, so I know it isn't anyone over there."

"What is your name?"

"Ali Kim."

Hope said "Ali Kim, all files, screen." On Hope's clear, see-thru desk was what looked like a clear piece of plexiglass. When Hope spoke, all of Ali's information began rolling across the screen. There were no inner workings to the screen, there was no projection mechanism he could see; Ali had no idea how the information was scrolling on the screen when there was nothing he could discern that would account for its being there.

Ali's information scrolled at a breakneck speed across the screen. Hope seemed to be reading it all, even though Ali had no chance of reading at that speed. Even though the information was about Ali, he still couldn't keep up with it.

"You have two disrespect write-ups, Mr. Kim. It seems you are quite the rabble-rouser." She still had the same smile on her face. It was like being called a trouble maker by an angel. Hope said a lengthy sentence in a language Ali didn't recognize.

"I'm sorry, I don't know what that means. Is that German?"

"No, Mr. Kim, it's Greek. It's from *Antigone.* Perhaps you've read it?"

"A long time ago."

"Well then, you should understand."

"It was a really long time ago."

"Are you saying you don't remember it?"

"I remember the basic point of it, I certainly don't remember any quotes from it. Not to mention, I didn't read it in Greek."

"It was written in Greek."

"But I don't read Greek. I read it in English."

"What a shame. You miss a lot by not reading the original. But still, you can use a second-rate translation and still learn everything you need to know." Hope seemed to be genuinely sad that Ali hadn't read *Antigone* in the original Greek.

"I suppose so."

"You don't agree?" asked Hope, her smile back and greeting Ali once again.

"Well, you can't learn everything from a book. Like Twain said, 'you don't learn everything in school.'"

"I think you mean, 'I have never let my schooling interfere with my education.' And that quote is not apropos to my point. I said that you can learn everything you need to know from reading, even if it isn't in the original and you lose a lot of the nuance. You seem to be suggesting that I mean that you can learn all there is to know from a book. I did not suggest that."

"I'm sorry, I guess I misunderstood."

"Experience is an important part of learning, don't get me wrong. It's just that without the theory behind what you are experiencing, you are likely to not know what you are experiencing."

"How do you learn the theory though?" Ali asked.

"By reading. The collective wisdom of the human race is in the written word; whatever you are looking for, can be found in a book. Don't you agree?"

"I suppose. Is there a book that tells me which boss to go see?" Hope was a nice lady, and Ali knew she was more well-read than certainly anyone in the building and probably knew what she was talking about, but he also didn't want to spend all day talking to her.

In the bunkers this was of course all the Philosopher Rulers ever seemed to do. The exception to this was the H-Ruler, who would disappear for long stretches at a time; no one ever seemed to know where he went during these absences either. The consensus among the other Philosopher Rulers was that he went to enjoy the benefits of the Deep Bunkers, where the other Others and the bat-like things live, since he was an absolute God there. They didn't ask because they really didn't want to know.

"In all likelihood Tutor is the one who is looking for you," answered Hope.

"Why is that?" Ali wanted Hope to be correct, Tutor was on the second floor, which meant he could leave the confusion of the BoI, which he didn't understand, and go back to the confusion of the Deep, which he did understand.

"He spends time with Deeplings, Almighty knows why he would do that. Still, be that as it may, I'd go see him."

"Thank you so much, Ms. Faith. I really appreciate the help." Ali looked up at the second floor. Having a glass building had its advantages in at least one regard, you always knew where people were because they didn't have a place to hide.

"His office is over there." Hope pointed up and behind Ali. He looked around to the general area where she was pointing. After a few seconds Ali thought he recognized Tutor.

"Yes ma'am, I think I see him." Ali hesitated as he looked around the BoI.

"What is it?" Hope asked. Ali was in a pickle; he could see Tutor but he wasn't sure how to get to him. Ali could backtrack and try to get on the air lift again, but he would have to admit he didn't know how. His T-badge was already proof of his stupidity, he didn't particularly want to add additional qualifiers to his resume.

"I hate to ask, but is there another way to get to the second floor? I've never been in here before and it's a little confusing." Ali didn't like admitting he needed help and, as always, he hated asking anything of an Upper.

You could always ask the Philosopher Rulers whatever you wanted; in fact, they actively encouraged it. While it was true anyone could speak to them, no one except a select few ever wanted to ask them anything. By the time they were done 'answering' your question, the questioner felt like everything she believed was garbage and if she didn't think like them, she was wrong. Which was particularly ironic since the Philosopher Rulers often didn't agree on things. There was a guy in the Deep Bunkers who was overheard talking about the Philosopher Rulers and the definition of piety. No one was really paying attention to him because he was absolutely smashed on red house wine.

Hope had continued reading her screen, the information blazing by at an almost incomprehensible speed. When Hope looked away from the screen and turned back to Ali, the text stopped scrolling and a word, presumably the one she had just finished reading, was blinking.

"Take the stairs, that's the best way to get to Tutor's office." Hope was still smiling.

Ali looked around. The stairs were also clear so Ali couldn't tell where they were. It was getting frustrating being in the BoI because he could clearly see where he needed to go but he couldn't figure out how to get there.

"You don't see them, do you?" If Hope hadn't been the one asking the question, it would almost certainly have been taken as a snide comment. Ali noticed many, many people looking at him. He could readily see the people on the first floor turn and look his direction; but the most troublesome experience was that the people on the floors above him were looking down at him. There was nowhere to hide and since everyone was connected to each other over unsecure earpieces, people at least knew what Hope was saying. Ali thought it must feel this way on gameshows.

In the Deep Bunkers, gameshows were very popular. While they were of unheralded popularity, all the Deep

Bunker gameshows were dangerous for the competitors, much like in *Running Man*, with the exception that there was no happy ending. There were no prizes to win or fame to be gained by playing; however, there was a forty-two percent chance of being killed while the game was being played. The games themselves weren't particularly difficult, but one of the objectives of all the games in the Deep Bunkers is for anyone not playing to kill the people who are playing.

This makes things extremely exciting in the Deep Bunkers during game time. Because anyone not playing in a gameshow is trying to kill anyone who is, most people don't watch the game, they go out to kill those playing. Those not watching the game who go out to kill those who are, actually begin playing as soon as they leave their house, as that is one of the rules of the game. This means that they too can be killed by those not playing. Anyone playing is allowed to kill anyone who is also playing, but not someone who is not playing. Anyone not playing who encounters someone who is, can kill the player if they want. If any player feels threatened then they can kill the person who is causing that feeling, regardless whether they are playing or not.

The actual objective of the games themselves seem exciting at first, when the objectified and sexualized hostess announces the rules, but as soon as the game actually starts, "it was on," as they say in Scotland and Peru. After the game, many of those that made it would meet in the

Deep Bunker bar, where they would discuss the objectives of the game they just played. Deep Bunker Fetch and Deep Bunker Q always had the best ideas; the Flush had a kill count that was unapproachable. Whenever anyone claimed she didn't kill as many as she said, she would kill them. If she asks, "You think I'm lying?" it's best to answer in a specific way, something like this.

"No, ma'am, I don't. I'm sorry, this is all so weird." Ali couldn't help but be honest with Hope.

"Deeplings. I will pray for you all. Light the way for him." When Hope said this last part the luminosity of the red light changed. The entire floor was still lit with a red glow, but there seemed to be a faint but redder glow along the floor. As Ali looked, he could see the glow lit a path out of Hope's office and towards Tutor's.

"That is tremendously useful. Thank you so much."

"You're welcome, Ali." Hope continued her reading, the information still blazing by on the screen. As Ali walked out, trying to follow the path, Hope said, "Ali."

"Yes?"

"I will pray for you child."

"Thank you."

Ali followed the path out of Hope's office and made his way through the invisible maze of the BoI. He arrived at the spot where the light ended. He looked around the floor and saw that the path light clearly stopped. He looked up into the second floor but there were no red lights shining above him at all. He could see people walking above him but he didn't see the stairs.

Ali stretched out his arm and felt the walls. He felt ridiculous as he stretched his foot out. His foot landed on the second step even though he couldn't make out the stair itself. He slowly climbed the stairs, gingerly placing his feet next to each other to make sure he didn't trip. As he was climbing up, an Upper passed him coming down the stairs. The Upper looked at Ali, said "I'm passing it now, should I push it?" and seemed to wait. Ali glanced around and saw many, many people looking at him. He could see them all talking, he could only hope enough of them voted "No."

When Ali finally made it to the second floor, it was worse than he could have imagined. First, he could see directly down into the first floor since the floor he was standing on was see-thru. This gave him a feeling of vertigo. The first floor was no longer lit by the red glow; however, the glow seemed to have followed Ali to the second floor because it was now awash in the red light.

Ali looked down for the path, getting slightly less dizzy as he became accustomed to looking down. Ali discovered that if he didn't look directly at the floor, he could see the path on his periphery and avoid getting nauseous. He slowly made his way to Tutor's office.

Tutor was sitting at his clear desk, wearing what appeared to be a skydiving jump suit.

"Come in Ali."

"Hello Mr. Carey, did you want to see me? I spoke with Ms. Faith and she said you would be the most likely person to have needed to see someone from the Deep."

"Normally she'd be correct, I often utilize Deepings for access to experiences to which I may not otherwise be privy."

"Finally." Ali said aloud, his excitement at having reached the end of his quest overcoming him momentarily. Composing himself, Ali said, "What can I do for you, sir?"

"I don't need to see you. I just said that."

Ali replayed the conversation in his mind, somehow having missed that part of it entirely. "Didn't you say you needed my help?"

"I said nothing of the sort. I said I often use Deeplings to gain access to experiences which I myself might have a difficult time securing."

"What can I do for you?"

"Nothing I can think of."

"Did you not need to see me?"

"No, I didn't. I have no idea who needs to see you. Why did you go see Hope?"

"Silas said the boss needed to see me and I have seen everyone in the massive BoA to no avail. It wasn't Hope, but she said it might be you."

"Well, unfortunately I'm afraid your quest continues. I need nothing from a Deeping at the moment. Is there something you wish to ask me?" Ali must have been looking more intently at Tutor's jumpsuit than he realized.

"No, sir; I couldn't help notice you are dressed a little differently than everyone else. I didn't mean to stare." Ali couldn't afford another write-up for disrespect; he didn't want to be terminated or lose his job.

"Oh, this," Tutor indicated his suit, "is my parachuting gear; I'm going skydiving immediately after work to test an experimental Company parachute."

"Wow!" Ali wasn't concerned about his excitement, testing experimental parachutes seemed *wow* worthy. "That's amazing, I don't think I could do that."

"It isn't quite as dramatic as it sounds. The parachute is experimental but it is perfectly safe. It has been tested and all the dangerous problems have been resolved." Ali considered asking who tested it before the dangerous problems were resolved but he thought better of it.

On Tutor's screen was a local Haitian news site; Tutor noticed Ali looking at it.

"Odd that I might be interested in Haiti?"

"No sir, are you planning a trip?"

"No, I've just returned. I'm reading about an incident I inadvertently found myself in while I was visiting. It seems I'm a sort of local folk hero of sorts."

"How so?"

"Well, I was visiting the island at the request of a friend, who is unable to travel herself. I collected some items in Jérémie and was set to travel by ferry to Anse-Rouge the next day. When I arrived at the dock the next morning, I found that my boat had already departed. Since I was unable to secure another berth to Anse-Rouge, I stowed away on a cargo ship bound for Baie-de-Henne.

"All was going well; I was tucked away behind some large crates, the seas were calm, the sun was bright, and the weather was lovely. I was content to remain where I was and steal away when we arrived in Baie-de-Henne. My plan was upset when the Capitaine ordered the boat searched. Apparently one of the deck hands had accused another of smuggling profane contraband.

"I slipped over the side of the boat and into the water, right as the men were about to search the area in which I was hiding. I began swimming to keep up with the boat, hoping to make enough noise and cause enough of a disturbance to attract the men who were now searching my vacated hiding spot.

"One of the men spotted me and called for the Capitaine to stop the boat. I was brought aboard and told the Capitaine and crew that I had bought a ticket to Anse-Rogue but the boat had left earlier than expected. I told the men I had searched for another passage but could not find one. I said that as the Capitaine was setting out, a dockhand told me they were bound for Baie-de-Henne. I knew I could travel by bus or taxi between the two and thought the Capitaine might be inclined to grant me a spot on his boat.

"I continued by saying that since I was a strong swimmer, I dove into the bay and swam after the boat. However, I explained that the Capitaine and his fine crew made good sail, and I was unable to catch them. It was sheer luck that the men on the side of the boat had seen me; otherwise, I might have had to swim the entire way to Baie-de-Henne."

Ali was speechless for a moment; it was the craziest thing he had heard. Ali didn't think he possessed the necessary moxie to pull off a trick like that.

"The Capitaine and the crew were so amazed that they granted me a hero's treatment for the remainder of the journey. However, when we set sail again, the men continued the search. Unfortunately, they found my bags, which contained some things the Haitian locals find very upsetting." Tutor didn't supply an explanation and Ali was completely fine with that.

"My bags were brought before the Capitaine, as was the crewman who had been accused of smuggling. The poor lad was an illiterate youth of fourteen and from a local region rumored to have ties to Black Magic. The boy was so terrified of the items he was accused of smuggling he was incapable of even explaining they weren't his; the Capitaine and the crew mistook the boy's fear for reverence and ordered him thrown overboard.

"I couldn't let the boy die yet I also knew that if I claimed the bags as mine, my subterfuge would be exposed. I told the Capitaine that since I was a traveler and was due to exit Haiti in less than three days, I would take possession of the items and they would be forever gone from Haitian soil. I asked for a moment alone with the boy, whose native dialect I also speak, and was allowed a private audience with him.

"I explained to the boy that the items were bound for a

voodoo priestess and told the lad that she was very proud of him and that he had played his part well. I explained to the boy that he must tell the Capitaine that he had been under a spell, which I had now cured. This the boy gladly did. Calm heads prevailed and the Capitaine spared the boy from a watery grave.

"We arrived in Baie-de-Henne, and I said goodbye to the crew. The Capitaine, to reward my deeds, presented me with a large sum of money. I was in Baie-de-Henne not more than a day when a very large native man accosted me and challenged me to a physical fight. The news of my deeds, and the Capitaine's generous payment, had travelled fast in the town and the man, a local bully and general cur amongst men, was there to prove his mettle and claim the money as his own. I told the man I would fight him in two days, in the local park. To this the man agreed.

"In the meanwhile, I visited the office of public records. After completing my research with regards to the bully, I had the young lad whose life I saved from the boat visit the local coffin maker, the local headstone engraver, and the local church, providing the proprietors of each establishment with a specific set of instructions along with a large payment in cash from the Capitaine's reward. The night before our contest I also visited the park and dug up the roots of two Royal Palm trees, which were situated roughly two feet apart. After I had cut up the roots, I arranged the dirt so as to cover my deeds.

"The next morning the appointed time arrived, and I

was in the park to begin our physical contest. The local bully, who was a giant of a human being, was eager to begin and prove his continued dominance of the region. I asked him if I might have a moment to prepare, which he begrudgingly obliged, succumbing to the pressure of the large crowd which had assembled to witness the event.

"As I sat meditating in the dirt, the local coffin maker arrived as I had instructed him. He was carrying a coffin and said he was to deliver it to the bully. The bully berated the coffin maker and sent him scurrying away. He was about to demand we begin when the tombstone engraver arrived bearing a tombstone that bore the man's name, his date of birth, and his date of death, which was set for that very day.

"The man was enraged and chased the engraver away. The bully was beside himself, what with seeing a coffin with his name burnt onto the wood and his own tombstone, which said he would die that day. The priest arrived as the man was looking at the tombstone and asked for the man by name. When the man announced that he was who the padre sought, the padre explained that he was to give the man his Last Rites. After the padre said this, I stood up and told the man I needed to stretch my arms and then I would be ready.

"I positioned myself between the two Royal Palms and pushed them as hard as I could. With the roots having been cut, the trees easily toppled. After the trees fell and as the dust was settling, I turned and announced I was ready to begin. The man simply had no idea what to make of all this and was scared witless. He turned and ran out of the town and apparently has not been back since."

"Why go through all the trouble? Why not fight the man?" Ali asked. The feat was almost unbelievable it was so amazing; in fact, had the story been told by anyone other than Tutor Carey, it probably would not have been believed by anyone.

"There was almost every chance the man would have killed me; this way I avoided having to fight him completely. As Sun-Tzu said, "Defeating the enemy without fighting is the true pinnacle of excellence." Tutor turned in his chair and began looking at his monitor again, clearly indicating that Ali's time was up and he needed to move along.

"Yes sir, thank you, that's certainly something to consider. Perhaps Ms. Goff wanted to see me."

CHAPTER 14

———————————

SUPPORTS.

SUPPORTS ARE, AS EVERYONE knows, the most underrated position in the game of Cheepee. The support is considered, by many, to be the playmaker on the Cheepee field; however, there are those who adamantly defend the box as the playmaker. Since the support cannot score, stop anyone from scoring, touch the rolling jum-jum ball (even if it has been killed), or use his/her sense of smell, many people do not want to play the position. The support's greatest asset is being the only person on the Cheepee field that can speak to another player, something the refs cannot even do. The fact that supports are forbidden to communicate with their own team after the tragedy of '91, does offset this "asset" a bit though.

The greatest support to play the game was Leah Mickey, Peaches '90. In her first match she manipulated a "rule" that said, "So welcome to the Company! Without your support, this would not have been possible." This "rule" wasn't in the abridged Cheepee rulebook, which was the rulebook used topside. The bunkers didn't have a rulebook because Cheepee was not a game there but a survival strategy, and losing meant dying.

The "rule" Leah was quoting was from the Company welcome packet. Many people thought this was cheating, which is allowed unless someone specifically says, "no cheating." If someone doesn't explicitly say, "no cheating," you can quite honestly do whatever you want on the Cheepee field as it becomes an instant State of Nature where there is no morality and the game is "solitary, poore, nasty, brutish, and short." Ask the NL-Ruler, he will tell you all about it while inadvertently making you terrified of everything.

The reason they thought this was cheating was because Leah did not bring it up during the pre-match meeting, conference, and, as the Company has repeatedly said, non-mandatory merchandise collection period. She said it during the game when the Peaches were ahead of the Greys. She stood in the middle of the field, atop the hangman's scaffold, and read the "rule." Since no one else was allowed to talk or ask questions, they all assumed she was reading from the rulebook. Everyone stood around until the lizard died, which always signals the end of a Cheepee match.

In the bunkers this "match" took place as well but it was between the residents of bunker modules one thru nine and the Greys, the little aliens with big heads and eyes, you know the ones I mean. The Peaches were winning until the Greys started atomizing people and using telepathy. That shit seemed unfair to everyone who was not a Grey. As I said, Cheepee is not a damn game in the bunkers.

Leah's subterfuge was discovered afterwards, when the abridged rulebook was consulted and the rule wasn't in there; however, since it was official Company literature it couldn't be dismissed. Leah decided to consult the official Cheepee rulebook for guidance. No one ever expected to see Leah again.

Leah stole off under cover of darkness into the bunkers, where she somehow gained entry into the Deep Bunkers, where the other Others and the bat-like things live, although no one is sure how. Leah was a disgruntled accountant who shouldn't have been able to pull it off at all. She managed to avoid Deep Bunker Fetch and the other Others but she lost a finger to one of the bat-like things; she didn't even know her finger was gone for thirty minutes, that's how scary the bat-like things are and one of the many reasons why they are called "The Unmentionable."

In the Deep Bunkers, where the other Others and the bat-like things live, she found herself completely lost in the dark. She was stumbling around in the pitch blackness where things ran over her feet while making a sound that caused her pelvis to vibrate uncomfortably. Whatever they were, the bat-like things loved to eat them. She found herself in a "cavelike dwelling," where there were prisoners chained to a wall. Above and behind them was a fire.

Shadows were cast on the wall by objects passing in front of the fire. The prisoners seemed to think that the shadows were real. Leah heard a "psst."

She looked around, there were two men in togas standing off in the shadows, one with a pig-nose and the other very broad-shouldered. She went over to them and they handed her a copy of the *Republic*.

Pig-nose said, "Everything you're looking at is in there, if you're curious."

The broad-shouldered guy whispered, "Isn't he dreamy?"

"Yeah, he seems nice," Leah whispered back. This was a white lie; she didn't think he was dreamy at all; broad-shouldered on the other hand wasn't too bad. Leah skimmed the *Republic* and got the gist of it. "So, it's hard work to get out of this cave because the exit is rough and painful." Leah pointed at a rough and steep ascent behind the fire, very faint traces of light coming through. The path did indeed look arduous and unpleasant.

"Yes," said the short guy. The other guy looked at him in a sheepish way.

"What about those?" Leah was pointing at a flight of stairs. "Where do those go?" The stairs led up into the dark, faint traces of light came through. They seemed to run parallel to the cave exit and to the same place. The only thing remarkable about them was that they were new, or at least not-well used. Of course, it was odd seeing a flight of stairs in the cavelike dwelling, but after losing a finger to the bat-like things, she was okay with weird as long as it wasn't dangerous.

"Oh, yeah, those go to the top too." Broad-shouldered said, looking at the ground in an embarrassed way, like a kid that peed itself.

"Why not take the stairs then?" Leah asked.

"You can, you just have to take off your hat and place it on the hat-rack."

"But I'm not wearing a hat."

"Then what is that?" Pig-nose pointed at her head. Leah felt and indeed she had a hat on her head. It was a plain cap; plain like herself. "Don't be concerned, no one notices it until someone points it out."

"All I have to do is take off this hat and hang it up, and I can walk up the stairs?"

"That's it."

"What's up there, the book kind of explained it but it doesn't seem to be all that useful to real problems topside."

"You have to see for yourself and then decide if you want to come back."

"Have either of you gone?" They both looked at each other for a moment, something passing between them.

"That isn't for us to say."

Leah was still looking for the official Cheepee rulebook and didn't have time to dally. "Well, I should take off. Here's your book back. Thanks." Leah went to the stairs and took off her hat. She noticed a flash inside the hat as she was hanging it on the rack. She looked inside; she did not cry out; her heart was not shaken. She did not see a devil's grimace or hear scornful laughter. She saw only her own reflection in a mirror that was inside the hat. She turned back to face the guys in the togas. She waved and said, "I'll tell you what all the fuss is when I get back." The gentlemen waved to her and went back to talking.

This, my friends, is going to be difficult to accept, for two reasons: first, the author didn't say if Leah took the steps or went the rough and painful way. It would appear that she took the steps, but he didn't specifically say either way, so there is a possibility she went the rough and painful way, some people are into that; and, so long as it's consensual, that's okay.

Second, you won't care how she got out of the cave, also for two reasons: first, both the rough and painful way and the stairs lead to the same place, just via different routes. The terminus of both points was a rickety door. Leah could tell the door led outside, and the smell of exhaust and copper hung heavy in the air.

When she walked through the door, she found herself in the Sub Bunkers under the Deep Bunkers, which resemble Precambrian Earth and where WWI, the Great War, is still being fought. I bet that you, like me, do not give one damn about whether Leah took the stairs.

The official Cheepee rulebook was located in the Sub Bunkers under the Deep Bunkers, which resemble Precambrian Earth and where WWI, the Great War, is still being fought. It was in the library in the middle of no-man's land, roughly halfway between the Centrals and the Allies. The strangest thing about all this was that units from all the wars in human history were engaged in WWI, the Great War. Because who fucking cares what you call it.

Leah, who had recently been promoted to Lieutenant in Napoleon's Hussars, was given the mission of leading a band of three other trusted Hussars to provide reconnaissance of the other side, a mere two klicks from the library itself. Her mission also included the proviso that, if they found any, they were to, "bring back some beer for the boys." This gave Lieutenant Mickey the chance she needed to get to the library and see if the Cheepee rulebook had clarification on whether supports made all this possible.

The best night to recon was the following evening, when the weather was supposed to get drab. That evening, a little before they were to set out, she sat across from Private Pierre Menard in the mess tent, the artillery having gone silent for vespers. Menard, as usual, was writing in his journal.

"What are you writing, Private?"

"A story about an errant knight and his faithful sidekick, ma'am," said Private Menard without looking up. Menard kept writing, obviously in the midst of a profound literary breakthrough. He put his pen in his uniform pocket and closed his notebook. He looked directly into Leah's eyes. "Ma'am, may I tell you something?"

"Of course. What is it?"

"I'm scared."

"Me too."

"Really?" Pierre Menard was a seventeen-year-old kid who shouldn't be in WWI, the Great War, Lieutenant Mickey thought. He was a boy playing at being a man, and he had thought that by holding a gun he could get there faster.

"Fear can be a good thing, Private. It means you're alive. If you learn to harness its energy, you can use fear to your advantage. Most people get nervous, successful people find a way to use that energy for something other than nerves. Take this here sniper rifle. I once shot a Roman Rock Slinger in Julius Caesar's Army at over a thousand yards; hit him dead center of the toga. I get scared; and I channel my fear into this here gun, and all is fine."

"Yes ma'am. I try to do the same thing with this." Menard held up his pen.

"I wouldn't count on that doing much damage, Pvt. Menard."

"With all due respect ma'am, this can do far more damage than what you're holding." Menard nodded at Leah's sniper rifle.

"How do you figure?"

"That gun can only take a life. This pen can do that too. I can also save a life. Or create one. This pen makes me an omnipotent being. Your rifle makes you scary, another limited god of death and destruction."

Menard was called away to help prepare the horses for the mission. As she watched him leave, Leah rolled a cigarette and thought about her conversation with the High Command.

"Congratulations, Lieutenant," said the High Command. The individuals of the High Command were hard to differentiate. They were many, their name was Legion.

"Thank you. I will do my best."

"We expect more than your best, Lieutenant, we expect 110%. This mission is of critical importance to WWI, the Great War." The High Command all nodded in unison, except the Z-High Command, he looked sad.

"Okay. How does that work?"

"What?"

"Well, both actually: how do you give 110% and how is this mission of critical importance to WWI, the Great War? First of all, you cannot actually give more than 100%. Watch this nifty little economic counterexample: if you give 110% of your money to someone else, then you gave that person all your money plus someone else's money. Here's a cool one from science: if you try to reach 110% of your heart's capacity, you will not make it. You cannot reach 110% without 110% being either the maximum possible threshold or a bump on your way to that actual threshold."

"It's a figure of speech."

"My ass, it's tied to my promotion sheet. That thing is full of numbers which you use to manipulate into a non-scientific statistic that's easy and fast to read. You then use this fictitious, "objective" yet scarcely-attainable, at best, criteria to justify your subjective opinions, thus keeping promotions and raises hostage."

"You are only a troop; you do not see the business of it."

"I'm sorry, of course I don't. You know what, it doesn't matter. I would like to say, since it's unlikely we'll be making it back, that this mission is not important to the success of WWI, the Great War."

"Why do you have such low prospects for success?"

"I did some intel research and the thing you want me to go recon is a fully-operational cyborg factory." That's right dear readers, even future wars make it into the Sub Bunkers under the Deep Bunkers, which resemble Precambrian Earth and where WWI, the Great War, is still being fought. "It's right beside a tank firing range and the route is through a sentient, AI guided mine-field."

"Your reconnaissance will allow us to make the correct decisions to finally bring an end to WWI, the Great War."

"You already have all you need to stop it."

"Dismissed, Lieutenant." As Leah was leaving, the Z-High Command caught her eye and something passed between them.

She finished her cigarette and went outside to where her Hussars were waiting. When she got close, Sergeant Ali called the Hussars to attention. "Hussars, a-ten-Hut! *Bon soire, mon Lieutenant.*"

"Stand easy." The Hussars relaxed but still stood tall and proud. There was Menard, Sergeant Ali, and Brigadier Houston, who had just arrived from the 1st Armor Division, Ft. Bliss, TX.

"Our mission is to go over there and see what's going on. Also, I need to stop at the library to look for a book. And we can loot and pillage so long as we bring back beer."

The Hussars nodded their approval of the verb pillage. Leah was a good leader, she did things in the correct order: mission, herself, others. She was sure to be successful.

"Ma'am, if I may, I'd like ta say I'm glad ta be here in WWI, which is *now* the Great War since Texas is involved." Brigadier Houston was wearing tanker boots and a Stetson hat; Leah thought the kid looked snappy.

"We're glad you're here too. We could use a little Texas help." Naomi beamed and nicked herself in the arm with a razor.

"Okay, enough talk, we get paid to work. Hussars, let's ride!" The Hussars let out a whoop that set the night air aflame. In Precambrian Earth, the only native life are single-celled organisms in the ocean and the dirty Paddi'u, who lived on the outskirts of no-man's land, not even worthwhile enough to be able to gain access to the meaningless death in that place. The little floaters in the ocean didn't seem all that impressed with the Hussar whoop but whole clans of Paddi'u beset upon other clans of Paddi'u and cannibalized them. This was because they thought the Hussar whoop was a command from some god telling them to do it.

Unbeknownst to the four trusted Hussars, the Allied forces had fielded military drones, complete with night-vision, infrared, thermal, telescoping lenses, and hellfire missiles. The combined weight of four adults and four horses is roughly 5122 pounds/2323 kilograms; one hellfire missile weighs roughly 125 pounds/57 kilograms, but only about 20 pounds/9 kilograms of that really matter, the rest simply gets it there. They never stood a chance; they were bested by technology and distance. The good news is the hellfire manufacturer was getting a bargain at one pound of explosive per 256.1 pounds of meat and bone. Invest in hellfire missiles, they are a sweet deal!

Before the hellfire killed everyone, Sergeant Ali saw Deep Bunker Fetch, who had slipped into WWI, the Great War, when Leah had left the door open because no one really avoids Deep Bunker Fetch. He was sneaking into a WMD depot, which was supposed to be empty but wasn't. Right before the hellfire announced its arrival, Deep Bunker Fetch caught Sgt. Ali's eye and winked.

Chapter 15

In which we meet a fountain of facts; a position regarding sex and objectification is presented; and the
least-liked person in the bunkers is allowed to roam.

ALI LOOKED DOWN, THE red path was no longer lit. He could see the people on the first floor, those who saw him looking sneered directly at him. He glanced behind him and noticed that Tutor was working on something and he didn't feel like asking him for help finding Calliope Goff's office.

Ali heard a "whoosh" noise immediately beside him and then plowed into a wall with his back. The Upper who had arrived on the air lift had startled Ali so bad that he had jumped back on instinct and collided with one of the invisible walls.

Ali heard many, many people laughing at him. The recently air lifted Upper who had startled Ali in the first place said, "Aren't Deeplings ridiculous!" He was laughing, "I know, right?!" as he walked away.

Ali was instantly happy and then immediately woeful. He was at the air lift, which meant he could use that to get to Calliope's office; the problem was, he had no idea how to use the air lift. The BoI Uppers all had earpieces and could talk to the air lift; workers in the Deep didn't wear earpieces, only Uppers did, which meant Ali had no way of communicating with the air lift.

Ali could see that his quandary was spreading throughout the building as more and more people began looking at him. He wasn't going to just step into the air lift and hope for the best; he didn't need the BoI to see him fall down an invisible hole in an invisible building. He decided to bite the bullet and ask Tutor how to get upstairs.

Ali turned and saw a Snail wiping the wall where he had left a smudge. Ali had no idea where the Snail had come from, everyone on the floor was easy to see and you can always tell a Snail when you see one. This had happened on the first floor too, when Ali had smacked into the wall face-first; a Snail had seemingly appeared, cleaned the glass, and then disappeared.

"Hi. Can you help me?" Ali asked.

The Snail looked at Ali in complete bewilderment. "Are you talking to me?" the Snail asked Ali in a hushed tone.

"Yeah. I'm trying to get to the third floor but I don't know where the stairs are and I don't know how to use the air lift. Can you help me?" Ali considered mentioning the Snail Way trip in the BoA but decided against it. He couldn't handle another trip like that, not here and not now, at least.

"I can walk you to the stairs to the third floor, but from there I can't help you anymore."

"Getting to the stairs will be fine with me. Thank you."

Ali followed the Snail as it led the way. Ali was amazed that the Snail, like the Uppers, could simply walk through the building as unhindered and free of crashing into something as confidently as someone would walk through an empty parking lot. Ali had to stay close because the Snail knew when to turn and Ali didn't. If he let the Snail get too far ahead there could conceivably be something in between the two of them that Ali would smack into again.

As the Uppers in the building were watching Ali, there began some commotion about how Ali was navigating the floor so quickly. Ali noticed people looking at him and clearly talking about him in their earpieces. He couldn't pay attention to them because he had to be diligent while following the Snail.

The Snail stopped and turned around; it pointed out and up with its left hand. "There. Those go up to the third floor."

Ali looked; of course, he didn't see stairs at all, just an empty space. He realized that he had one advantage now; the red light was only lit on the floor he was on; any floor where there apparently wasn't a Deepling wasn't lit with a red light. It wasn't a trail of breadcrumbs but it was an advantage when, and if, he found stairs.

"How do you find your way around so fast? I can't tell where anything is in here. I keep running into things."

"I've been here a long time; I know where to go."

"Oh."

"I need to go back to work, good luck." The Snail walked off. Ali looked at where the stairs were and then looked up to see if he could locate Calliope. Ali had never met her and he only knew her from her Cheepee information. He had heard stories about her and he was not looking forward to encountering her at all; if any single one of the stories were true, Ali had to be careful not to invoke her wrath and get another write-up for disrespect.

Ali decided to walk up the stairs as if he could see them. In a moment of blind faith, he closed his eyes and stepped up. His only error was in not knowing how many steps there were; he guessed twelve. He guessed wrong; however, luckily there were only eleven stairs and not thirteen, otherwise he would have kicked the last step and gone sprawling. Ali noticed that the red light came on as soon as he alit on the third floor and that helped him realize he was on the last step. He looked down, he noticed that floors one and two were no longer glowing red. The second floor Snail was nowhere to be seen.

Ali scanned the third floor looking for Calliope. Most of the people on the floor were looking at him and talking into their earpieces. Ali had an idea; he smeared his hand against the glass wall in front of him.

"Excuse me, sir, I need to clean that." The Snail said from behind Ali.

"Goodness gracious, where did you come from?!" Ali

nearly screamed from fright. The Snail retreated, making Ali feel like an ogre. "I'm sorry, you scared me."

"My apologies, sir. Please don't kill me."

"What?"

The Snail looked at Ali and saw the T-badge. "You don't work here, do you?"

"No, I work in the Deep. My name is Ali, I need to find Calliope Goff, can you take me to her?"

"I can, but I need to clean that first," the Snail was pointing at the smudge.

"Oh, sorry about that. I didn't know how else to get you to come over here."

"It's okay, sir; it's why I'm here." The Snail cleaned the wall to a see-thru polish in an instant. "Please, follow me."

The Snail led Ali along the third floor. Ali could see down two floors, and while he wasn't acro- or agoraphobic, the effect of looking down into the first floor from the third was still uncomfortable. The Snail walked along, not touching anything; Ali followed close behind. As when the Snail on the second floor had led Ali along, the Uppers continued the commotion about how Ali was navigating the floor so quickly.

The Snail stopped and pointed to the left. "She's right over there." Ali looked to where the Snail was pointing. He could see Calliope looking directly at him from about fifty feet away and talking into her earpiece. Ali turned to thank the Snail but it was gone. Ali scanned everywhere but he did not see the Snail at all. He was tempted to smear the glass again but he could feel Calliope's eyes on him.

Ali slowly made his way to where she was, his hand out in front of him all the while. As he approached her, he heard her talking.

"Not so much painful as annoying. No, not like getting a shot. There are three, not two. Your job, your own well-being, and your community support."

Ali guessed he had reached her office, she was sitting at her see-thru desk, the same as Hope and Tutor. Ali wasn't sure how to knock without looking foolish.

"Ms. Goff?" Calliope stood when she was greeted.

"Calliope Goff, Bureau of Information Keeper of Facts. Introduce yourself Deepling. Because she's a burden to you. She doesn't love you. Don't know, haste, DDT."

"Uh, my name is Ali Kim, I work in the Deep."

"It depends on where you get it. Yes, and the size. That would be community support. No, you can't use that because it's part of her job. Where is your badge Deepling? She belittles you. That's not love, it's spite. Sees, epees, error." Calliope was looking directly at Ali but he wasn't sure what she was talking about; he knew she was talking to him at least part of the time, but it couldn't have been the case that she was talking to him all the time.

"I lost it while…."

"The ribs hurt. Meaty areas aren't bad. That's okay but ask if there's anything better. Make sure you use version three. Shut up. What do you want? You shouldn't feel guilty. She didn't love you before she got dementia. Leaves, hosted, atv."

"Silas told me the boss wanted to see me and…."

"That depends on the size and location. They work with you. Two weeks ago. Not much, formatting mostly. It is preposterous to think that anyone would want to see you. Her retirement check should cover the cost. Bye. Bonders, Erato, nabob."

Calliope continued to speak into her earpiece, effectively ignoring Ali. She continued her other conversations but she was no longer talking about badges or Deeplings. Both Bunker Calliope and Deep Bunker Calliope were black market traders with the mongrel Paddi'u. One would expect this in the Deep Bunkers, where the other Others and the bat-like things live, and where anything at all goes. How Calliope interacts with the disgusting things is a complete mystery. No one in the Deep Bunkers knows Calliope interacts with the Paddi'u; she tells people she fashions the things she trades. This is believed because Deep Bunker Calliope is very distantly related to Tvastar and she disappears into the mezzo-tunnels with "The Other Unmentionables" and the real Others for weeks at a time. The fact that she is extremely useful to everyone, and no one knows she deals with the Paddi'u, are the two reasons no one bothers her; she is the only safe person in the Deep Bunkers.

One would think that the Philosopher Rulers would discourage interactions with anything topside; however, Bunker Calliope's activities are tolerated to a degree. This is the one time the Bunker Dweller Speaker swayed the Philosopher Rulers. In a speech, the Bunker Dweller Speaker had said that sending a person topside to explore was practically useful in that information about conditions topside could be gained and resources could be located and possibly retrieved. While the risks were great, the rewards too could be great.

The Bunker Dweller Speaker concluded by saying the only real problem the Philosopher Rulers were facing was allowing Bunker Calliope to re-enter the bunkers once she left. As anyone was free to leave whenever they wanted, or were required to leave after the bunker census, that was not an issue; Calliope could simply leave on her own at any time.

She should be allowed to return because she above all people was willing to endure the conditions topside of her own volition and, since she was the least-liked person in the bunkers, it would actually be better for her to be gone. If she made it back, then the Bunker Dwellers may gain some useful information; if she didn't make it back, that was equally useful. There was no danger of anyone "following in her footsteps" because, seriously, she was the least-liked person in the bunkers.

The Philosopher Rulers agreed to let her go, on the condition that she would be decontaminated thoroughly upon her return and the Philosopher Rulers would be allowed to speak to her first, in private. This was not well-received by the Bunker Dwellers, for they thought there should be more transparency. The Philosopher Rulers said that the horrors likely encountered would be both many and easy to misunderstand; therefore, she should speak to them first so they could help her understand her own experiences. The Bunker Dwellers begrudgingly agreed. The Philosopher Rulers didn't say it, but they knew she was the least-liked person in the bunkers, even amongst themselves, and it would actually be better for her to be gone.

Ali left Calliope's office by doing a one-hundred-eighty degree turn and walking back fifty feet to where the Snail had left him. By sheer chance he saw Fetch looking at him from above. Fetch motioned for Ali to come over to him. Fetch was about two-hundred feet away and clearly on the fourth floor because he was bathed in white light, not red. Ali didn't know how to get to where Fetch was so he smudged the wall to bring out the Snail again.

"Excuse me, sir, I need to clean that," the Snail said from behind Ali.

"Shit fire, man!" Ali yelled and spun around. The Snail cowered in fear.

"My apologies sir, please don't kill me."

"Dude, what are you talking about?"

The Snail looked up at Ali. "Oh, it's you. How may I help you?"

"Do you see that guy over there on the fourth floor?" Ali pointed at Fetch.

"Yes, sir."

"I need to get over to him. Can you lead the way?"

"Yes, sir. I need to clean that first," the Snail indicated the smudge Ogre Ali had created to bring it out of hiding.

"Oh, sorry about that. Is there another way to get your attention? I hate creating work for you."

"It's okay. If you don't like smudging the walls you could throw down some trash and I'll get it."

"What?"

"You can throw something on the floor instead of smudging the glass."

"Why would I do that?"

"To get my attention."

"You're joking, right?"

"No sir, that's why I'm here. Please, follow me."

The Snail seamlessly navigated its way around the third floor, close to where Fetch was standing. It stopped and turned around to face Ali. Ali could tell by the lighting that he was at a staircase.

"Go up, turn right, and walk straight one-hundred feet; you won't hit anything. Good luck." Ali heard Fetch call his name from above.

"Ali, get up here," Fetch called from above. Ali turned to thank the Snail but it was gone. Ali scanned the entire floor for the Snail but it was not there.

"What are you doing?" Ali turned and looked up the stairs. Fetch was standing there, waiting for him.

"Hello, I was looking for the Snail."

"There are no Snails here."

"I'm sorry?" Ali was standing beside Fetch when he realized he had climbed the stairs without even noticing it. The lights on the fourth floor were now red; a quick glance down showed white light all the way down to the ground.

"There are no Snails here. Where is your badge?" Fetch was looking at the dishonor clipped to Ali's shirt.

"I went running and I lost it somewhere. I have the paperwork for a new one, it should…."

"Shut up. This is exactly why no one likes Deeplings. Why are you here?"

"Silas told me that the boss wanted to see me, but he didn't say which one. I've seen almost everyone and I still don't know who wanted me. It isn't you, is it?"

"Why would I want to see a Deepling in the BoI? I don't like red light, dude."

"Maybe it was Acrimony."

"Careful Mr. Kim, you're on probation."

"Yes sir, no disrespect intended, I meant Ms. Taylor."

"Better." Fetch scanned the fifth floor looking for Acrimony. Into his earpiece he said, "Acrimony? That's right, man. It's all cool, thanks." Fetch looked at Ali, "She's not here today."

"Really? Do you know if she wanted to see me?"

"Why on earth would I know that, man?"

"Will she be back tomorrow?"

"Am I your freaking secretary, man?" Into his earpiece Fetch said, "She'll be back tomorrow, right? Cool, alright." To Ali, Fetch said, "Yeah man, she'll be here tomorrow, but you'd better be here super-early, she has a meeting all day tomorrow and won't be available after 7:00am."

Ali looked at his watch. "Okay, it's time to go home anyway."

"Cool, I'll go out with you." Ali couldn't believe his luck; with Fetch walking out with him he could get out of the building simply by following him. They began walking to the air lift, Ali letting Fetch lead so he could follow; also, Ali shouldn't be walking directly beside an Upper anyway.

"Do you have any plans tonight?" Ali was taking a risk here, he shouldn't be getting personal with an Upper in the BoI, even though Fetch was his Cheepee teammate.

"Yeah man, I've got a date."

"That's nice. Any plans?"

"After we have sex or make out, we may go do something, hard to say really. She's supposed to be into necromancy, so maybe something to do with that," Fetch was as nonchalant as ever. They had reached the air lift and Fetch said into his earpiece, "Lift, fourth floor to entrance." A *whooshing* noise signaled the arrival of the lift.

"Do women ever get upset with your forthrightness?" Ali asked as he entered the lift and they descended.

"Why would anyone be upset?"

"It seems a little disrespectful, doesn't it?"

"Is it disrespectful to ask for your check when you're done with dinner?"

"No, I guess not."

"Is it disrespectful to tell someone you want a size ten shoe and not a size eleven?" They had arrived on the bottom floor and were heading out the building as they talked. Ali could see via the X-rays that Fetch had several piercings; the thermal monitors showed Ali that Fetch was getting excited about his date, or at least the conversation.

"What does that have to do with anything?"

"It's not wrong to tell people what you want. It's also not wrong to want sex. It's disrespectful to not be up front with people about what you want."

"It seems like you're objectifying them."

"Not at all, man. I respect people and I show my respect by being straightforward. There's no objectification there; I would only be objectifying people if I weren't honest with them up front. It's disrespectful and objectifying to lie and try to weasel into someone's pants without their knowing that's what you're doing."

Ali and Fetch had made it outside the BoI and were standing near the security grotto. Fetch removed his earpiece, turned it off, and put it in his pocket.

"Don't you think it's a bit misogynistic to tell women up front you want sex with them? Seems to me that you are using them as a warm spot to park yourself." This would have been grounds for instant execution per Company law had Ali said it to Fetch in the BoI or if his earpiece had been in and other people could have heard him; however, since Fetch and Ali were outside, Ali could adopt a more convivial attitude.

"You make it seem like I'm a follower of Hesiod, Paul, and Schopenhauer. It isn't misogynistic to enjoy sex; it's misogynistic to think women are only good for sex. I find being in the presence of women both enjoyable and entertaining. And that's not from, or for, the sex.

"I have plenty of women peers and I respect all of them. I listen to them, I consider their opinions, advice, and arguments, and I treat women as human beings, no different than men. I don't see how you get that because my penis fits into their vagina and I enjoy the sensation of it that I am misogynistic." Fetch wasn't angry, he seemed genuinely confused that Ali didn't understand him.

"I think that it seems crass is all."

"Don't even start with me. You want Maggie, don't you?"

"That's not the same thing at all." Speaking of crass, Ali was getting a chubby thinking about sex with Maggie.

Nope, I got this dear reader, if I miss anything, feel free to jump in when I'm done asking the author about this.

"I think it would be beneficial to you to perhaps reread chapter three," I said.

"What do you mean?"

"I thought that Ali was female when it came to Maggie? You tried to run me through with an illegal epee when we 'discussed' this earlier."

"That's still true." The authored furrowed his brow and did an open palm gesture; the international sign displaying that the person to whom you're speaking is a jackass.

"Okay, listen to this, 'speaking of crass, Ali was getting a chubby thinking about sex with Maggie.' I'm not an OB/GYN specialist or anything, but I don't think women get 'chubbies.'"

"I don't think they do either; well, at least not a penile chubby."

"Thank you for walking straight into the problem, I hope you weren't injured."

"What problem?"

"That Ali has a chubby because of Maggie and we have just established that women cannot get penile chubbies."

"But Maggie isn't there, they are only talking about her. It would be stupid to suggest that Ali was a female when thinking about Maggie. That doesn't make sense at all."

"And it makes sense that Ali's sex changes when Maggie is present?"

"Yeah, because of my artistic endeavors."

Ali and Fetch were waiting for the trams to come. Ali's tram would be first since he lived further out on Company grounds than Fetch.

"Because I find Maggie sexually attractive doesn't mean I objectify her." Ali said.

"I agree. You have a hang-up about sexual liberalism or something, doesn't make sense to me." Fetch lit another cigarette, his ninth since leaving the BoI. "I want a relationship that includes sex. There's nothing wrong with wanting that."

The trams and the maggots were on very tight schedules. Upper management likes to stress that using the tram is not a requirement for a positive employee report and you will not be hobbled in the way of Annie Wilkes if you don't use the tram and/or maggot.

There was one important exception to the non-requirement of taking the maggot. Bunker Calliope was required to walk everywhere she went because she needed the cardio for her topside explorations. She was also not to be followed. No one could interact with her between the time she left for topside and before she was debriefed by the Philosopher Rulers. Also, since she was the least-liked person in the bunkers, no one really wanted to follow or talk to her anyway and it was actually better that she wasn't allowed to ride in the maggots.

Her first three topside excursions were mostly uneventful. She found contaminated and unpotable groundwater, very little naturally growing food, all inedible, and vast stretches of parched land. She didn't know if it was the peoples' negligence or their arrogance that had caused it; it's not like it mattered, either way.

The Philosopher Rulers contemplated disallowing Bunker Calliope to travel anymore, but she was so disliked they allowed her to go again. The Philosopher Rulers thought the bunkers were demonstrably better, and they meant by any ethical standard that can be used.

While exploring much further than she had planned, she was ambushed by a band of Paddi'u in the early morning hours of her sixth day in the actual-empty wastes. The Paddi'u rendered her unconscious and carried her to the Paddi'u President. When she awoke, she was in a furnished room, laying on a feather bed. The door opened and what might have been two Paddi'u females were standing there.

"Did you sleep well?" the first woman asked. She was tall and had skin of the deepest ebon. Her companion was almost stark-white.

"I did. Where am I?"

"You are in the palace of President Lucas of the Paddi'u. My name is Imgur. This is Kašušu." Imgur was very broad at the shoulders and was a formidable figure in breadth; Kašušu was much taller and Calliope could see her musculature left nothing open for debate about her power. Both were vastly bigger than Calliope and she knew that if anything went sideways, she was in trouble.

"You are to see President Lucas, if you are ready," Kašušu said. Both Paddi'u were wearing what looked like minimal togas, which they called an *anpa len*; Imgur's was scarlet with white piping, Kašušu's was white with lapis lazuli piping.

"I'm ready to go," Calliope said. She was about to get out of bed when she realized she was completely naked. Her clothes must have been removed while she slept.

"Do you know where my clothes are, I seem to have lost them. And my bag, do you know where that is?"

"Your belongings are safely locked up in the armory. They will be returned to you when you leave. In the meantime, while you are here, you may wear the *anpa len*." While being publicly naked in the bunkers was commonplace, Calliope didn't want to be so exposed among the Paddi'u.

The *anpa len* that Imgur indicated was terra-cotta colored and similar in both fit and design to the ones the Paddi'u were wearing. The *anpa len* was sitting on a chair across the room. Neither Imgur nor Kašušu made any move to give Calliope privacy so she could get dressed.

Calliope got out of the bed and crossed the room to retrieve the *anpa len*. Once she had it donned, she told her escorts she was ready to see President Lucas.

"Very well, please follow," Kašušu said. She then turned and began walking down the corridor. Imgur moved to the side to let Calliope follow Kašušu. When she had entered the corridor and was following Kašušu, two hooded Paddi'u wearing teal blue and white *anpa len* flanked Calliope on either side. She could tell that Imgur was walking directly behind her. No one said anything as they moved along the corridors.

While they were walking, Calliope could not help but notice that there were no windows. The bedroom didn't have any and she didn't see any in the corridors. Odorless and smokeless wall sconces lit their way.

Kašušu arrived at a large double door and stopped. She turned to face Calliope.

"Inside is the President of the Paddi'u. As you are not one of us, you do not need to offer supplication; however, please be honest with any answers you provide. Please do not be disrespectful. Do you have any questions?"

"Not at this moment. I may later though," Calliope said.

"Very well. Please follow." Kašušu opened the door and walked into the room. Calliope followed her, the flanking, hooded figures keeping perfectly abreast with her as she moved. When they had all five entered, Imgur closed the door.

Calliope caught her breath; the room was gigantic and

there were at least a thousand *anpa len*-clad Paddi'u sitting in chairs like they were attending a lecture. The chairs were arranged in a semi-circle, auditorium style, with stadium seating. The Paddi'u in the room were seated according to the color of their *anpa len*. There were at least thirty different groups and she noticed none of their *anpa len* was terra-cotta. Within the groups there were all types of Paddi'u, all ages, sexes, colors, and sizes; the only thing that provided continuity among them were the colors of the *anpa len*. When the door closed and the party walked down the main aisle, every eye turned on Calliope and no one made a noise.

Kašušu led the group to the stage in the front of the room and stood erect as an obelisk. Five heavy, booming knocks were heard throughout the whole room, causing Calliope to start. At the end of the fifth knock, Kašušu, Imgur, and the two escorts dropped to their left knees, placed closed fists on either side of their right foot, and placed their foreheads on their right knee. All one-thousand and four Paddi'u bowed and began to hum in a very low, guttural way.

Calliope watched horrified as a man entered. He was wearing a very heavy robe which extended past his legs and created a train like on a wedding dress. The sleeves extended well-past the hands.

The color of his robe and the color of his face were exact matches and the line where the neck ended and the robe began was seamless. The effect was so completely unexpected Calliope thought her brain was going to forego the polite two-week notice and simply quit on the spot. The man walked to the center of the stage and sat on a chair, his fleshy-robes draped about him. She realized it was fabric, but the imagery was almost sickening.

"Friends, please." At these words the entire room became silent and the seated Paddi'u raised their heads. The hooded-Paddi'u on Calliope's flanks rose and stepped away from her, both turning to face her. Kašušu took two steps forward and turned to face her. She heard Imgur take two steps back. Everyone was now looking directly at her.

"I am Stan Lucas, President of the Paddi'u. We welcome you. May we ask you some questions?"

"Yes sir, of course."

"Thank you for your courtesy. What do you prefer to be called? Please spare no formality, choose as you wish to be called and we will call you that."

Calliope had never been given the opportunity to select a name before. She quite enjoyed her own name, so she said, "My name is Calliope Goff, but please call me Calliope."

"Thank you, Calliope; and again, welcome. How is it that you have come to be here?"

"I'm not sure. I woke up here. To be honest, I'm not sure where 'here' is."

"Thank you for your honesty, Calliope. Honesty is very highly valued here. Please allow a clarification question: how did you come to be in a position to be brought here?"

"I was exploring topside and I made camp for the evening as normal. I went to bed in the actual-empty wastes and awoke here."

"Thank you, Calliope. You said 'topside' and 'the actual-empty wastes.' Do I understand that those terms are synonyms for you?"

"Yes, we call them the same thing."

What happened next was so fast it was almost over by the time Calliope consciously registered any of it. Imgur grabbed Calliope's feet from behind her and lifted them high into the air. Calliope would have face-planted into the floor had the hooded-Paddi'u beside her not caught her arms and held her. The way she was positioned against them, if they dropped to a knee, they would have broken her wrist and elbow and most certainly removed her arms from the socket at the shoulder.

Kašušu had stepped forward and was holding her by the hair. She had a sharpened blade against Calliope's throat. There was not an ounce of doubt in Kašušu's eyes that led Calliope to believe she would not kill her; Kašušu's hands were steady as stone.

"Friends. Please." President Lucas stood up, his robe-self spilling onto the floor. Calliope's legs were released and the hooded-Paddi'u at her sides moved to catch her legs with theirs and gently lowered her to the ground. Kašušu had released her hair and was again standing two steps away. Whatever had been at Calliope's throat was no longer visible.

"Our apologies, Calliope." President Lucas turned and faced the Paddi'u. "Friends, a reminder that Calliope is not one of us and therefore is not bound by our rules. She is not subject to our approaches. I will remind us of our rules about these matters if I must, but I don't think that will be necessary at all. Will it?" Every head lowered as one. "Friends, thank you." President Lucas sat down and every head raised as one.

"Calliope, again, our apologies. If you like, I can explain what just happened; however, we can assure you it will not occur again, unless you pose a danger to us, through deed or illocutionary act. Do you understand? It is very important you do; whether you would like an explanation is solely up to you."

"I, I, uh." Calliope was shaking. Beside her, to the left, the hooded Paddi'u presented her with a cup of clear liquid.

"It is water, Calliope, and it is completely safe to drink. Any of us would take the first sip, should you desire."

Calliope took the cup and drained it. The water helped her calm down. She handed the cup back to the hooded-Paddi'u. She took a deep breath and exhaled.

"I understand, I'm not a threat to you, I swear on my life. Please don't let that happen again." Calliope was scared to death and on the verge of tears.

"It will not," President Lucas smiled.

"Okay, I'm really sorry for whatever I did. I'd like to know."

"I understand. I asked if topside and the actual-empty wastes were synonyms to which you said, 'yes, we call them the same thing.' You are not qualified to make that claim, since there is no 'we' here."

"I don't get it." Calliope didn't know what he was talking about at all.

"You are from the bunkers, are you not Calliope?"

"I am, how did you know?"

"You are not Paddi'u, no one can live in the actual-empty wastes alone, and only someone who lived underground would call the actual-empty wastes, 'topside.'"

"Oh, that makes sense. But what did I do to deserve whatever just happened?"

"Here, in this place, it is punishable by death to speak for the group without the group being present to give its consent. When you said 'we' you were speaking for a group that wasn't present."

"Wow! I don't want to sound rude, but that is a lot different than how the bunkers work. It's also completely against Company policy." The Company promotes groups, although, as Upper management likes to stress, being a member of at least ten groups is not punishable by demotion or chemical castration. They stress this non-punishment a lot.

"We are sure it is."

"May I ask you a question?"

"Certainly, Calliope."

"Why do you keep saying 'we?' Come to think of it, you

have personally referred to both yourself as an individual and as part of a collective. Why is that not punishable by death since you're talking about a group?"

"That is a good question, Calliope. I can say 'we' because this is all of us." He motioned with his arm to the room. "The entirety of our group is present in this room. I am the President by unanimous decision so I can speak for the whole; since I am still me, I can speak for myself too. I do not confuse the two; nor do we."

"I think I get it, seems pretty inefficient though."

"It is not inefficient; if anyone disagrees, they need only stand up and say their piece. Calliope, may we ask you one more question?"

"Yes."

"Why were you topside?"

Calliope explained about the bunkers and the Company and, the author says, showed him a copy of this book, which is apparently a smashing success in the mostly-empty wastes between the actual-empty wastes and the Company grounds. Deep Bunker Q is said to have a copy of it on Snail Pages and the thing is said to be amazing.

"Do you think there's a way for us to trade with each other, maybe learn from one another's culture? Who knows, maybe find a solution to our collective woes?" Calliope was hopeful. She thought that whatever good the bunkers had done and whatever good these Paddi'u had done could be combined for everyone's good.

"We thank you Calliope, but we cannot accept."

"Why?" Calliope said. She thought at worst they would say, "let's think about it," or a promise of future cooperation; she hadn't even considered she would be outright told "no."

"Calliope, from what you have said, your own group doesn't cooperate amongst itself. You would not be able to work with us."

"You're missing a great opportunity." Calliope wasn't ready to present a full set of reasons; she was hoping the opportunities were enough to sway him.

"I once lived in a town, and then I had to leave. I was exiled from my home for reasons I was never myself given. I have something for you, it may help." President Lucas reached into his flesh-robe for something. To Calliope it seemed as though he had reached his hand into his own body and was digging around in his chest cavity. She was hoping he wouldn't pull out his own heart and show her.

From his robes, President Lucas produced a book. He handed it to Kašušu who handed it to Calliope. She looked at it; the book was called *The Arrest*.

"We are all here because we didn't want to be a part of that anymore," he indicated the book with a pointed finger. "We have what we need; it is too bad you think you don't."

"What happens now?"

"You will be getting drowsy in a little while; the water you drank will make you sleepy, but it is not harmful or dangerous in any way. When you awake again, you will be where you set up camp last night."

"But I don't know where I am or how to get back here to see you again."

"I know. We think it's for the best. There are other groups topside, as you call it; perhaps what you are looking for is with them."

"I hope you get what you are after." Ali said.

"Thanks, man." Fetch lit another cigarette and took a pull from a handle of whisky. "She's pretty awesome and likes to bang, so it'll be all good."

CHAPTER 16

───────

READERS ARE TEASED WITH A SIGHT OF THE PENTAGARCHY; ALI ENDURES A COLD AND SWAMPY STANDOFF; THE BUNKER EXPERIMENT WITH THE RULES; AND THE PROS AND CONS OF EXCESS.

ALI WAS RUNNING MUCH earlier than usual, which meant he wouldn't get to see that flash of light on top of Ditch Peak. He wouldn't be running this early but he had to be at the BoI to see Acrimony. Fetch had said that he would let Acrimony know he was coming to see her. Maybe Fetch thought he was doing Ali a favor.

As Ali approached the Statue of Progress, it occurred to him that he had never been this close to the guard shack without there being any light. That weighed heavy on his mind as he approached the turnaround.

He was tempted to turn around before he even got to the guard shack and had made up his mind to do so when he noticed that there were no lights on in the shack itself. No security lights lit up the outside either. Ali hugged the far shoulder as he slowly approached the Statue of Progress.

From the look of it, there was no one there; the guard shack was unmanned. Ali thought that was fairly odd, since you typically guard things at night and not exclusively during the day. Whatever the reason, Ali considered himself lucky the shack empty; he took a drink, stretched, and ran to catch the early tram.

Ali was surprised to see Q on the tram. "*Hola*, Q."

"*Hola, Ali. Como estes?*" Q wasn't smiling her happy smile. She looked upset and tired.

"I'm fine, thank you. You don't look very good. Did you have a bad night?"

"*Si*. I had a bad dream." Ali counted his blessings because she said 'bad dream' and not *pesadilla*, which was a nightmare; a good thing since Ali was still trying to erase the disturbing mental image of Q's terrifying swing-set. The Company had buried the intern who had died upon hearing it and that other one is still somewhere in the mighty, mighty Pacific Ocean.

"Oh, I'm sorry." Ali specifically did not say, "do you want to talk about it." Unfortunately, Q must have heard him say it anyway because she started telling Ali about her dream.

"I was in a room. A light was shining on me like I was on a stage and the center of attention. Cinco figures stood before me, on a platform. They had neither arms nor legs; their bodies were *tubos* covered in course hair.

"The skin on their heads was a dark clay brown. Four of them had eyes, all glowing orange: one had eyes on the end of *tallos largos*...."

Dear reader, I think the author had a bit of demonic possession and I stopped taking notes. I don't think anything he "said" was pertinent to the plot or that any of it was meant to be heard by the living. I pretended to take notes because he was freaking me out pretty bad.

Ali was doing everything he could not to listen. He even went so far as to try to isolate this moment in time from himself, which he thought might be possible, given his conversation with Antoinette.

"Yeah, that is bad. Hey Q, would you mind signing me through the security grotto?" Ali indicated his T-badge and hoped she wouldn't smite or curse him.

"Oh, you haven't heard the bad part yet. You never found your old one?"

"No, it hasn't turned up yet. I keep looking for it while I'm running, but no luck."

The tram stopped and they got out. After Q signed Ali in and they went through the grotto, she asked Ali if he wanted to hear 'the bad part' of her dream.

"I'd love to Q, maybe later. Right now, I have to go to the BoI and see Acrimony Taylor."

"¡*Ay*! What for?"

"I'm still looking for whomever it is that wants to see me. Silas told me the other day to go see the boss and I've been trying to find out which boss."

"Too bad. Buena suerte, Ali." Q walked away toward the Deep as Ali headed to the WDC.

Ali walked into the *ridículamente aterrador cuadrado*, descended the escalator, saw he might have a cavity, and headed to the air lift. Although he didn't understand how, the air lift took him directly to the fifth floor when he entered it; as he rose in the lift, he watched everyone in the building as they went about gathering and passing information. He tried not to look, but he noticed two people were in the slightly opaque. It struck Ali as weird to see every move everyone made; he watched as they effortlessly moved about, never once colliding with anything.

Ali supposed that once you knew the layout, even an invisible labyrinth can be navigable. While there is no labyrinth in the Deep Bunkers, where the other Others and the bat-like things live, there is a Minotaur. No one seems to know if it's *The Minotaur* of ancient fable, or a different, non-fabulous one. There is, however, absolutely no question that it is an actual minotaur. It is the only thing Deep Bunker Fetch ever deliberately tries to avoid. When it doesn't eat a Deep Bunker Dweller who misjudged where it was, it is said to dine with Deep Bunker Q.

Ali was on the fifth floor and needed to get to Acrimony's office. There were few people in the building, of course Ali could see all but the two in the opaque, so there weren't many people to sort through to find her. From what Ali remembered about her, she was always wearing a parka, and indeed there was a parka-clad woman about three-hundred feet from Ali. She was talking into her earpiece and looking at her monitor, she had either not noticed Ali or was ignoring him.

Ali could summon a Snail, he knew that; he could also do the ridiculous looking shuffle with his hand out and taking tiny steps. Ali heard the *whoosh* of the air lift and a woman got off on the fifth floor.

"Good morning," Ali said to the woman.

"Deepling?" she asked, looking at the T-badge, the indicator of Ali's revulsion.

"Yes ma'am, I work in the Deep. Can you…?" Ali never finished his question. He was going to ask her if she would mind walking him to Acrimony's office; instead, he was watching her walk away from him.

The good news was that Ali watched her as she walked away. He very carefully watched as she seamlessly navigated the floor. She passed Acrimony's office and said good morning. Acrimony said, "Good morning, Hanna," without ever looking up at her.

Ali carefully walked ahead, following Hanna's path as he remembered it. He arrived in front of Acrimony's office without incident, which made him so happy he committed the way back to the air lift to memory.

Ali was standing in the entrance to Acrimony's office; it was like a Carolina swamp in August. It wasn't the heat so much as the humidity; Ali could smell the change in air density, he had no idea how Acrimony could stand being in the office. The fact that she was wearing a hooded, military-style parka was dumbfounding.

"Ms. Taylor?"

"What do you want Deepling?" Acrimony never looked at Ali while she talked to him. She continued to work on whatever she was doing without ever registering Ali was actually there.

"Silas told me…."

"That you needed to see the boss. Did he say you needed to come see me?"

"No, ma'am, he didn't know who was looking…."

"That is because Deeplings are the epitome of ineffectualness. That Silas did not know who was looking for you is not surprising. No one expects anything of any of you, so I shouldn't be surprised you're wasting my time."

"I'm sorry, ma'am. I'm trying to do what I was told to do. Do you know…."

"You were not seriously going to ask me if I know who wants to see you, were you?" Acrimony continued to work on her screen. Ali was pouring sweat from just standing in the door, he felt dehydrated even though his clothes were sticking to him.

"Yes, ma'am. I have seen everyone else in both…."

"That does not concern me, what does is that you think I should stop what I am doing to find out who wants to see a Deepling."

"I didn't…."

"Mean any disrespect? It would not be worth writing you up. But just as a dog cannot be disrespectful, neither can a Deepling."

Ouch. Ali didn't know what to say. He wondered if, "drop dead, you fucking cunt," would be bad-mannered or simply doggish. Not wanting to find out, Ali instead said, "Yes, ma'am."

"After all, they don't know any better."

"How's that?" Ali asked.

"A dog."

"A dog what?"

"A dog doesn't know it's being disrespectful. It isn't smart enough to recognize its betters; after all, it's just a stupid dog." At the term 'stupid dog,' Acrimony looked up at Ali, the first time she directly acknowledged his presence.

"No, ma'am, I suppose a dog doesn't know any better." Ali kept his eyes locked on Acrimony's. Upper or not, he didn't like being called names. As it turned out, comparisons to a dog were not all that high on his list of likes either.

Ali wondered if the semifinal match had anything to do with this stand-off. First, Acrimony, as the Yellow co-groove, may or may not have had consensual sex with Fetch during the match; that they had sex was not in doubt. Second, they had lost to the Olives which meant that Acrimony had been subject to a disinfecting and/or delousing, and with Fetch she should have asked for both, because of Fetch's use of the rules.

These kinds of rule massages have never worked against the Philosopher Rulers; although, the High Command loves playing with the rules. The reason the Philosopher Rulers were never tricked by any use of the rules was because they did not issue any rules. It is true there were policies in place, namely the schedules for the maggots and the bunker cleaning schedule, but these were not things that could or could not be followed like rules.

There were also policies about the distribution of resources; however, these too were not things that could or could not be followed. The Bunker Dwellers were fully aware of their resources, its use, and its distribution. As there is no "out of sight, out of mind" mentality in the bunkers, there is also no notion of unlimited resources and overconsumption without consequence. Everything was in clear view and effects were immediate and individualized to the offender.

There was also the pillory policy, because the sum total of happiness achieved by having the pillory was an order of magnitude higher than not having it. The three times someone wondered aloud whether the pillory policy was a good idea, all three times they withdrew the question as soon as the U-Ruler stood up to speak.

The Philosopher Rulers were experimenting with the idea that rules do not actually help you, that the function of a rule is to hinder progress for the enrichment of a few. As there was no money in the bunkers, and resources were known to be limited, there was very little need to gain an advantage, because there wasn't one to be had. If you used more than your share of the collective resources, in such a way that the collective would survive without your re-source depletion but not survive with it, you had to leave. Excess in the bunkers was not valued.

In the Deep Bunkers excess reigned. Even though it was a collective, there was no collective mentality in the Deep Bunkers, so there was every reason to horde. Natural re-sources were almost nonexistent, so there was every need to horde. Manmade resources were abundant, especially gunpowder and alcohol, although people still horded the former in case they found themselves on a gameshow; the latter because it gave them the audacity to play at all.

"Say again?" Acrimony said.

"I said, 'No, ma'am, I suppose a dog….'"

"Yes, ma'am." Acrimony was communicating into her earpiece, still locked gaze with Ali. "Yes, ma'am."

"It's your lucky day; Ms. Russell wants to see you." Acri-mony was talking to Ali again, still staring at him.

"Really?" Ali had blinked and he knew it. Even though the ice in Acrimony's bones didn't thaw an iota and she didn't smile, an icy gleam passed over her eyes.

"You are being called to the sixth floor. Did you want me to walk you?" Movement from below caught Ali's eye and gave him a way out of this conversation.

"No ma'am. Oh look, there's Fetch."

Acrimony's internal temperature plummeted to -102.6 degrees in a parody of the fire of anger. She returned to her screen.

"I wouldn't keep Ms. Russell waiting, Deepling."

"Yes ma'am, thank you." Ali turned and, by memory and sheer force of will, made it back to the air lift without putting out his hand or hitting anything.

When Ali got to the air lift, he knew he had the same problem as before, he didn't know how to use it. There was a *whoosh* noise that signaled the arrival of the air lift. Ali looked down; Fetch winked at him from the floor below. Fetch gave Ali the thumbs up gesture and pointed at the air lift.

Ali entered and whooshed to the sixth floor.

CHAPTER 17

BOXES.

BOXES ARE CRITICAL TO the game of Cheepee, especially since a box is the only position that can stop anyone from scoring. To play without a box is very risky, although an obscure rule that isn't much used is that if you have two grooves, one of them can sacrifice him/herself "for the love of the Company game" by climbing the hangman's scaffold and plunging to his/her death. When this happens, the game is considered a tie and that employee is considered for a promotion.

The box is considered, by many, to be the playmaker on the Cheepee field; however, there are those who adamantly defend the cover as the playmaker. During the season where boxes were required to play blindfolded, the crème de la crème of the box position was Ximena Garcia, Chartreuses '97. Although the Chartreuses never won a match, the opposing team never scored when Ximena was on the playing field. It was rumored that she kept bacon in her pockets so the rolling jum-jum ball would always come directly to her. Everyone knows rolling jum-jum balls have a penchant for bacon.

Ximena had accepted a job with a company in another city, this one being a mecca for all things American and the supposed center of three of the four known universes and five out of a whole bunch that we know absolutely nothing about, except that one thing I just told you. This city, being the hub for all things American, was an alluring place for those looking to make it "big." If it didn't happen here, it might as well not have happened at all. The saying was that if you could make it big in this city, you could make it big anywhere. Ximena had heard this, and like so many others, went to go make it big.

And she did indeed make it big. Ximena became enormously successful. She was famous for being an athlete, a musician, a fashionista, an artist, a writer, and a model. She wasn't particularly good at any of it; you don't need to be good to be famous, only in the right spot. Ximena became the doyenne of the city's powerful, wealthy, and other-famous. The talk of the town, so they say.

Ximena decided to return to the Company to show everyone that she had "made it big." As she travelled west, Ximena became lost in the even-further outer-wastes of the sordid Paddi'u. That despondent lot had never heard of Ximena. She was captured near the South Dakota/Wyoming border, which is mighty convenient since regardless of where you think this is happening, either in the Midwest or the Pacific Northwest, this does not mess with the reality of the situation. The author consulted a map and showed me to verify this.

Ximena was a very pretty woman by at least one standard; she was very symmetrical. Most people aren't perceived as really beautiful unless they possess a symmetric morphology, especially in the face. The absolute most perfectly symmetrical face to be found within nine AUs actually belonged to Deep Bunker Q. This should actually come as no surprise to anyone but Deep Bunker Q's symmetry was not natural. In order to achieve the effect, she relied on a spell that caused the astral connection with both Bunker Q and Q to remain open full-bore for several days; this increased Bunker Q's French vocabulary making her seem inordinately intelligent because she would use the most obscure possible word for anything; the effect on Q was her *pesadillas*.

Ximena had near perfect symmetry; had an autopsy been performed they would have found that her left nostril was 1mm larger than her right and the right ear was slightly more protruding. This did not affect the way those parts tasted in any way.

Her symmetry was the only thing that saved her from being tasted to death on the spot when she was overcome by the group of roaming Paddi'u. This non-tasting did not apply to her right foot, which everyone considered too gamey, like 'gator. The Paddi'u, having staunched the bleeding with sand, effectively ending her modeling and athletic careers, gagged her and carried her to the Paddi'u king. After prostrating themselves before the king, they turned Ximena loose.

"It will speak," the king said.

"What the fuck!" Ximena was visibly upset, as was probably a pretty normal reaction, I would imagine. "Who do you think you are, you freak?!" For her questions, Ximena received a slash across the back with a sharpened epee.

Dear readers, I have to tell you that I have confronted the author about the epee fight from earlier. As noted, only a bunker alarm stopped it and as described, my question about Ali's sex started it. I asked him what the necessity of the epee fight was in the first place.

"It was necessary to demonstrate my point."

"What point?"

"That people resort to violence when reason fails."

"When did reason fail? I asked a question about Ali's sex. And I'm not convinced you needed to pander with lesbianism in the first place."

"You were going to say that the reader was going to be too confused and that I should not have that part in there at all. Then you were going to say I could easily make the point by making Ali a woman to begin with and avoid succeeding at failing to be clever."

"I would not have said that last part like that at all; but I'm fairly certain that I would have conveyed the same idea."

"I know, and I would have disagreed with you because while I'm not trying to be clever, I am trying to do something unconventional. I am not particularly interested in commercial success, so I am not looking to do things normal and to do those things that generate success in the short term."

"You could still cut the nonsense and make the point."

"What if the point is nonsense? You couldn't write something absurd without the thing being absurd. If you did that, you would be writing about the absurd. And to address your point about the readers, readers generate their own nonsense." This of course was true in the bunkers because of the pillory and the conspiracy theories people would have the pillorite read. Some of the cockamamie garbage that people would make the guilty read while in the pillory was quite elaborate and bizarre. I won't get into any of them because that's propagating nonsense; it's bad enough I have to propagate the author's nonsense.

The Philosopher Rulers decided, mainly because they were getting fed up with the people being in the pillory for way longer than was necessary, that if you wanted to comment about someone in the pillory then you had to do so in person, there was no "phoning it in" in the bunkers; you had to defend your comments. This greatly cut down the amount of time most people spent in the pillory because bravery and accountability have a sexy inverse relationship with one another.

"Readers will either canonize, demonize, or ignore a

work. The function of the critic is to facilitate this decision. Of course, critics are only people and they have their biases, so in the end, like with Ximena's lack of talent, sometimes you just have to be in the right spot."

After she had received the epee lash across the back, Ximena's attitude changed dramatically. Funny how pain and fear will make people compliant.

"Why has thou come?" demanded the king.

"I was trying to get back to the Company and show them I made it big." Ximena whimpered.

As before, her symmetry was the only thing that saved her from being tasted to death by the Paddi'u king and his court. It did not apply to her left hand, which everyone considered too chewy, like squirrel. They also had niblets of her right eye, her nose, and her ear lobes; no one complained about these niblets. All this tasting effectively ended her musician and artist careers. She did not die however, despite all the cannibalism. In fact, Ximena was given to the Paddi'u king as a trophy wife to signify that he had conquered one who had "made it big." This made him bigger.

Ximena, with all the boisterousness that infects the people of that other city, demanded she have a proper wedding, replete with a ceremony, a ring, and a cake. The ceremony and cake were easy, even for the desolate Paddi'u: the king was authorized to appoint a Justice of the Wastes who had civil authority to marry any two Paddi'u; however, they did not participate in the religious aspects because they didn't see the point since a religious marriage is none of the government's goddamn business and even the ridiculous Paddi'u know the difference between a controlling institution and the love people share between themselves.

The cake wasn't all that difficult to make either, except you really don't want to see the recipe; oftentimes it's best not to know what you're eating, or in the case of the cannibal scourge that is the Paddi'u, who you're eating. After all, if you don't know where it came from or the conditions in which it is kept before being harvested, you have no moral responsibility for it whatsoever; or so I've heard it said.

Finding a ring was much more problematic; however, Ximena was absolutely set on it and the king was constantly harassed about it. Desperate to please his new queen, and hoping to get her to be quiet for five minutes, he sent out a band of the least-incompetent scout Paddi'u to locate a ring for Ximena.

Dear readers the author has again stepped out to check the weather. Everyone knows he smokes except him. I honestly don't get why he hides it. I'll be brief because it's cold out and that means half a smoke; I'm not sure why he is telling you this. I do think I know what he is setting up here, I can tell you that. He's about to get into a Ring of Gyges example. If the ring turns someone invisible, then it is definitely the ring of Gyges. If something else happens, then I am as lost as you as to what is coming next.

In the *Republic*, Book II, Plato's brother Glaucon talks

about a Lord of the Rings-style ring (but let's be honest, Plato said it first) that turns the wearer invisible, he sleeps with the queen, they kill king, yadda-yadda-yadda, you get the gist of it. The point of the story Plato tells is, "what would you do with a ring that turned you invisible and allowed you to act with impunity?" Your answer determines, basically, the overall fate of mankind.

So, I will keep true to my task here and present the story as he is telling it, but seriously, if someone disappears after fiddling with the ring, I'm done. He's back:

"You have a smoke?"

"No."

"You smell smoky."

It was smoky outside when the scout Paddi'u set out to find something Ximena would accept as a wedding ring. They wanted to see their new queen happy; then she might stop having them killed at random, probably not though. There was a great earthquake, and the scouts feared the end. The earth heaved and shuddered; when all was calm, there was a fissure in the ground, which led to a small opening. Climbing through the fissure, one of the scouts found a hollow creature with a corpse inside. Upon the corpse's hand was a golden ring, which he took for Ximena.

As the scouts made camp in the desolate wasteland, fearing the flying things they call "the U'mentio," the scout with the ring examined it. He saw a small decoration on the ring, a collet, I believe it's called. The Paddi'u, fearing the U'mentio, secured the ring in a bag and presented it to Ximena the following day.

The wedding ceremony was sheer bliss. The king declared the day a national holiday, political rivalries within sty-like Paddi'u culture were set aside, and whole tribes beset and cannibalized other tribes and then were told about the wedding, it was magnificent.

Ximena was happy as the Paddi'u queen for a very long time; it was wedded bliss. Despite her many amputations, she had again found her place; she had again, made it big.

Despite her bigness in both that other city and in the even-further outer-wastes, Ximena knew that she was still not as big as she could be because of the Paddi'u king. The Paddi'u king was a traditionalist in the common usage of that term. Ximena was a traditionalist only insofar as she would follow traditions, if they coincided with her independent values. Patriarchal control was not a value they shared in common.

The king was content for Ximena to be happy "in her place," but any time she expressed her independence, which was fine so long as that independence stayed within acceptable limits, i.e., it coincided with his own dominance, she was belittled and scorned. Much like how a pet is treated when it gets out of its cage.

Ximena was too strong-willed a woman to allow this to happen. Late one night, she stole away from the Paddi'u and headed west.

After a while, she again found herself desperately lost.

She was driven into a cave by a fierce storm that blotted out the sky and released a tempest like she had never seen. The cave entrance was slick with dump and mud. When she crossed the threshold, she plummeted down a natural slide for what seemed an eternity. The slide terminated at a hole about thirty feet above the ground. She landed on her back with a mighty thud and lost consciousness.

When she came to, she was lying on a floor in a cavern. She stood up and looked around. She saw that she had fallen from about thirty feet. There was no way she could climb back up. Ximena heard a noise like footfalls echoing in her direction. She looked around but there was nowhere to go.

"Who are you?"

"I'm Ximena." She hesitated to identify herself as Queen of the Paddi'u. Depending on who this stranger was, that might not be the best way to identify herself. She could always go for a grand reveal later; she still had on her ring to show as proof.

"How did you get in here?"

"I fell. Who are you?"

"Fell from where?"

"Up there." Ximena pointed to the hole with her right hand. Deep Bunker Fetch followed her finger. He smiled.

"You don't say." Deep Bunker Fetch looked Ximena up and down. "You look a little worse for wear. If you don't mind my saying so."

"Who are you?"

"You know, no one's asked me that in a long time." Deep Bunker Fetch looked up at the hole. "Where were you going? Before you fell from," he pointed at the hole, "up there?"

"I was going back to the Company, to show them I made it big. I'm sorry, I didn't catch your name. Who are you?"

Deep Bunker Fetch looked at Ximena and smiled. "And did you?"

"What?"

"Make it big?"

"I am the Queen of the Paddi'u." Ximena held up her hand to display her ring. Ximena was only used to dealing with sheep and fake wolves. She had never met someone like Deep Bunker Fetch, a real wolf.

"That's a lovely ring. A toast to honor the Queen of the Paddi'u. Welcome, Your Majesty." Deep Bunker Fetch pulled a flask from his pocket. He nodded and held it out for Ximena.

Ximena reached out her hand and took the flask. As she did, Deep Bunker Fetch ran his thumb across the ring, turning the collet around to the inside of Ximena's hand. The flask fell to the ground.

"Well, isn't that something." Deep Bunker Fetch said. He reached down and picked up the flask. "Ximena, if you had any idea what you possess, then you would indeed make it big." He put the flask into his pocket and walked toward the cavern exit. He stopped before leaving the cavern and turned back around. She didn't know how he did it, but Deep Bunker Fetch looked directly at Ximena, even though she knew he couldn't see her. "Thank you, by the way. You have been very useful." Before he left the room, and still looking directly at her, Deep Bunker Fetch smiled and winked.

I told you. Read the *Republic*, II, 359b-360b; and good luck with your answer.

Chapter 18

The Statue of Progress.

Nothing you will ever see, dear readers, no matter how long you live, will ever compare to the Statue of Progress. Should you become a multi-centenarian, visit all the planets, see all the sights of the Milky Way, should the last thing you see be the completed Statue of Progress, you would gasp with your last breath. You would forget everything else your eyes had captured. No matter what beatific fate your family tree meets, no offspring's accomplishments; nothing, *mi amigos*, is like it.

The entire complete Statue of Progress is composed of three separate parts. The statue proper stands upon a pedestal, upon which is affixed a plaque. Each component was designed by a different master, each the most excellent practitioner of her profession.

The plaque is inscribed in the most perfect of languages. The two Truths which the plaque announce are nothing short of divine revelations. To read it is to see directly into the mind of the Almighty. Those who have read the inscription have been immediately altered by its message, became the best of humans, exemplars of the world.

The Icelandic master linguist and inscriber, Birna Jorgensen, was commissioned to complete the plaque. Birna collected enough poudretteite to form a 1cm raised lip around the edges of the plaque. The main bulk of the plaque is composed of pure tanzanite, giving it a sapphire purple-blue color which, combined with the pink-purple edges of the poudretteite, is such a joy to see, if one never even saw the pedestal or statue proper, they would die happy.

The inscription itself, those two sentences given to man by something far better, is composed of rich, deep green jadeite, commonly called Imperial Jade, with the minutest traces of yellow. These colors perfectly complement the pink/blue plaque base and edge, causing each to glow with a radiant energy visibly noticeable. The plaque shines like neon without any help from electricity or gas. The effect has made grown adults weep like little children.

Birna Jorgensen, upon being commissioned by the Company to complete the plaque, mined the minerals herself, which took close to thirty years. After the mining processes where complete, including the requisite treatments, Birna began forming the uninscribed plaque. The plaque is 107cm long, 56cm high, and 7cm thick in the middle, 8cm thick at the raised poudretteite edges.

Upon completing the uninscribed plaque, Birna went

to sleep. When she woke up, she locked herself into a primitive hut in Raufarhöfn, Iceland, removed her own tongue so as not to sully the message by using human speech to utter it, and completed the plaque. Her dream had contained a vision in which she was revealed the inscription on the plaque. Her missing tongue precluded her telling anyone about the dream. The only reason people even know what happened was she pantomimed it to a fisherman before renting a small fishing vessel and setting out into the Greenland Sea. She was sailing north. The man was recompensed by the Icelandic people for his boat; it and Birna were never seen again. She had the plaque with her when she disappeared.

The Mauritian master architect, Alika, was commissioned to complete the pedestal. Alika discovered three large blocks of alexandrite and she fashioned them into a helix spiral which was used to cover an incandescent light source. This incandescent light source was solar powered and the luminosity of the light changed with the intensity of the sunshine it absorbed. The ambient air temperature, atmospheric pressure changes, and humidity also affected the brilliance and luminosity of the incandescent light.

When the sun hit the light source itself, it effectively cloaked it, rendering it functionally invisible. This made the pedestal appear to be a single, spiraling piece of alexandrite. Since alexandrite changes color from green to red depending on the light source that is passing through it, the visual effect was that the spiral column appeared to be continuously drilling into the ground.

To support the weight of the statue, rods of magnesium alloy were strategically interspersed. A fully-fueled jumbo jet carrying all the whales and elephants on the planet could crash into the pedestal and not move it. These rods were hidden from view as not to occlude the aesthetics of the pedestal itself.

Alika finished the pedestal and moved it into the open light of the remote village near the shores of Mare Longue Reservoir, where she had lived while completing her work. The effect was so dazzling it caused her and the villagers to go blind. The pedestal's pulsating light was accompanied by a sound. Unlike the visual manifestation of the pedestal, which appeared to be drilling down into the earth, the sound was not one that accompanies a drill. As the pedestal pulsated, it began to speak. Alika and her fellow blinded villagers began to supplicant themselves before it and then they listened.

When the pedestal had finished giving the blind Alika and her blind cohorts its commands, she and the others chartered an expedition to Ethiopia. The pilgrims carried the pedestal, which was covered and placed in a sound-proof and airtight coffin, to the summit crater lava lake atop Erta Ale. The congregants, being certain they were alone, placed the pedestal on the rim of the caldera and uncovered it. Again, they listened.

One by one, the villagers walked over the edge and fell into the lava lake. Alika, the last one left, went to the pedestal, kissed it and said, "I understand." She hugged the pedestal in a mother's embrace, and they both went into the lake.

The Romanian master sculptor and preeminent geneticist, Ioana Popescu, was commissioned to complete the statue itself. The Statue was not made, it was not created, it was not sculpted; it was born.

Ioana began her quest for the female components of the Statue. She visited the Vatican, where she chipped a piece of Mary from the *Pieta*. She also visited the Mamayev Kurgan in Volgograd for a piece of *The Motherland Calls*. Her final stop was Paris, where she went to the Rue de Rivoli for Jeanne D'Arc and finally to the Louvre for pieces of *Nike of Samothrace* and *Venus de Milo*.

To collect the male components, Ioana had traveled to Rio de Janeiro where she chipped a small piece of the statue of *Christ the Redeemer*. She travelled to the mountains of Bhutan and chipped a piece from the *Buddha Dordenma*. From there she visited Malaysia to acquire a piece of *Lord Murugan*. From Florence she obtained a piece of *David*, and then finally travelled to Zurich for a piece of Rodin's *Thinker*.

All artists give birth to their creations for they come from the minds of the artists. The Statue, as mentioned, was born; however, not in the sense that it came from the mind of anyone. After she had collected all her materials, Ioana returned to her home in Constanta. She took all the pieces of material from the statues and liquified them into a mixture of water, hydrogen, methane, ammonia, and carbon dioxide. She took this primordial soup and chemically infused it with a piece of granite which was four-million-years-old.

Ioana went to sleep and the next morning the Statue was sitting where the piece of granite had been before she went to bed.

"Good morning, Ioana." Its voice was the velvet touch of pure love.

"Good morning." Ioana experienced agape for the first time in her life. She sat down across from the Statue and looked into its eyes. It was absolutely perfect. Tears of joy, love, and pride began to run down her face.

"I'm sorry," she said.

"You do not need to be sorry," the Statue said to her.

"You can't stay, can you?"

"No. I have to leave."

"Can I go with you?"

"You will not be able to return. Do you understand that?"

"That's okay, I would rather go with you." Ioana and the Statue travelled to the Arabika Massif, of the Western Caucasus. The Statue carried Ioana to the Game Over Chamber at the bottom of Voronya Cave; they were standing 6824 feet below the surface. At the bottom of the cave the Statue opened a door.

"Go inside and wait for me. Do not be afraid. I will be behind you in a moment."

"I am not afraid," Ioana said. She walked through the

door without hesitation. The Statue closed the door and waited. Another door opened across the cave and someone exited.

"You know what's funny, I really thought you would look different."

"You look exactly like I thought you would. You are even holding what I thought would be in your hand," the Statue said.

"You trying to get out? You should be safe below; but then again, you do not have to worry about the…," Deep Bunker Fetch looked at the warhead detonator in his hand, "…after effects."

"There is no out."

Deep Bunker Fetch looked toward the Game Over Chamber exit. "Where does that lead then?"

"It leads up."

"You mean out."

"No. I mean up; there is no out."

"Not for them." Deep Bunker Fetch triggered the detonator. The ground vibrated slightly. A finch took flight somewhere. The eyes of the statues of the holy were dry; their tears ran out long, long ago.

"You know, I have other tools. Tools that might not be so harmless to you."

"I know."

"You aren't scared?"

"No. You present me no threat. There is nothing to fear from you."

"Too bad no one is going to hear your wise words, if that's what you're trying to sell."

"I am not alone."

Deep Bunker Fetch smiled and looked at the door behind the Statue. "You know, I'd be willing to bet that you only managed to get one to come with you."

"That is all I need."

"Well, good luck with that, I better let you get to it. Until we meet again?" Deep Bunker Fetch winked at the Statue.

"This is the end. We will not meet again."

Deep Bunker Fetch left the chamber as the Statue closed the door. Deep Bunker Q was unaffected by both the radiation and the blast, she had anticipated Deep Bunker Fetch's move. Q had a dream she never wanted to talk about. In the Sub Bunkers under the Deep Bunkers, which resemble Precambrian Earth and where WWI, the Great War, is still being fought, the High Command took the blast as an unfortunate occurrence of collateral damage, a small, unnecessary evil to stop an even greater and more unnecessary one.

CHAPTER 19

ALI FINDS THE BOSS AND IS GIVEN A LESSON IN HISTORY; SOME COMMENTS ON THE BEVERAGE TEA; ALI GETS A SURPRISE; AND THE AUTHOR TALKS ABOUT THE DIFFERENT TYPES OF DEAD.

ERIN RUSSEL, THE KEEPER of Information, had a surprisingly Spartan office. In front of a window sat a medium-sized writing desk with a high-backed chair in front of it. The desk was situated before a window; the view was of the mountains. In the middle of the room were three chairs and a table. On the table sat a porcelain tea pot and two matching cups and saucers. Erin was sitting in one of the chairs. She was an old woman, her downy hair white and thin with age. Although she was very old, her eyes were those of a young woman. Ali could tell her mental prowess was still well in its prime.

"Hello Ali, would you please sit down?" Erin said. She had slightly risen as a sign of politeness; she hadn't fully risen because she was an Upper and Ali was a Deepling and those things matter, especially to one of those sides.

"Yes ma'am. Thank you." Ali hurried over to the proffered seat and sat down. It was nice having a floor he could see under him and nothing to smash into while walking to his seat.

"Would you care for some tea?" Erin asked.

"No ma'am, thank you though. You wanted to see me?"

"Yes, thank you for coming. I will get right to the point Ali, and then we can chat for a spell. Will that be alright?"

"Yes ma'am."

"Ali, I would like to offer you a job. I would like you to be the Manager of the Deep."

"Wow, that is quite a promotion. What about Silas and Helen? Wouldn't either of them be the next person in line to manage the whole Deep?"

"Positionally, yes one of them would be, 'next in line,' as you say; however, we have been watching you on the Cheepee field and we think you are a good fit. Would you like the job?"

At Ali's level in the Company, vertical promotions were rare, although lateral "promotions" happened with ease and regularity. In fact, Ali was unsure of his job title more often than not. Every time he signed his employee report, he had a different title, even though he was never told this himself. Every time he had business cards made, they were obsolete by the time the printer was finished spitting them out. Not only was his position different, his office telephone number and email were constantly changing.

"I didn't think I would be getting a promotion."

"Because you lost your badge?" Erin was a very direct woman. She was looking directly at Ali as though she were a schoolmarm, resting bitch face and all.

"Yes ma'am, it fell off when I was running the other day. I didn't mean to lose it. I've looked for the old one, but I didn't find it."

"It doesn't matter. Would you like the job?"

"If it's available, of course."

"Very well, it is yours. Congratulations Ali; or should I say, Congratulations Manager of the Deep."

"Thank you, ma'am." Ali puckered his lips and twisted them to the left.

"What is it?" Erin said.

"You said the badge doesn't matter. Why not? I thought that losing it goes into my employee report."

"It does."

"So why doesn't it matter?"

"No one really reads them. We already know what we need to know."

"Then why bother with the reports? We spend an incredible amount of time on those things."

"As Manager of the Deep you will realize quickly that the reports are a way of keeping people busy. Do you know who to go to when you need something specific?"

"What do you mean?"

"When you need a specific task completed, or a specialized job, do you know to whom you should turn to get that accomplished?"

"Yes ma'am, I go to the people I know who have the qualifications."

"As do we. The reports allow us to justify those decisions."

"Oh."

"Don't worry Ali, you will understand. Tea?"

"No thank you." Ali was thinking about something else.

"What else?" Erin asked.

"There's a road that leads past the Statue of Progress, it goes off to the northeast of the Company grounds. Where does that lead?"

"It goes to the cemetery for the useless dead," Erin said. "Would you like some tea?"

"No thank you." After a few seconds of brain processing, Ali registered what Erin had said. "I'm sorry, what did you say?"

"You asked about the road, the one that goes out past the Statue of Progress."

"Yes."

"It leads to the cemetery for the useless dead."

"I don't understand, what is that? I've never heard of the 'useless dead.'"

"It's not all that surprising, most people have neither heard about them or even know that there is a cemetery out there."

"Have you been?" Ali asked.

"To the cemetery?"

"Yes, have you ever been out there?"

"Almighty no, there's no reason to go out there."

"Why not?"

"I just told you." Erin said.

"You told me what it was, but that doesn't explain it or why there's no point in going out there. What are the useless dead? I don't even know what that means."

"The useless dead are the people who have been swallowed up by the machinery of the Company or steamrolled by their own lives."

"And those people constitute the useless dead? They are just buried and forgotten in some distant cemetery?" Ali was aghast.

"Not exactly."

"What do you mean?"

"They aren't buried out there."

"Cremated?" Erin shook her head. "If they aren't buried or cremated, what happens to them?"

"They are left in a field and are forgotten."

"What?!"

"You heard me."

"That's unconscionable."

"Why?" Erin seemed to be completely unaffected by what she was saying.

"You can't do that to people."

"They aren't people."

"They were."

"I agree, and the operative word is 'were.' They aren't people now; now, they're the useless dead, so there's no problem."

"They just throw the bodies in a field?"

"It isn't as primitive as all that. They cover them with lime to reduce the smell. They didn't used to do that, I hear. Those were not good times; the old timers, when I first got here, said it reminded them of a dairy farm, only much worse." Erin casually sipped her tea. Ali thought she looked quaint, somewhat like the Queen of England. Ali wondered if Her Majesty talked about such awful topics with the same air of nonchalance. To see Erin talk without hearing her, you would think she were casually chatting about the weather, not about the useless dead.

"They should have markers or tombstones. They should have something for the families."

"Why?"

"It's the right thing to do."

"It might be the polite thing to do, but there is no right or wrong to it."

"What exactly is the useless dead?" Ali's morbid curiosity had asked this question without his brain's permission or his mouth's consent. His ears wanted to jump off his head and throw themselves over a cliff.

"The useless dead are the dead that exist for our reference only. Families pay homage and lip service to them, as is proper, but the useless dead do not require our admiration, our respect, or our attention."

"What do you mean 'reference only?'"

"Families appeal to their dead often, but it isn't that much different than referencing a character from a play, book, tv show or movie. The more time passes between the living and the dead, the more the dead become fictions. Would you like some tea?"

"No, thank you. How do the dead become fictions?"

"Here, have some tea." Since he was tired of being asked, Ali finally acquiesced. Tea had been a commodity more precious than gold in the Deep Bunkers, where the other Others and the bat-like things had lived. Tea was so highly sought that the easiest way to get someone killed, call her X, was to tell anyone, call him Y, that "X had tea." Y was guaranteed to try to kill X. This applied to all tea; none in particular was coveted. For example, Chamomile and Black Russian Caravan were equally treasured. An ethical egoist would never tell anyone she had tea because that someone was guaranteed to try to kill her, and being dead, in general, is not in your own self-interest.

The exception was that Chai tea had been universally loathed. In fact, an easy way to get yourself killed was to accidently be correct and X did in fact have tea, but it was Chai tea. If that happened, after Y had killed X and then found the Chai, Y was guaranteed to try to kill you.

Everyone knew Deep Bunker Fetch had tea, but no one was willing to try to go get it from him. The same was true for Deep Bunker Q. There was a probably true rumor that she could put the idea in your mind to go get tea from Deep Bunker Fetch, which was nigh a death sentence.

"Let me tell you about my great-great-aunt, Mildred." Erin poured Ali a cup of Chai tea, his favorite. "Do you know about the Underground Railroad?"

"A little."

"My aunt Mildred," Erin began, "was a South Carolina Belle. Her father, a state senator, owned the third largest plantation in the state. His total slave population was over four-hundred souls." Ali whistled at the impressive number of evil. "That's right, four-hundred individual pieces of biped property. He sent my Aunt Mildred on a tour of the North, so she could see how the treacherous Yankees lived but also to get a sense of American history. While visiting the many historical landmarks in the North, Aunt Mildred found herself amongst a group of Quakers, members of the Religious Society of Friends.

"While there, and unbeknownst to her, the Friends took her to an anti-slave rally. Appalled at first, Aunt Mildred became despondent when the slaves were asked to remove the burlap sacks which covered their backs.

"Being a Southern Belle, Aunt Mildred had led a mostly sheltered life. While she was friendly with some of the house slaves, she never mingled with the field slaves. She had heard tales of overzealous slave drivers, and had been witness to many conversations amongst her father and his friends about the disposition of insolent slaves; she had never entertained the idea that these things did take place. She had certainly never seen the aftereffects of 'slave discipline.'

"Upon seeing the immense scarring on the backs of the recently escaped slaves, she knew that the worst of the stories were true, that slaves were sometimes killed without regard or worked to death or treated as nothing better than upright livestock. The sight of the slaves' backs never left her mind.

"Upon returning home, she did some subtle investigative work and discovered the true horror of that practice. I will not get into the details of her journal, but as you can imagine from the depiction of accurate historical accounts, descriptions of the times, and even movies about the subject, her acceptance of the practice diminished with each tale told.

"Aunt Mildred asked her father if she could make a return trip North, ostensibly to view more historical sites; her real aim was to contact a known leader of the Underground Railroad and offer her services. This she accomplished, much to her delight. But as Voltaire said, 'She was sensible of her triumph: but she was not yet sensible of its extent.'

"The mission she was given, and swore to complete, was to free slaves from South Carolina. To be exact, slaves from her father's plantation."

"Wow, that's quite a mission." Ali was genuinely impressed.

"That it was. Aunt Mildred was given information she needed about getting the enslaved to the 'station,' a safe-house where her part would be over and another 'station-master' would escort them North.

"She was told that she would have assistance from a local who was sympathetic to the movement. She was given a pass phrase, which, upon hearing, would signal that the person speaking to her was the trusted agent. The phrase was, 'I love my sister; are you my sister?'

"Upon returning home, she went about her daily life. Now a covert Abolitionist, Aunt Mildred began becoming familiar with the people who worked in the house. She finally treated Anne Marie, her 'personal slave,' as an equal, although to keep up appearances she feigned an air of superiority when others were around.

"Aunt Mildred was certain that a beau of hers, Lance Smith, was the agent. Lance had said some things on occasion that made it seem as though he shared her commitment to end slavery. Many times she had overheard him in her father's parlor saying, "Slavery is coming to an end," and "I tell you, in ten years there will be no slaves." These snippets of conversation made her excited. She was very fond of Lance and the idea of them dashing off to fight for freedom, evading slave chasers and dogs, getting married, and raising equality-loving children was very delightful.

"Many nights she was tempted to ask Lance if he was her sister, but she remembered she was told that first contact would be made by the agent and should not be attempted by herself. As she and Lance took a carriage ride one moonlit evening, he declared his love for her. He said, 'I love my mother and I love my sister. I love you too Mildred.'

"Aunt Mildred was anticipating the question of 'Are you my sister?' If Lance was going to ask her, he was planning another night. After she told Lance she loved him too, they exchanged idle talk about family, local trifling matters, and other such niceties as visit young people in love. Like Turgenev said, 'Young people who spend much time amicably in each other's company are often visited by identical thoughts.'

"After arriving back home, Aunt Mildred was at her evening toilet as Anne Marie brushed her hair. Aunt Mildred recounted the events of her evening with Lance. She confessed that she was hoping that Lance would ask her something else. Anne Marie tucked Aunt Mildred into bed and blew out the lamp.

"'Good night, missus.'

"'Good night, Anne Marie. Perhaps I will get my question another time.'

"'Yes miss, I'm sure Mr. Lance will be asking for your hand directly.' It occurred to Aunt Mildred that it made sense Anne Marie thought she meant she wanted Lance to propose to her. She had kept her intentions of assisting the Underground Railroad a complete secret.

"As she lay there, she could feel Anne Marie's presence still by the bed. She asked Anne Marie, 'Are you okay?'

"Yes missus, I wanted to tell you that I love my sister; are you my sister?'" Aunt Mildred sat bolt upright in bed.

"'What did you say?'

"'I love my sister; are you my sister?' Aunt Mildred's head was spinning, or the room was spinning. She fumbled for the matches to light the lamp. In the lamplight Anne Marie looked very focused and intent.

"'Yes, I am your sister,' she said.

"'We don't have a lot of time left. The escape is in two days.' Aunt Mildred and Anne Marie spent much of the night discussing the plan. They were to lead the fleeing group through the swamp on the far east side of the plantation. It would be a treacherous fifteen-mile trip to the station. A boat was being brought in to smuggle the newly liberated people to Massachusetts, where they would be given a new chance. There was room on the boat for both Aunt Mildred and Anne Marie."

Ali was hanging on every word coming from Erin's mouth. To think this woman had the blood of someone so noble and brave coursing through her veins lent her a new air of regality.

"The night of the planned escape was running like clockwork, until tragedy struck. Her father, upon Lance's insistence, bought a new McCormick reaper, an invention that would reduce the number of slaves needed on the plantation. Lance had told Mildred's father on several occasions, 'Because of industry and technology, slavery is coming to an end.' He had also told him that 'In ten years there will be no slaves; there will be teams of good white men driving the reapers." I guess Turgenev was wrong.

"The night of the escape, Lance decided to bring the new reaper to the plantation. Instead of surprising her father, Lance surprised Aunt Mildred, Anne Marie and the fleeing slaves. Aunt Mildred admitted the plot, after the blades of the new reaper were tested on the feet of the fleeing slaves; Lance did this to ensure that everyone knew this was no game.

"When her father arrived, he slapped Aunt Mildred and spit into her face. He told her she was no longer his daughter. After she and Anne Marie were horsewhipped, their hands and feet were severed, they were tied together at the neck and waist while facing one another, and then thrown into the swamp for the alligators."

Ali looked like a ghost. He felt the color evaporate from his face. He was on the verge of tears; Erin had finished her cup of tea and was looking toward the window, lost in thought or memory.

"I am so very sorry that happened to your great-great-aunt. You must feel proud that a member of your family was that brave."

Erin smiled and snapped out of her haze. "And what about you, Ali? Who are your people?"

"I don't have anything as grand as that. Both my brothers were in the military. My older brother was killed in Afghanistan and my younger brother died two days later in Iraq."

"Are you not going to expand on that?"

"I hadn't planned on it. Why do you ask?"

"You are missing an opportunity."

"How's that?"

"If you elaborate on their lives and make the stories moving and flattering, then the circumstances surrounding your brothers' deaths would benefit you."

"But I don't know the circumstances. We got a letter saying they were killed somewhere but that their deaths were for a very good cause."

"You see, that works."

"How?"

"Your brothers dying for a good cause. You can fill in the details and use that to engender a usefulness from them, a usefulness to yourself; otherwise, they too will become the useless dead."

"But not all dead are useless. What about the pictures of the Cheepee players who have died during the game? The relics containing their bones are in the Multi; they aren't forgotten."

"They aren't the useless dead."

"What are they?"

"The famous dead. They are the ones who are remembered by everyone, but they cannot be used to function like the useless dead. That wouldn't work because too much is known about them. Too many facts are verifiable and the veracity of claims to them are confirmable or deniable. The famous dead are for public use."

Ali didn't know what to make of all this. He was also beginning to question whether Erin even had an Aunt Mildred. According to her, she could have whipped up that story for her own ends. Ali couldn't imagine using his brothers' deaths to promote himself.

"Do you have anything else you'd like to talk about, Ali?"

"Well, I guess maybe one more question."

"Of course, what is it?"

"Do you know what's on top of Ditch Peak? I see a flash of light from the peak when the sun is coming up and I can't figure out what it is."

"Oh, that. That's kind of interesting. You should go see for yourself. This will get you past the guard shack." Erin reached into her pocket and brought out a badge that she handed to Ali. It had his picture on it, the same dopey smile from before. This badge said "All Area Access."

Erin stood up, "There are two more things, Ali."

Ali was on his feet as well. They were walking toward the air lift. "Yes ma'am."

"I would like for you to be the Red cover. I know the finals are tonight and this change will not take effect until after the game, but we think a change is overdue."

"What about Hope, she's the Red cover."

"We are moving her to the Olives."

"Oh." Ali wasn't overly excited about this, even though he acquiesced to her request. At least he and Maggie would be on the same team now.

"What was the other thing?" Ali asked her as the air lift went *whoosh* to announce its arrival.

"Your promotion will be effective at noon on the day after the finals, but please do not mention it to anyone yet. We will send out a message making the announcement. This will give us enough time to make the logistical arrangements. I hope you understand."

"Yes ma'am, I do. I won't tell anyone."

Erin shook Ali's hand. "Congratulations again Ali. On your promotion and joining the Reds. Best of luck in the finals."

"Yes ma'am. Thank you for the opportunity, I'll do my best."

"We expect more than your best, Ali, we expect 110%."

CHAPTER 20

CHEEPEE FINALS.

NAOMI WAS LATE FOR the pre-match meeting, conference, and, as the Company has repeatedly said, non-mandatory merchandise collection period; no one knew why and she didn't offer any explanations. She strolled in, sat down, and said, "Texas is here ya'll! Hell yeah!!" Before the match began, the obligatory names of recently retired employees were read aloud. Those were followed by the names of employees who had died. Finally, employees who had been fired were burned in effigy; those who were still in the Multi for whatever reason were burned in actuality. The crowd always loved that part.

When the players were released from their pre-match cages, everyone saw why Naomi had been late to the pre-match meeting, conference, and, as the Company has repeatedly said, non-mandatory merchandise collection period. Somehow or another, Naomi had built a perfect 1:25 scale replica of the Alamo in the middle of the field.

Its walls extended across the entire playing surface, even covering the out of bounds moats where they dump the fat from the cows that become hamburger and the fat from the pigs that become porkchops; don't be grossed out, you eat most of it so there isn't a whole lot of fat in there, just enough to form a surface jelly and smell bad.

The game was a defensive contest; at half-time the score was 1-1. Through either error or subterfuge, the refs had released an undomesticated rolling jum-jum ball and that thing was so feral most of the players ran away from it. This one also still had its teeth and spiked tail so that little thing was all business; and by all reckoning, it was seriously pissed. For those interested in why either side was able to score with an undomesticated rolling jum-jum ball on the field, technically it ran into each goal of its own accord so they actually didn't. But the Western side of the stadium could not understand the score nil-nil so the refs counted the goals.

After half-time the refs had corrected the error and they were now playing with a domesticated rolling jum-jum ball. While Naomi was defending the Alamo in the middle of the field, Ali was doing what covers do best, which is why they are covers. He caught glimpses of Naomi from time to time but she seemed to be defying both logic and physics. I'll start with physics: things larger than subatomic particles cannot be in two places at the same time. Naomi seemed to be in at least two places at all times, though she wasn't "everywhere at once," which is a turn of phrase and if you hear someone say, "I was literally everywhere at once" then you should start worshipping that divine being.

The reason Ali could verify that Naomi was sticking it to physics was because he could clearly hear two different guns firing and from two different places. One was a bolt action rifle that Naomi needed almost no time to reload; the other must have been a Tommy Gun judging from how many rounds as were coming out of it. Since Naomi wasn't using live ammo, the guns were allowed; she was, however, using dead ammo.

After sauntering into the pre-match meeting, conference, and, as the Company has repeatedly said, non-mandatory merchandise collection period, and sitting down, Naomi had asked if live ammo was allowed. To this she received a slap in the face and a 'no.' This was how they did things: you ask a question, you get slapped in the face and then the answer. This has drastically cut down the number of questions, except for questions from Fetch, who seemed to really enjoy this rule change because he would not stop asking questions.

The Philosopher Rulers, instead of giving a slap to the face, demand a toe from the questioner. Despite the fact that their reasoning was sound, this made the Bunker Dwellers really mad. The bunkers have not been cleaned since the policy was adopted. The Philosopher Rulers are in charge of the cleaning schedule but they haven't released it. No one is willing to lose a toe for it either. No one takes the initiative to clean the bunkers because the Philosopher Rulers said the schedule they produce is a perfect synchronization of utility, Kantian ethics, and hedonistic materialism. What is really impressive is every Philosopher Ruler agreed with the schedule. The Philosopher Rulers don't seem to understand that this has the bunkers slipping dangerously close to an oligarchy, and then you know what happens!

Naomi had then asked, "Is dead ammo allowed?" After another slap to the face, the refs conferred and agreed that it wasn't expressly prohibited therefore it could be used. The Gingers knew this was bad because they only had live ammo. Naomi nicked her arm with a razor and said, "Texas!" No one was sure where Naomi had actually gotten the dead ammo. The obvious answer seems that she would have gotten it from Deep Bunker Q; however, the author said, when I asked, that Deep Bunker Q made undead ammo, which is apparently something too awful for words. Upon my insistence the author said he didn't know where Naomi had gotten the ammo, she hadn't told him. I asked him if he knew how preposterous what he said was. It was illogical.

Naomi's defiance of logic was that she was violating both the law of excluded middle and law of non-contradiction with her simultaneously being in multiple places. Look it up, or if you are feeling a little lazy: A or ~A; and ~(A and ~A), respectively. The law of identity was still intact, for the most part. A = A.

Naomi was hooting and hollering at the top of her lungs. By the volume you would think she had three lungs. Deep Bunker Q had three lungs, which was necessary for one of the more lethal and unpredictable spells that even she was hesitant to use. Q was in a fight for her life. Booster Mathis was trying to set her on fire. Since she was allowed to use her feet, Helen Henderson was working magic with the rolling jum-jum ball and continuously kicking it into the side of Q's head. This didn't give the Gingers any points, but the crowd simply could not get enough of it. Q was putting up a valiant fight, but she was getting overwhelmed and it was only a matter of time.

Naomi#1 was using a bolt action rifle, which was a Mauser M1903 Springfield, to keep Mildrew pinned down. Mildrew was wearing a suit of armor which Ali swore was empty. He said he saw into the helmet, right before the last two minutes, right before they turned the emus loose, and that it was blackness. It didn't move all that human-like either, more like a lame robot. No one was sure if that was because it was a really lame robot or that's what it would be like if it were a suit of armor with Mildrew in it. If it was just a haunted suit of armor, then no one knows where Mildrew was during the match. Regardless of any of that, since Ali didn't actually see him, for the purposes of hide-and-seek, Mildrew is technically still hidden. With two minutes left, the refs released the emus.

Naomi#2, the one firing the Tommy Gun, which was a Model 1927A5 Thompson submachine gun, was trying to kill Tutor Carey. Tutor was behind an Alamo outhouse and was very clearly speaking emu because the birds were running to him like he was saying, "come here." He should have been screaming, "run for your bird lives!" because Naomi#2 simply could not miss with the Tommy Gun. It was not all that clear if they would run out of emus before she ran out of bullets but she was mowing those things down with ease; emus apparently do not understand the rules or the point of Cheepee.

Ali saw a flash of red light and smelled burning hair. Naomi#1 was dead, a laser blast having melted her head. The ghost of Sam Houston came to collect her spirit; the two of them held hands and walked into that great Texas in the sky. Most people took off their hats and stood; it was nice.

Ali rushed up to the top of the Alamo chapel, which Naomi Prime had situated so that it guarded the ladder to the top of the hangman's scaffold. He grabbed the M1903 and saw he only had two rounds left. He aimed at Helen Henderson and pulled the trigger; Q was no longer being kicked in the head by the rolling jum-jum ball. Ali figured that Q probably wouldn't be completely consumed by the flames and that she would be, more or less, okay.

Ali looked around for the source of the blast that had killed Naomi#1, Naomi#2 still dropping emus with impunity, shouting out, "And that's for Lubbock" or "And that's for Ft. Worth." It was not all that clear which would run out first: emus, bullets, or the names of cities in Texas. He saw Fetch with the rolling jum-jum ball, running toward the goal. Ali noticed something in Fetch's hand. It looked like a toy ray gun.

Everyone could see that the lizard had only moments left to live, which was odd because it seemed sicklier than was natural. Booster was about to throw gas on a burning and heavily concussed Q when he noticed that Helen had failed the Company. He looked around for the rolling jum-jum ball. He saw Fetch with it, getting ready to score for the Olives.

Booster looked at the scoreboard, 3-3. The Olives were going to score, even if Fetch tried to stop it, the rolling jum-jum ball itself was rolling towards the goal, as in the rolling jum-jum ball was intently going to the goal of its own accord. Booster had a way to tie it. He looked up at the hangman's scaffold. He ignored Q's screams of "*¡Agua, por favor, agua!*" and ran towards the Alamo.

Ali watched in the scope as Fetch kicked at the rolling jum-jum ball; it was quicker than he was and easily avoided his foot. It kept heading for the goal, speeding up to get away from Fetch. Ali was still looking at Fetch through the scope. When Fetch missed the rolling jum-jum ball he turned; Ali saw his face. It wasn't Fetch.

An emu was running for the rolling jum-jum ball because emus don't understand the rules or the point of Cheepee. Deep Bunker Fetch aimed the gun at the emu and pulled the trigger. A flash of red light emitted from the gun and the emu was aflame and melting, apparently not being able to handle a laser blast. The emu let out a terrible cry that made all but one group of deplorable Paddi'u run into the Deep Bunkers, where the other Others and the bat-like things had lived, unaware of the situation there. Deep Bunker Fetch looked up at Ali and aimed the ray gun directly at him. Deep Bunker Fetch winked at Ali.

Booster was almost to the top of the Alamo when he heard an emu scream. "Lasers," he thought. The Olives were good, he had never even thought about using lasers. Still, he had to tie the game; he kept climbing. As he mounted the top of the chapel, he saw Ali and heard a shot.

Ali saw Deep Bunker Fetch's ray gun turning red and he shot. Deep Bunker Fetch went down like a sack of hammers before he could pull the trigger. The rolling jum-jum ball took to its feet, which it always did with a minute left, and ran for its sorta-life into the goal. The Olives were ahead, 4-3.

Booster saw the rolling jum-jum ball take to its feet and run for its sorta-life into the goal. The Olives were ahead 4-3. He could only tie the game, the rolling jum-jum ball was probably already asleep in the goal; whatever it was doing, it wasn't likely to come out again. He saw Ali looking through the scope; he didn't know Booster was there. Even though Ali was a cover and couldn't stop him from scoring, he could stop him from tying the game by not letting him up the ladder to the scaffold. Booster had only one chance.

Booster rushed Ali before he even knew Booster was there. Booster threw Ali off the Alamo where he landed on an emu that was pecking at the suit of armor that might contain Mildrew. The emu lurched from the surprise of a rider now atop its back. It started running and Ali grabbed its long neck to stop from being thrown. The emu took two steps and Ali heard a shot. The emu dropped to the ground. Ali heard, "And that's for El Paso!"

Booster was on the top of the hangman's scaffold, ready to tie the game. He swan dove off the scaffold without hesitation and screamed, "For the Company!" Deep Bunker Q, in an effort to finally rid herself of Deep Bunker Fetch, used her third lung to initiate a lethal and unpredictable incantation capable of reaching topside. The incantation was indeed lethal; the incantation was indeed unpredictable. All Deep Bunker Q managed to do was kill the lizard. It died seconds before Booster could tie the game.

CHEEPEE SCOREBOARD

Olives 4 Gingers 3

Chapter 21

The top of Ditch Peak.

ALI WAS RUNNING ALONG the road toward the Statue of Progress. The Cheepee finals were over and the Olives were the Champions. He was no longer the Olive co-cover. At noon he would be in charge of the Deep and all the Deeplings. The bunker cleaning schedule had been posted and a breakdown into an oligarchy was prevented, although they still seem to be on a slide to the same sad fate as those topside, before they had to go to the bunkers. The Deep Bunkers, where the other Others and the bat-like things once lived, were still a poisonous wasteland of radioactivity because of the warheads that somehow got there. There is no resolution for the Paddi'u; they remain the unlucky ones, the heavy-clothed.

Ali watched the sun rise, his new badge proudly clipped to his shirt, his dopey smile beaming over his heart. He saw the flash of light on Ditch Peak. His new badge would get him past the jerk guard who wanted to kill him, if the guard was even there, and then he could see the source of the flashing light. He ran a little faster at the thought of one mystery solved. As he ran, a breeze picked up and the wind blew through the bushes. Something under a bush caught Ali's eye and he stopped. It was his old badge, having somehow made it back from that place where things go that are lost forever. Now maybe he could get that blemish off his employee record, if it even mattered. He picked up his badge and began running again, happy that one more thing was fixed.

He ran past the "No Standing," "No Stopping," "No Waiting," and "No Loitering" sign; he never bothered to look at it, he didn't notice it now also said, "No Running." Ali stopped and stretched at the Statue of Progress, the most magnificent thing ever produced by human hands. He looked down the road to the right, the Company cemetery unseen, many miles away. He felt a wave of sadness at the thought of what was out there, baking in the sun covered in lime; forgotten until they were necessary, and then as easily forgotten again.

To his astonishment the guard shack was unmanned, which was mighty convenient because he wouldn't have to get shot right away. It seemed unlikely that kid-Commando would listen and let Ali through, even though his new badge gave him access. Ali didn't know why the shack was unmanned. He wasn't early like the other day, when he arrived before the rising sun.

Ali jogged past the barricades and began climbing the

hill to Ditch Peak. He could tell by the steady and substantial grade that he was in for a real workout; his tight right quad was giving him trouble. He definitely needed to take a break from running to give his body time to heal. After all, he had recently been thrown onto an emu. Company insurance did not pay for any injuries, illnesses, or deaths caused during a Cheepee match because, as Upper Management likes to stress, Cheepee is a voluntary activity. Ali knew that ice, elevation, and rest were the best things for his leg. This was going to be his last run for a while.

As he ran along, he began wishing he had worn his other shorts, the ones with pockets. It was annoying having to hold on to his old badge while trying to ascend the hill, which was getting steeper by the step, something which his right quad found regrettable. He had to start walking.

He walked up the road, not thinking about anything and not even noticing the clop, clop of his shoes. Ali turned a bend in the road and saw the top of Ditch Peak was a very long way off; the road switch-backed up the mountainside. It was too steep to run and too long to walk. He knew he wouldn't be making it to the peak today. It wasn't that big of a deal since his new badge would let him explore later.

As he stood there, stretching his quad, Ali tried to see if he could tell what was on the peak. He was on the west side of the mountain, the rising sun illuminating the peak itself. It was too far away. He could not make out any discernable features. Obviously, Ali would have to actually go to the peak to see whatever was flashing.

He resigned himself that the peak was not in the cards. He heard the sound of a vehicle approaching, fast. The car was coming from up the road, from the direction of the guard shack. On instinct, Ali looked around for a place to hide. He positioned himself behind a boulder as he saw a security car turning the bend at high speed. The lights were on but not the sirens. Ali didn't recognize the guard. It looked like the kid-guard, but then again, it also looked like the grotto guards.

Ali thought about why he had hidden in the first place. He could talk to the kid-guard at the shack and explain that he had a new badge, one that gave him access to the area. He could explain this while safely on the other side of the red line at the guard shack; he might not have that opportunity where he was standing now.

He watched the silent but flashing security vehicle as it sped along to the top. Ali saw the car disappear at the summit, a tiny speck in the distance.

Ali heard something familiar yet very out of place. The sound was of a very heavy door opening and closing. The door was loud enough to make a thudding echo. Being on the side of a mountain made the noise sound alien. Ali stood up and turned to face the sound, which had come from further up the road, toward the summit.

The road to Ditch Peak was unprotected on one side and ran near-flush along the mountain on the other. Although it switch-backed several times along the way, the whole road was visible until it crested the peak. The sound definitely came from the mountain itself, but Ali wasn't sure where. He was also confused about why a door would be in a mountain.

He walked up the road, crossing over to the right side to get a better view of the side of the mountain. He glanced over the side, wondering why there wasn't a guardrail; there was no surviving a fall down the side, either in a car or on foot. Ahead of him, coming down the road, Ali saw someone walking his way. He couldn't see who it was because of the shadows and distance. The walker stopped short of exiting the shadows when it saw Ali.

The person waved a badge high in the air and wiggled it, pointing with their left hand. They motioned to their badge with their finger in a jabbing motion, like they were demanding to see Ali's badge. Ali raised his old badge high in the air, thinking the person wouldn't be able to tell it was his old badge from this distance. In two steps Ali would be able to see who it was.

"Freeze asshole!" Ali stood frozen; he knew he was lucky he wasn't dead already. He had never even heard the kid-guard walk up behind him. "Put your hands in the air! I am authorized to kill you where you stand. If you don't show me your authorization I will shoot. Keep your badge in the air and do not turn around."

"Officer…"

"Shut up! Do not speak! If you try to talk to me again, I will kill you as authorized by the use of deathly force." Ali knew this was it. He could not explain to the officer that the badge in his hand was his old badge, which did not authorize him to be there.

"Spread your legs." Ali spread his legs.

"Place your right hand between your legs." Ali did so, his old badge hanging between his legs, like the swaying *bolas* under the dress of Q's nightmare swing-set. He wanted to laugh at the absurdity of it all.

"Drop your badge." It hit the ground.

"Take two steps forward and lay on the ground with your hands behind your back." Ali took two steps forward and saw the figure in the shadows. A tear ran down his face. Deep Bunker Fetch winked at Ali.

"Charlie One for High Command, come in."

"High Command for Charlie One, go ahead."

"Charlie One for High Command, unauthorized intruder. Advise."

"High Command for Charlie One, use of force is authorized. Repeat, use of force is authorized. Your mission is of critical importance to WWI, the Great War."

"Charlie One for High Command, order confirmed. Alpha Papa."

"Delta Bravo Foxtrot."

Somewhere in the Sub Bunkers under the Deep Bunkers, which resemble Precambrian Earth and where WWI, the Great War, is still being fought, the High Command raised their glasses, celebrating being one mission closer to bringing about the end of WWI, the Great War.

Ali put his head down on the asphalt, closed his eyes,

and thought of nothing at all. Ali Kim, Manager of the Deep, former Olive co-cover and current Red cover; and now one of the useless dead.